Anopheles

a novel

John. J. Smith

All Rights Reserved

Published 2015 by Progressive Rising Phoenix Press, LLC

www.progressiverisingphoenix.com

ISBN: 978-1-940834-96-2

Visit John online @
www.progressiverisingphoenix.com
and www.writersalcove.com

Printed in the United States of America

1st printing

Dedication

Joan Lundholm.

Acknowledgement

First to Annita Paniagua for her editing expertise, incredible input and suggestions, I thank you and will forever be in your debt. Anything found out of sorts, is all mine.

My special thank you to Joan Lundholm, Julie Glowney and Sharon Smith for their front line editing, and as that of a beta reader, I thank you and will forever be in your debt.

To Fred Hoffman (wherever you are), Cedric Lee, Christine Lowe, Jackie Smith, Shirley McCleskey, Terri Preston, James Poon, and Debbie Tarabay for your advice and support throughout the first edition and other projects.

Then to CL Stegall for the excellent design and the creation of the Anopheles cover. Your creative mind continues to amaze me and I feel honored to be able to read your work as well as display your art, thank you.

Introduction

Dear Reader

First allow me to thank you for taking the time to read Anopheles; I hope you enjoy reading the story as much as I enjoyed writing it and knowing that you are reading this makes it all that more important.

Please note I am not making light of such a horrible virus and what it can do to those who are exposed to HIV. Although there have been great strides in dealing with HIV, it is still a silent killer, and it still is not in check, meaning there are thousands who contract HIV each year.

Anopheles was first written around twenty years ago when a co-worker contracted HIV. While talking to him, he said he was infected with the virus from a mosquito. I didn't question him (agreed or disagreed and never will) and I'll be honest, it frightened me.

After he passed away, dying from AIDS, I took it upon myself to research the virus, wondering if there were other ways other than intravenous drug usage and unprotected sex, and found there are other "possible"—possible meaning it hasn't been proven/disproven—ways to contract HIV, which I depict in Anopheles. Is it possible that a mosquito could pass along the virus, I am not sure, but it would help explain the high HIV rate in the mosquito belt in Africa. It is also in the same family as malaria, and we know mosquitoes can pass malaria, so?

I am certain there will be debates as to the information I researched, and have updated from its original conception and writing, elated that there has been tremendous strides in fighting HIV from twenty years ago. Again, please be certain I am not making light of it, but it is still there and it seems to be a subject we do not like to talk about, and frankly, HIV frightens me.

After the first release of Anopheles, I put it to rest, never wondering if I would ever dust it off. Of course with the Ebola scare (outbreak) in Dallas, I had to dust Anopheles off; not to capitalize on the horrible incident in Dallas but to show there are other virus' that are around that we never dream could be an outbreak. Could HIV could be one of them? Is it possible? Who knows? My hope is we never find out. My hope is it will go away and never harm another person.

Again, thank you. Without you, Anopheles would be just another story told but not heard.

Chapter 1.

July 1. 2:35 A. M.

Violent rain slashed fiendishly against the windshield, blinding the driver of the Peterbilt eighteen-wheeler as large, skeletal-fingers of lightning danced the dark sky, casting a surreal silvery sheen of glitter across the dark asphalt that extended in front of him. The beams from his headlights disappeared within a few feet of the truck, hiding in the darkness behind a thick curtain of rain.

The driver yawned. Then stretched. The noise of the CB radio, the roar beneath the tires, and the pounding of the heavy rain barely kept him awake. It was hypnotic. His head nodded forward then bounced up. He wiped the heel of his palm across his eyes, yawned again, and tried to shake away the sleepiness.

"Break one-nine," Wayne shouted into the CB microphone as if trying to will himself to stay awake.

"You got a break, driver. Come back."

"I'm driving westbound on this here Interstate 30 and comin' up fast on Sulphur Springs. I'm looking for the quickest route to Tyler, come back."

Lightning illuminated the darkened sky again, revealing huge slate-gray clouds and then turning the windshield into a silvery mirror. Deafening thunder buffeted the truck.

The truck careened from the high winds.

The canvas tarp tied over the trailer slapped against the tractor tires that Wayne Shackelford Trucking was hauling as cargo.

The right wiper struggled and stopped. It started again a few seconds later, but finally stopped midway across the windshield.

The CB crackled as another streak of lightning raced across the horizon. There was a long static-charged screech before, "The quickest route to Tyler would be south 154 to west 37 to south 69, come back."

"That's a big ten-four, driver. I surely do appreciate your help," Wayne answered with a grin.

The radio went silent.

The right wiper started again, and then stopped midway across the windshield.

Pressing down on the accelerator, Wayne didn't know, and had forgotten to ask, how far it was to Tyler, but he had already changed his log records to show that he had stopped for the evening. He really should have stayed and rested for the night at the truck stop where he had fueled up, but the ship bringing in his cargo had been late arriving at the Norfolk, Virginia shipyard and he was already behind.

As luck would have it, for Wayne, the inspector who usually checked the cargo understood his personal needs once the two twenty dollar bills exchanged hands, and the tires were loaded without the inspection. It wasn't his fault the tires had been docked in some unknown port for some unknown amount of time in Africa. It wasn't his fault the delivery was already late. Besides, his wife was waiting for him at her sister's house in Tyler. Two weeks was a very long time to leave a woman waiting.

He had had a fight with her just before he left and so she went to visit her sister until he came to his senses. He did. He had never been to Tyler and never wanted to, but those old amorous feelings grabbed at him like a magnet.

He felt a tingle in his groin.

He came to his senses all right. Two weeks alone on the open road can do that to a man. And Wayne was certainly all man.

"I'm coming, Puddin," Wayne sleepily mumbled. His eyes grew heavier with each mile. He tried to stretch as he yawned and adjusted his NAPA baseball cap lower on his forehead. Only a few seconds later, his head nodded forward then sprang back up. "Damnit..."

The right side of the windshield was a white mask of condensation as the humidity thickened inside the cab.

He turned on the defroster and slowed down as he reached the exit for State Highway 154 and then quickly sped through the yellow light. As Wayne's tongue moved a toothpick from one corner of his mouth to the other, he read the clock on the dashboard. 2:35 in the morning; surely the local police would be elsewhere.

Thirty minutes later he crossed over Lake Fork, ignoring the heavy fog that enveloped the windshield as larger drops of rain began to pelt.

He pushed down on the accelerator. The engine roared as thick gray smoke escaped the twin exhaust pipes. The truck whined and backfired as he downshifted; the Peterbilt's engine complained more about his driving than about the slight incline that lay ahead.

When Wayne reached the top, he quickly turned right onto State Highway 37 and again pushed down hard on the accelerator. The trailer drifted a little, but cooperated. The truck's tires sizzled as they rushed over the standing water. The huge tractor tires strapped to the trailer behind him groaned as the stagnant water within them sloshed from side to side. The inhabitants of the once still, stagnant, water were now waking up.

Wayne drove past the Governor Hogg Shrine State Park and slammed his foot down on the pedal as he shook his head and laughed aloud at the name. Gaining speed and racing through another small town that he knew nothing about, Wayne sped past its cemetery.

Eyeing the graveyard with heavy, burning eyes, he missed seeing the faded-gray Oldsmobile pulling out in front of him from a driveway just beyond the graveyard.

The Peterbilt slammed into the back left side of the opaque object, toppled left and jerked right, weaved, and then slammed into the back of an abandoned car. They both bounced. The cab finally toppled over on its side as the trailer fishtailed and skidded across the slippery three-lane blacktop highway, slamming back into the cab and hurling it and its unfortunate driver back across the road.

The cab slammed into the Oldsmobile again as if to put an exclamation mark on the sentence. BAM! The Olds flipped, landing near the rain-swollen shoulder.

Huge drops of rain fell in thick masses that deadened the impact.

Sparks flew from the legs of the trailer. It flipped over and rolled as it crashed through the Crystal Lake Resort Restaurant and then stopped when it landed in the small lake behind it. The straps holding the cargo of tractor tires snapped and they catapulted in every direction imaginable.

Thunder roared above the Olds as its driver, Tommy Johnson, lay draped through the shattered windshield. Large sinister droplets splattered against his broken face as he gazed up at an elderly stranger.

Only moments after witnessing an odd mist that fluttered from the pretzeled trailer in a chorus of humming, the stranger carefully pulled the driver from the wreckage and lay him on the cold, wet asphalt.

The driver's last breath fluttered before everything went black.

Chapter 2.

July 4. 7 A. M.

Jennifer was astounded with the crowd that filled her small diner. For the past six weeks, Quentin, Texas, home of the largest Big Mouth Bass, had been hit with torrential downpours. Even when it wasn't raining the air was thick with humidity. The diner's air-conditioner groaned above the chatter, as if begging for relief. It cooled as much air as it possibly could, which wasn't really very much but with the diner filled to capacity, she felt a bead of perspiration trickle down her back.

The small breakfast club, which met every weekday morning, was enthusiastically discussing the events for today's Independence Day gala. Quentin took pride in being a small town in the good old U.S. of A. Her sons were among those wounded and killed in every war or conflict fought since the time that America declared independence from England.

Jennifer could not believe her eyes and her good fortune. Even in this horrible weather, everyone who had the day off work had flocked to the diner this morning. Surely, it wasn't because of the atmosphere. Decorated in an early western theme, the rustic diner accommodated twenty-five people at best. A wagon wheel adorned the far wall below vintage wanted-posters that she had bought at the First Monday flea market in Canton. Pictures of women from the 1800's festooned in long elegant gowns hung around the room. She almost wished she had lived during that time except for the fact that air conditioning had not yet been invented. Or hair coloring and make-up.

On another wall was a 1924 painting of Quentin, its painter unknown because the signature had faded years before she purchased the diner. The front wall had oblong windows that faced the Quentin Courthouse, the most regal building in town.

The tables and booths were adorned with red and white gingham tablecloths and matching linen napkins. They sat beneath knock-off Tiffany lamps that reflected sparkles of red, yellow, green, and blue against the old weathered wallboards that she swore she was going to replace until the crowd held a small revolt, saying the wallboard gave the place an ambiance that made the place a home.

The aroma of coffee and bacon mingled with the lingering scent of stale tobacco and heavy perfumes. Jennifer wouldn't have it any other way. This was her life. The Diner and Quentin were her true loves. Nothing, except her three-year-old son, Jasper, meant more to her.

Jennifer had opened the eatery six months after she divorced the man who treated her as his personal punching bag. It took her those six months to convince her father to invest in the dream that she knew might fail and leave her just as stranded as she had been the day she and Jasper left Sulphur Springs in search of a new home. Now, two years later, she was amazed at how well she was doing. She was not rich by any means, and was usually late with her bills, but she had paid her father back the small loan she had used as a down payment to the bank and, other than the monthly payments to the Quentin National Bank, she believed the diner was hers.

She picked up the coffee pot from a hot plate that sat on a corner counter and slowly made her way around to the tables and booths, pouring coffee for the people she had grown to love. They were more than customers, they were extended family.

"More coffee, Bernard?" Jennifer nearly sang as she began pouring. Her long slender fingers playfully massaged the back of his thick flabby neck.

Her soft perfume drifted toward him in a light floral fragrance. Bernard loved being around Jennifer and he struggled to keep his feelings secret and never once allow her or anyone to know how he felt.

"Now what if I said no?" Bernard Talbert chided, barely holding back a smile while inhaling the sweet scent.

"Because I know you. Whenever you finish off a big breakfast—"

"But he's been a good boy, Jennifer," Winona wisecracked as she sped behind Jennifer with another pot of coffee. "How much do you weigh now, Bernard, if you don't mind my asking?"

"I'm down to about three-thirty-five, three-forty," Bernard replied, happy that he was making progress with his new diet. He longed to feel the intimacy of a woman, but his weight kept every woman he ever met out of reach.

"You're doing just wonderful," Jennifer said with one of her warm smiles, and then kissed his cheek. "I'm proud of you."

"Bringing your van in this afternoon?" Bernard asked Jennifer quietly, somewhat embarrassed at the attention. His garage serviced nearly all of the cars in Quentin. Most of the breakfast club rarely paid for car parts, and paying for labor was unheard of. These were his friends, and extended family as well, and he took care of his family, especially Jennifer. Once made fun of and not particularly socially accepted, Bernard's world had changed when Jennifer moved to Quentin. She immediately befriended him and in doing so, brought the rest of the breakfast club, and then eventually the town into his circle of friends.

"Right after lunch and before the festivities begin," Jennifer replied. "I promise." She leaned in and patted his hand as he returned the coffee cup on the saucer. "Claude and I have prepared some really good meals for this week. You're going to love them. He guarantees it'll help with your diet," she whispered, "I'll bring them by as well."

"Thank you," Bernard said. "Between you and Claude, I never knew dieting could be so good."

She lightly brushed his shoulder, her way of showing support.

"Claude promised he'd have you courting all the single women in town before December," Jennifer continued. "And I believe him. You're looking great."

Bernard blushed, all the while thinking how much he wished that were true.

As Jennifer started to leave, Monica, who sat at the next table, gingerly touched her hand and whispered, "I like your new waitress. She's very pretty. Such a lovely figure and creamy complexion."

"Only because she is of African descent," Chauncey, her good friend, interrupted. His thick British accent blended perfectly with Monica's Texas drawl.

Monica smiled, and continued, "I'll have you know, Professor, that in all of my years of teaching, I never favored a child simply because they were black. Being a black woman has left me with the civility to tolerate cretins such as yourself."

The entire room burst into laughter as Chauncey turned red from embarrassment. He embraced Monica's fresh opinions and trivial remarks, and enjoyed her getting the best of him.

"Is that so," said Chauncey as he recovered from the embarrassment, laughing. "You'd be heartbroken if I decided to have my coffee at McD's," but in fact, he loathed the mornings Monica missed coming to the diner and joining them in their daily conversations. She was the only joy in his life since his wife of fifty years had passed on. Monica was more intelligent than he was, but rarely demonstrated it in a manner that would embarrass him. She, the ever-loving teacher, and he, a professor for most of his adult life, had a lot in common and not one time did their opinions differ.

Monica adjusted the gold chain that held her glasses. She perched them on the end of her nose, peered through them into Chauncey's aging eyes, and smiled. She knew she had the best of him.

"I love you, too, Chauncey," Monica rebutted, and it seemed everyone in the diner howled again.

Jennifer, laughing as well, started to walk away, but stopped when everyone in the diner stood as Amy Newcomb jogged by.

Amy's husband, Travis, stood and jumped as his finger hit the stopwatch. "I'll be damned. I'll be damned! She did it. She just beat the Boston Marathon pace!" Travis roared, holding the stopwatch above his head.

Nearly everyone in the diner cheered as Amy paused for a brief second, jogging in place, her hands raised over head and her fists pumping toward the sky, with a large beaming smile stretched across her face. She knew she had just surpassed her previous record, and knowing even more so that everyone in that diner was cheering her on.

"You did it, baby. You did it!" Travis shouted over the din through the windowpane. "Woot! Woot! Woot! Look out Boston!"

Amy was proud that she was running an average of 30 miles every week as she built her stamina and improved her pace. As she turned and continued down the path that she took every morning during her run, she began to think about expanding the route to get closer to the 26-mile Marathon distance. That would take about eight laps all the way around Quentin!

Growing up as a sickly child, Amy had always dreamed of competing in the Olympics. It was Travis' idea to train for and run the Boston Marathon as a possible stepping-stone. He knew she could win; she just needed someone to discover her and he had reached out to every organization he knew to get her the recognition she needed to get the attention of the Olympic Committee. She still had time. Amy was only 25 years old and had the energy and determination of a teenager.

Travis sat back down, shaking his head. He had never been more proud of anything as he was at this moment and the excitement showed as his hands trembled. "Yeah... she did it," he mumbled. "She sure as hell did it."

He glanced across the table toward Brett Jackson, who grinned and said, "Next year?"

"You bet," Travis exhaled in excitement. "She's going to win Boston, then on to the Olympics."

"Well, she couldn't have done it without you," Brett continued. He knew Travis was worried about the age difference. Amy, an exceptionally attractive, petite woman, was fifteen years younger than Travis, which was something he seemed to worry about since the first day they had met. However, Amy knew it was Travis who brought her to where she was today.

Travis, a naturally shy man, dated very few women in his life, single digits to be exact. He'd met Amy at Brett's birthday party and was surprised that she even talked to him and it was

Amy who invited him to dinner. During that first of many dinners—she wouldn't yet call it a "date"—Travis learned of Amy's dreams to grow from that sickly child to an athlete who could wear an Olympic medal.

Travis liked Amy better than his postal truck—that postal truck meant more to him than his own truck, and he loved his truck—almost as soon as he met her. As one dinner turned into two, then three, and then a date and eventually to marriage, he had promised himself that she would wear that medal and he would do everything in his power to make it happen.

Travis exhaled a nervous sigh, ran his fingers through his slightly gray, tinted brown hair, and said, "Yes, she could. She can do anything she puts her mind to."

"Go'n hunting with me this season?" Brett continued, hoping to change the subject. He and Travis had been friends for as long as Brett could remember. Brett knew that Travis was sensitive about the age difference with Amy and had stopped the "cradle robber" comments as soon as he saw it might turn into a serious relationship.

"Probably," Travis groaned. "But only if you promise not to win all the stuffed animals from the shooting gallery tonight."

Although both men laughed, they knew Brett was an expert sharpshooter and was the best in Quentin, probably the best in East Texas. Although a quiet man, Brett's shooting prowess had landed him on television shows and the covers of magazines touting his skilled marksmanship, hunting, and competition ability. Like Amy, Brett had his own dreams, and took to the woods like the animals he hunted. He loved being out in the thicket where not even the deer and turkey saw him hiding.

The racket inside the diner continued until almost eight o'clock. Then, one by one, the breakfast club disappeared. Today, that suited Jennifer just fine. It was Independence Day and there would be a great excitement during the afternoon and evening.

"That's it! Let's shut everything down and get out of here!" she shouted to Winona, Marco, Jess and Claude as she turned the door sign around to read 'CLOSED'.

Chapter 3.

While Marco, Jess and Claude moved around the kitchen cleaning the grill and putting the food away, Jennifer sat back in her favorite booth, the one that faced the courthouse, watching people come and go, and secretly wondered what had happened to Cameron. He usually stopped in before seven.

"You really like him, don't you?" Winona asked as she passed the broom beneath Jennifer's feet, breaking Jennifer from her reverie.

"Yes, no," Jennifer replied nervously. She just didn't know. She did not need a man in her life. Her last one had been enough.

"I'm sure he ain't like your ex. You might want to go ahead and go out with him and find out for yourself. I mean, you've had the man over for dinner, what, three, four times?"

"I don't know. It's not worth starting something, when you know it's destined to fail. You, of all people, should know that."

Winona sat down opposite Jennifer, and sat in silence for a moment, dropping deep into a reverie of her own; recalling the husband who had beat her senseless and left her near Lake Fork to die. She remembered crawling along that dirt path to State Highway 154, barely alive, calling out for someone, anyone, to help. Then, through the fog of her swollen eyelids, she saw the compassion and concern in the sparkling blue eyes of a very pretty woman looking down at her. The woman pulled a wet wipe from her pocket, opened it and wiped it across Winona's badly beaten and bruised face as she assured her that she would be okay.

"Why'd you help me?" Winona asked, surprised as the words spouted out without truly thinking about them. "You could have just as easily walked away."

"What kind of question is that?" Jennifer asked. She was just as surprised at the question as Winona was.

Winona nervously played with her napkin. "I don't know. You saved my life, took me into your home, fed me, and brought me back from death. You gave me this job and then found me a place to live—"

"Because I like you," Jennifer interrupted.

What else could Jennifer say? Winona was a person. A real human being left to die by a man that claimed he loved her.

Jennifer looked at her with a warm smile. "What should I have done, left you by the lake? Taken you to the hospital, left you there, alone, and frightened. Maybe let you leave the hospital, only to go back and give him another chance to do it again. At least I had my father to turn to. You had no one."

"But you can't afford me. Marco. Jess. Claude. Nor yourself for that matter."

"Is this about money?" Jennifer asked. "What, like I can't afford to have someone to help me run this place?"

Winona smiled, and her dark beautiful eyes sparkled as she continued, "I don't know what it's about. I'd just like to try and figure out why you seem to help everyone except yourself. Cameron really loves you. You should give him a chance."

"Nope. I am happy with my life the way it is" Jennifer answered without a pause for thought.

"But he could make you happier," Winona sheepishly grinned.

Jennifer was quiet for a moment as Winona resumed sweeping. It was curious, even to her, how could she be with a man who walked away from the life of a doctor to become a deputy in a small town like Quentin? What would make a man walk away like that, from that type of awesome responsibility to a job where there was almost none?

Was that it? Did she think he was a failure, or did it bother her knowing he could save lives as a doctor instead of taking a life as a gun-toting dep- uty?

No. She didn't need a man like that in her life, especially a cop.

Chapter 4.

Cameron piloted his beat-up multi-colored Ford F150 pickup truck down Main Street, praying that it would make it to the station, just as he prayed every evening that it would make it back home without leaving him stranded on the road. Thick plumes of black smoke billowed from the exhaust pipe in between showers of sparks.

He slowed, as he turned right onto Goode Road, then again when he turned left onto Goldsmith Street and into the Department of Public Safety parking lot. He turned off the engine and sat as the truck rocked and creaked. Then he listened to the pounding of the backfire from an engine he was sure was way past its life expectancy.

He stepped out of the truck, slammed its creaking door and meandered toward the entrance of the small but quaint building that resembled more of a prefabricated home than a police station.

"Morning, Cam," Shirley blurted in her normal fluttering way when Cameron came through the door. "Mindy miss the summer camp bus again?"

Cameron smiled and winked his deep blue eyes in an expression of pain. "Couldn't get the truck started."

He made his way down the narrow hall, pulled the duty roster clipboard from a long thick rusting nail in the wall, grinned and mumbled, "Thank God, no duty tonight. Only on standby." He glanced around the dark paneled walls and thought about how safe he felt in Quentin.

Before moving to Quentin, Cameron Nickels had been an ER doctor in Washington, DC. One day, while working the emergency room, a gang shootout had occurred inside the ER and Cameron took two bullets to the chest. There was pandemonium everywhere for only several minutes and Cameron nearly lost his life while the DC police and hospital security guards allowed the gunmen to escape, leaving two nurses, an orderly, and a patient—a senator's son—murdered only a few feet from where Cameron lay, slowly bleeding out. The figure stood over him and said, "Wrong place, wrong time, Doc. Lay still, they'll think you're dead." Cameron then felt a second bullet hit him seconds before the gunman fled the hospital. Luckily for Cameron, the shooter that stood over him knew just where to put a bullet that wouldn't kill him, something he wondered about from time to time, knowing in the back of his mind that the shooter had a mission that included Cameron's patient, the senators son, and not Cameron.

"I hear Jennifer's doing the kissing booth tonight," Shirley continued in an excited richness (a tone that Cameron had grown to like) when he came back to the counter. Her cheeks flushed with abashed excitement as if she were embarrassed to be bringing up the subject. She nearly knocked her glasses off her petite nose as she swiped at strands of hair that fell onto her glasses.

"That's what I heard. Got me twenty—count 'em—twenty, one dollar bills just waiting to be spent," Cameron joked worse than a schoolboy in love for the first time.

"When are you two gettin' married?" Shirley continued in an excited cackle that Cameron loved. He treated her like his mother and she treated him like a son, a son she never had; a bond that started almost immediately when Cameron showed up the first day as a deputy. He, Shirley, and Mindy had spent many weekends, while Cameron did odd chores around Shirley's place, while Shirley spoiled Mindy. She knew more about Cameron than anyone in Quentin, and knowing he had been more than he led everyone to believe made her love him even more.

"Come on, Shirley. We've never even been out on a real date," said Cameron looking over his shoulder to see if the chief, Buster Givens, was listening in.

"Cammy. Cammy. Cammy. I keep telling you. Quentin just ain't like the big city. Once you've started proper courting, and you have, the rest just comes natural."

Cameron frowned as he glanced back down the hall to Buster's office. He then softly replied, "She really doesn't want to get involved, Shirley. She seems to be perfectly happy..." He shrugged his shoulders as his words trailed into preoccupied thoughts while a frown creased his forehead.

"I'll have you know, when a woman invites a man to dinner..." Shirley continued as she patted Cameron's hand—

"—Now, Shirley, that was before she knew how I felt," Cameron interrupted.

Shirley waved her hand as if swatting at him and continued, "Like I said, if you'd stop interrupting me and let me speak. When a woman invites a man to dinner and proceeds with proper courting, the rest just comes natural."

"She called me a Yankee, do you believe that?" Cameron excitedly whispered. "A Yankee."

Shirley howled in her cackled laugh and continued, "Her diner is a miniature United Nations, being a Yankee don't matter none."

Cameron leaned across the counter, kissed her on the cheek, and whispered, "It's a shame you're married."

Shirley broke out in a roar, "And twenty-some years older than you." She snorted. "If she knew what was good for her, she'd grab you up and lock you in her house. Why a rugged, good looking man like yourself—"

Cameron blew a kiss at her and quickly stepped out the door, letting it shut behind him. He darted to the unmarked Ford Crown Victoria parked next to his pickup and jumped inside.

He glanced around the peaceful parking lot and thought how nice it was to live in a small town. No blaring sirens. No one standing outside the hospital, nervous, wondering whether their loved ones were going to survive after being shot during a drive-by. No one standing inside the hospital worried that a gang would open fire on people already in fear. No one raising hell just to take over the drug sales in a neighborhood.

He fingered the two bullet scars, then smiled. Living in Quentin was so far the opposite of DC, he felt he would never again have a fear of dying except due to old age.

He glanced around the small parking lot and thanked God that this town only needed and operated six cruisers. Four marked in full colors with Quentin stenciled in large blue letters across the doors. His and Buster's were the only unmarked vehicles and to this day, he could not understand why any small town would even need a plain-clothes officer. It had been six months since he'd written a ticket, and twice that since he'd responded to a call. He believed Buster had probably given him the job only because Cameron's friend from the Metropolitan DC police, Captain Zollor, had recommended him. Zollor said it was the least he could do as Cameron prepared to leave the hospital where he'd been a patient rather than a doctor for several weeks. Two bullet holes to the chest turns even the best ER physician into a code blue in mere seconds.

A single bead of sweat trickled down Cameron's cheek.

He started the engine, turned on the air-conditioner, and quickly glanced at his armpits, hoping the humidity hadn't already ruined his shirt.

"God, I'll be glad when this stuff breaks. If it isn't the rain, it's the humidity. The mosquitoes are going to be so thick tonight, it'll be miserable as hell," Cameron said to himself as he piloted the cruiser out of the parking lot and drove toward Main Street, slowing so that he could read the banner draped across the unusually heavy traffic area. The bright red, white and blue sign advertised the day's activities and their times; twelve noon the picnic would begin, followed by softball, volleyball, sack races, and then there would be the craft show and a carnival midway. Supper was at six. Baking cook-off at seven. Eight-thirty, fireworks. Every business, store, and shop would close down as everyone in Quentin would be walking the fairgrounds and looking for a place to sit for the fireworks.

He stopped at the light on the corner of Main Street and State Highway 154, turned right and drove toward Lake Fork and the town limits. He quickly glanced toward the diner, disappointed when he saw the CLOSED sign. He wondered if the Yankee remark was genuine or just a product of Jennifer's humor that he adored.

While waiting at the next light (Quentin had maybe three), an image of Jennifer came into his mind's eyes. He could visualize the beautiful woman with whom he had fallen deeply in love. Her golden-blond hair, her perfectly shaped face— at least he thought her face was perfect—laced with freckles, the blue star tattooed behind her right ear, and her thick Texas accent that drove him absolutely insane; he'd never been exposed to an accent that sounded so warm and intoxicating in his life and the newness alone was driving him crazy. And at last, those damned big deep blue eyes, God, did he love those eyes. Her eyes were bluer even than his, which was a first. He had it bad, and she was on his mind almost every waking minute and most of the times in his dreams. Yes, he had it real bad.

The song, 'Lost in Love', flowed from the radio, pulling him deeper into his private fantasy.

While he envisioned a soft caress of her lips at the kissing booth, a blaring trumpet sounded behind him. He glanced in the rear-view mirror and saw a frustrated hand pointing at the traffic light. He glanced up, waved, and then sped through it.

He had to get that woman out of his mind.

Impulsively he piloted the cruiser to the side of the road and quickly made an illegal U-turn. He pressed down hard on the accelerator and sped toward the diner.

He really had to get her out of his mind.

Cameron eased the cruiser to the curb, parked, climbed out, and then sprinted to the door as if expecting a new thunderstorm. He knew the door would be unlocked because her van was still parked out front. Sure enough, the bell at the top of the door announced his arrival as he stepped inside.

"Hey, Cameron," Jess Everhart bellowed from the kitchen. "Killed any crooks lately?"

"No, just shooting them in the foot as a warning, Jess," Cameron joked.

He heard Jess and two other voices laughing at the joke.

"What's the word on the truck driver," Marco shouted.

"Nothing new. He was driving a load from Norfolk, Virginia to Dallas, but intended to stop in Tyler. I guess he fell asleep and didn't see Tommy's Oldsmobile pulling out in front of him. I believe the funeral was yesterday."

"Tommy going to make it?" Marco continued.

"Yeah, but he'll be sore for a while," Cameron answered. Although standing at the entrance and answering their questions, he couldn't take his eyes off Jennifer's favorite booth.

"What are they gonna do with all them tractor tires?" Jess Everhart asked. "I'd like to have me a couple of those for my 4 Runner."

"Deliver them I guess, and if you can get those big ole things on your 4 Runner, have at it," Cameron answered. "I promise you, I'll look the other way and no one will be the wiser."

"Shoe! I was afraid you'd be lobbin' a couple of them 9 millies at me from that big Glock of yours," Jess continued. "I took a few of those over in the desert wars, and I don't want no one shoot'n at me here in the good old U S of A."

Jess, Marco, and Cameron laughed with a little banter as Jennifer signaled for Cameron to come on in. He sat at Jennifer's favorite booth and smiled as she sauntered toward him with the last of the coffee.

"Morning, officer," Jennifer said in a sultry timbre that she knew drove him insane. "Running a little late this morning, aren't you?"

Cameron blushed. "A little."

"Oversleep?" Jennifer continued, pouring him a cup of coffee. "Claude still has some croissants in the back. Want to try one?"

"No, just coffee." *God is she ever beautiful,* he thought. The French apron was snug around her thin waist.

She sat across from him, smiling, thinking that he was a nice looking guy: rugged, cute, but in a boyish way. He wasn't very big, but he wasn't out of shape, either. His hair, light sandy-blond, combed back but spilled forward over his forehead. She liked the look, but she wasn't really too sure about him. She wasn't used to shy men.

"Going tonight?" She asked, her voice soft, her eyes batting, teasing him.

"Yes... Well." He struggled, looking for the right words. "I was wondering, if—"

"Spit it out, Yankee. I ain't got all day," Jennifer joked. She really enjoyed teasing him. Her inflection and accent made the words spill out in thick syllables that nearly made her laugh. Soft, with a song-like melody.

Winona stood behind him, making faces, kicking her feet and pretending she was shy.

"I was wondering if Mindy and I could join you tonight. You know." He hesitated, as if he was still looking for the right words. "Uh..."

"Yes, you may pick us up at four."

Cameron smiled. "Okay. Four. Sure. Yeah. Four is good." He stood up and backed toward the door, unsure of what else to say on his way out. He scratched his head and continued, "Good. Okay. Uh, see you at four."

Claude, Jess, and Marco were laughing and whistling in unison from the kitchen while Winona leaned against the counter howling in laughter.

When Cameron stepped outside and headed to the cruiser, Jennifer ran to the door and called out to him, "Cameron, could you do me a favor?"

His face turned serious as he thought, *Oh, God, here it is. The big let down.*

Jennifer joked, "Don't look so glum, Yankee." She smiled as she waited for him to calm down. "Would you go by and see Mahowee? He's upset about the celebration tonight."

"Something wrong?" Cameron asked, smiling, relieved but then tried to answer with a serious expression and manner. This woman really got under his skin and he had no way of getting himself under control.

"He said he isn't going and told me not to go, either. He has some crazy notion that something bad is going to happen. He's been telling everyone not to go, and is starting to upset everyone, especially the Mayor. He likes you, and..."

"Sure," Cameron said as if completing her sentence. "It will be my pleasure. I'll call you later and let you know."

She shook her head as she watched him back his way to the sedan, and then laughed as she closed, and this time locked, the door. "That man is as shy as a little kid," Jennifer said to Winona.

"And as lovable," Winona said as she tried to regain her composure.

"Go easy on him," said Marco as he walked out of the kitchen, drying his hands on a towel. "I like him. He would be good for you and Jasper."

"Oh, really," Jennifer replied. "And how would you know?"

"Any man who would raise a small child alone is a good man," Marco answered. "When I left Mexico, my heart weighed heavy until my family came to join me. Other's... Well... Others see it differently. He raised that child from birth by himself. That is someone you should really get to know."

Jennifer glanced out the window and watched as the cruiser hit the crest of the small hill and then disappeared. She smiled to herself. He was special. Different from any man she had ever met. Special.

Chapter 5.

While Cameron drove northeast on State Route 154, he thought of his deceased wife, Amanda. The pain, although fading after twelve years, gnawed at him from time to time and usually when he least expected it. She died so that Mindy could live. Complications during the birth had left him a widower to raise a newborn on his own. The first two or three years, although bad, were not as bad since he had to spend every waking moment taking care of Mindy and competing with the hours spent in an ER. Once Mindy was able to walk and close to actually feeding herself, Amanda's ghost would appear without warning, and it's still the same today.

He named Mindy after Amanda's nickname, Mindy, so that neither he nor his daughter would ever forget what a wonderful woman Amanda had been. He knew Amanda would approve of Jennifer, because, although they didn't look alike, they had the same survival spirit, and that was the real attraction. Jennifer was independent, reliant, and she put others before her own needs, which was something Amanda had always done.

"You'd like her, Amanda," Cameron said aloud as if Amanda were sitting next to him. "She has all of the same qualities you did, and I couldn't help but fall in love with her... please don't be mad at me, it's been twelve years, and although I still think of you, see you, and talk to you, I think you want me to move on and be happy." Of course, Amanda would never respond but Cameron honestly knew what her response would have been.

He came to a clearing totally out of character for Quentin; cattle ranching and farming filled most of the surrounding land, but this tract lay in a thick carpet of lush green grass with a cabin under twelve hundred square feet, which counted both front and back porch, sitting back about thirty yards from the roadway.

He turned right into the long gravel driveway and proceeded to the cabin that sat deep in a canopy of oak and pine trees. Their thick branches and boughs blocked the glare of the summer sun well enough so that the house felt cooler than most air-conditioned establishments. In the fall, Cameron and Mahowee trimmed away a lot of the clutter so that the cabin would capture the sun's heat during the winter.

He stopped, turned off the ignition, climbed out of the unmarked sedan, and stood by the door.

"Mahowee!" Cameron called out, admiring the natural beauty of the seven acres of land.

"Come, my friend," Mahowee replied in a deep accent. "What brings you here at this time of day?" He continued, walking out from behind the house.

"Came to see how you're doing, my friend," said Cameron with one of his famous smiles and manner, as he started up the flag stone walkway to the front porch.

"For a man reaching his seventy fifth birthday next month, I do well. Not like it was when I was your age, but I'm good, better than you are, my children are old enough to take care of themselves." Mahowee answered and strolled over to a line of azalea bushes and began slapping them with a thin, hand-carved paddle. "Too much standing water," Mahowee mumbled. He then looked at Cameron. "Too many trips to the bathroom at night, and my prostate is now the size of a Florida orange, but I'm okay. Much better than you'll be at my age."

"You said that already, or did you forget," Cameron said, shaking his head, laughing. "Alzheimer's, I'm sure. Do you even remember where the bathroom is or did you take a leak in the closet?" Cameron loved it when Mahowee rambled like this and the banter would go back and forth; it made the trips out here worth it.

Mahowee bent over to slap at another bush and his thick dark black hair fell forward, exposing deep streaks of gray. He then looked back and said, "Quit the laughing and goofing off and pour us a glass of lemonade while I tend to these," Mahowee continued seconds before his voice broke into a native chant.

Cameron walked up onto the porch, poured two glasses of lemonade, and sat down. Moisture squished from the plastic cushions, staining the legs of his cotton pants. Although somewhat cooler, a bead of sweat cascaded down his cheek and another down the middle of his back.

"Man, this humidity sucks," Cameron mumbled while watching Mahowee slap at the bushes. He loved this man like a father but he often wondered if he wasn't a sandwich short of a full picnic, and he couldn't figure out what he was doing. Cameron had never seen someone slapping at bushes as Mahowee was doing. "Why in the world are you slapping your bushes, surely they didn't keep you awake all night."

"Is this a social visit? Or are you here on business?" Mahowee asked.

"When have I ever been here on business?" Cameron asked, surprised.

Mahowee stopped for a moment, moved a thick branch, slapped it, and then continued onto the bush next to it.

Waves of heat rippled up from the asphalt road out past the yard. A Volvo station wagon drove north; its roar faded beyond the crest of the large pines. Moments later two Chevrolet pickups drove south.

"Well?" Cameron asked. That comment was unlike Mahowee and it bothered Cameron. Most of the people in Quentin thought Mahowee was a little odd, eccentric perhaps, but Cameron had liked him from the beginning. He had never met a real Native American Indian before. He felt foolish, but the novelty had never worn off. At first, he would visit him once every other week. Now it was two or three times a week, and then that didn't seem to be enough.

Mahowee glanced up. "You never grow tired of me. Why?"

"What the hell?" Cameron said, perplexed. "What kind of question is that?"

Mahowee smiled. "How is Mindy?"

"She's fine. What did you mean by that?"

"I'm babbling. I'm an old man. I'm allowed to babble," Mahowee finally answered and slapped another bush. Pausing as he saw an unusually large mosquito flutter by nervously. "Mother Earth is angry."

"About what?"

Mahowee turned, swept his hands in odd gestures. "Too much concrete. Too many bricks. Too many man-made lakes. Too much. Much too much." He stood still as if in a daze. "No marsh land to clean our water. Chemicals seeping into our rivers and streams." He paused. "Exhaust polluting our air." He looked at the mosquito that fluttered by. "Insects growing larger each year, developing their own defenses. New ones finding their way up from the South or from lands across the Oceans..." He continued with a list of activities that amazed even Cameron.

"Okay, now that you got that off of your chest, are you going to stay stuck in the sixties or are you going with us to the celebration tonight?" Cameron asked, hoping to get Mahowee to talk to him. When Mahowee rambled on in a negative mood like this, it seemed to last forever, and sometimes it got even worse.

Cameron glanced at his wristwatch hoping that 4:00 was just a few minutes away. It wasn't.

His fingers nervously tapped the metal arm of the chair and then on the slightly battered wooden table that stood between the two lawn chairs. Jennifer crept into his mind. She was beautiful. Full of life. He was nervous and anxious.

"No," Mahowee snapped, his anger now obvious, jerking Cameron from his brief reverie. "And neither should you."

"You're kidding. I thought you enjoyed it when the town got together?"

Mahowee slapped another branch with enough force that he broke a branch and the leaves of a healthy bush scattered across the yard. He mumbled a few choice curse words that he didn't want Cameron to hear, and then slapped another. He turned to Cameron. "Because Mother Earth is angry, that's why! A cleansing is about to begin and I don't want to be one of the chosen!"

Cameron gawked at him, perplexed, and needless to say, worried. He saw anger in Mahowee eyes, which was a first. The sharp creases near Mahowee's eyes and around his mouth appeared to deepen. His swarthy complexion looked like leather. He looked older now than he had just two days ago.

"Are you feeling okay? You're not sick, are you?" Cameron asked.

Mahowee laughed. His shoulders bounced slightly. He slapped another bush and stepped back as droplets of water flew as if trying to escape the impact. Larger mosquitoes danced away, out of reach.

"I am well. But I can tell by your face that you think I have gone crazy. But believe me, I haven't," said Mahowee, defending his mood and outburst.

Cameron laughed along with him. "Are you still smoking that evil weed?" Mahowee didn't answer and Cameron continued, "So, you gonna let go of the sixties and join us tonight?"

"No... and global warming is no laughing matter, doctor turned deputy," Mahowee said in a manner that should have told Cameron to shut up and let it go.

"Oh, damn," Cameron said in a near whisper.

When Mahowee still didn't answer Cameron changed the subject and asked, "When are we going to paint the trim around this place?"

"In the fall," Mahowee answered. "When the rains give way to pleasant winds."

Mahowee walked up to the porch, stopped when he reached the top step, and watched as Amy jogged by on her way back to town. He remarked slightly above a whisper, "She is a beautiful sight to see." He paused, smiling. "Every day she runs past here. Her beauty adds charm to an ugly world."

Cameron didn't understand that statement and wasn't sure if he should pursue it. Mahowee appeared to be in a rare, dark mood that he had not seen before, and honestly, he didn't know what to do.

"Have you given her an Indian name yet?" Cameron asked, hoping to change the mood.

Mahowee smiled, and then finally laughed and said, "You watch too much television, Mr. Nickels."

Cameron blushed. "Yeah. As a child, I suppose I did."

"Go home, Cameron... go home and take care of that beautiful daughter of yours... stay home tonight, Mr. Nickels. Mother Earth is very angry."

Chapter 6.

July 4. 2 P. M.

Jennifer drove her light blue Dodge Caravan into the parking lot of Talbert's Gas, Garage and Mini-Mart. A large Texaco sign stood on the corner and Bernard's official name was above the door. Although officially closed in honor of the day, Bernard left the doors to the garage opened for Jennifer's van.

Cans of Texaco oil lined the large window of the mini-mart. An old swimsuit calendar peeked out from behind a cataract haze in the far right corner near the garage.

Jennifer stepped out of the van and walked around it, opened the door, and helped Jasper out of his car seat. "Be good. Okay?" He giggled as she kissed him on the forehead before she put him down. "Stay out of Marlene's hair if she's busy."

Jasper smiled. He loved the mini-mart and ran there as fast as his little legs would carry him, hoping that Marlene would give him an ice cream, which she usually did. Whenever Jennifer came in, Marlene became an instant aunt, spoiling Jasper beyond his wildest dreams. When he walked out after a visit, he'd have lipstick on his cheek, ice cream on his shirt, a toy in his hand, and the silliest grin you'd ever seen on a little boy.

Bernard appeared from nowhere, smiled and didn't say a word as he opened the hood. He seemed to disappear inside the engine. For a large man, he certainly had a way of maneuvering his body around the tight space.

For what seemed an eternity to Jennifer, but only a few minutes to Bernard, she waited. "Just what I thought. Water pump is about to go. Can have her done, say... this time tomorrow." Bernard said seconds after poking his head out from under the hood.

Jennifer glanced around the parking lot, worried how she would be able to pay for the work.

"Don't worry, Jen. It's not going to cost you a dime," Bernard continued.

"Bernard. You can't—"

"Sure I can. I own the joint," interrupted Bernard with a smile and then he continued in his normal I care a lot about you manner and tone, "Get what you need out of the van and I'll take you home."

Jennifer blushed.

"You're the only person who has never taken advantage of me and has treated me like a human being," Bernard continued, "You don't honestly think I would ever charge you, do you?"

Jennifer didn't reply, she merely smiled an embarrassed smile. Not for one minute, would she ever use or take advantage of Bernard and she hoped he knew she never would. Jennifer never realized that it was she who had pulled Bernard into her family of friends. Before Jennifer and the Diner, Bernard struggled socially, and at times, financially. It was after he became a member of the breakfast club that people started going to his station. Soon word spread and he now had the most profitable station in Quentin and in some of the outlining areas. He knew, and owed her a debt of gratitude that he believed he would never be able to repay.

"Friends like you are truly hard to find," Bernard continued, his thick lips stretching into a wide, beaming smile.

Jennifer kissed him on the cheek, wondering what she would ever do without his friendship.

Chapter 7.

Chauncey sat on the front porch of his small, but quaint house, reading a book that his wife had given him on their thirtieth wedding anniversary; a leather-bound book filled with short love stories written by various unknown authors of that time.

He adored the short story collection as much as the German Lugers he had managed to hold on to all these years; semi-automatic pistols that he had taken off dead soldiers during one of their invasions near his family's vacation home in Boulogne, France before his parents were able to sneak across the English Channel into England. They were on holiday when the Germans struck and nearly did not make it back, but before they did, Chauncey grabbed as many weapons as he could carry and managed to hang onto three Lugers in perfect working condition. Of course, he hadn't fired the pistols in ten, maybe fifteen years, but he checked and cleaned them on a regular basis. Even more often than he read the short story collection. He hated the German people, almost as much as he hated Hitler and his SS. Even today, when he came upon a man dressed in black, a shiver would race up his spine, reminding him of the horrible German SS squads. He always thought, if the kids today knew what their Goth clothing and manner represented he knew they would shed that God-awful apparel. The Third Reich represented the Devil and the SS dressed in black represented death.

Tall, thin pines circled the house as if guarding it with their heavy boughs, blocking the summer sun that shone brightly over him.

Chauncey removed a pair reading glasses that he wore on the tip of his nose as he wiped away a tear with the handkerchief held in his liver-spotted hand. His arthritic joints appeared larger today due to the humidity and they burned mercilessly; pain that sometimes appeared far away and then would burn as if his hands were ablaze. Today the burn was much-much worse than he could ever recall. He flexed his fingers and grimaced. Oh, God how they hurt.

He missed those days with Jocelyn. He missed her dearly. Each time he read these stories it would bring back many amorous memories. Memories of two young lovers in love with each other and the world. She had been gone long enough that her ghost had finally faded away, but his precious long-term memory held the treasures he refused to give up. He no longer saw her sitting at the table in the morning but he held her hand often when he closed his eyes at night.

He had met Jocelyn in a bomb shelter during World War II. Hitler's Luftwaffe was pounding London, and life felt like it was nearing an end. Hidden deep in a far-darkened corner of the basement with her hands covering her ears and her eyes tightly closed, was a lovely woman of only sixteen. He was seventeen and fell madly in love with her on the spot. When the bombing finally stopped and the war came to an end, they were married and lived in Liverpool until he was offered a teaching position in the US. During a cross-country trip, Jocelyn fell in love with Texas. After months of searching for a quiet place to retire, they ended up in the house where he still lived. Yes, her ghost was gone but the trinkets, what-nots, furniture, and even her clothes were still where they were the day he returned home from the cemetery.

He wiped his eyes again, and sighed. He flipped to the next story with trembling hands, a story that he had read at least a hundred times. He read all of them repeatedly just to recapture those vivid memories.

He longed for those days.

He longed for his Jocelyn.

He wiped his eyes again, and when he made a fist, the arthritic pain jumped up his arm from holding the heavy book. He often thought about purchasing a bookstand when his monthly retirement and social security checks arrived, but usually found more worthwhile and much-needed things to spend his money on.

He glanced across the yard, smiling at his memories and the short stories as the humidity danced across the scarce lawn, and wondered when the humidity would break. He watched as a swarm of mosquitoes fluttered in and out of the dense foliage, which made him think of using, or at least taking, some bug spray with him tonight. Who knows, maybe all of the excitement would chase the bugs away but he didn't think so. Now if Jocelyn were here she would get right up and go get the bug spray and pack it into the basket before she'd forget. She was like that, always taking care of the little things, something he had never learned to do, even after all these years. Jocelyn took care of the little things, and he the larger, and today the little things would pile up until they became big things, but that was okay with him, little things were never important. Even the bug spray wasn't a big thing to him...

Drifting away from that thought, he looked down at the page and suddenly felt warm inside. A thick teardrop welled, and clung to his bottom eye-lid until the weight of the tear forced it in a thin stream down his cheeks.

He sighed as he finger-brushed the tear away.

The stories were about his Jocelyn.

He forgot his bug spray.

Chapter 8.

Brett Jackson stared out of the second floor computer room window of Quentin Telephone at a small clump of trees behind Talbert's Garage. His handsome reflection stared back at him but he didn't notice and couldn't have cared less; the trees had his full attention. He made a gesture as though he were holding a rifle in his strong hands, and then whispered, "POW—POW. Gotcha."

"What are you looking at?" Joan, the computer operator, asked as she looked out of the window; she noticed her lovely image staring back at her. She straightened her soft summer-cotton dress and then gently brushed back her short blond hair, stopping long enough to smooth out her lipstick.

"A dove," Brett answered. "Could have nailed her from here." He grinned. "And had her for supper tonight."

"Where?" Joan asked as she strained to see what Brett was looking at. "I don't see crap over there, Brett!"

"In those trees behind Bernie's garage," Brett answered.

She looked at Brett with amazement. "You have the eyesight of an Eagle, dude, and I bet the moment you step foot in those woods every animal within hearing distance runs the other way." Brett laughed. He liked Joan; she had a good sense of humor. "Well, I'm outta here, Hardware Man. The party has already started, and we're missing all the fun. It's bad enough we have to work on a holiday but I sure ain't working late. You coming?"

Brett loved the outdoors, and when he wasn't hunting, he was dreaming about it. His uncanny eyesight gave him an edge over most hunters he knew, and his marksmanship was the best in Quentin, and notably one of the best in east Texas. Although a quiet man, Brett's reputation had taken him to television shows and in magazines for his skilled marksmanship, and hunting and competition ability. He only hunted what he needed, but the joy of hunting far outweighed the bounty that resulted from it.

He ignored Joan's question about the celebration and looked back at the woods, and then in a volume that was meant for only him he mumbled, "Only better to see you with, my dear." Then, raising his voice, he replied, "Yep. Just let me put this computer back together."

He moved from the window and mumbled, "Just can't wait for hunting season. Better than sex..."

Joan stopped in her tracks and turned back to Brett. She could see it in his eyes, his hunting meant more to him than anything she could imagine.

"Later, gator," said Joan in the middle of laughing and shaking her head. She would drop everything for just one date with Brett but he acted as if he never even knew she existed. *Damn him.*

He watched Joan for a moment as she took two steps at a time down the stairs and then he looked back out the window, at the trees. The dove that sat on one of the branches was unaware that a bullet had its name on it. "Won't be long..."

Excited about the doves behind Talbert's, he hadn't thought much about tomorrow other than trudging through the woods, looking for game. As a hunter, Brett was more prepared than those serving in the armed forces on foreign soil; however, for a simple night of fireworks and fun, the thought of being prepared never crossed his mind.

Chapter 9.

Monica Parker sat and watched two of her third grade students stumble and finally fall over. The brown burlap sack was wrapped around them all the way up to their small chins. The cheering of the kids and parents made it virtually impossible to hear the two children cry out in pain and frustration, but not for Monica. Her large-boned frame raced toward them with the grace of a running back of the Dallas Cowboy football team. She quickly snatched up the two boys and then let them loose as they stumbled around, trying to catch up with the rest of stumbling, sack-wrapped kids.

She frowned. Then laughed. Strange mixed emotions overwhelmed her. They were hurt, but still having fun. Just what was an overly protective woman supposed to do?

She had never borne children of her own, but the children of Quentin had somehow become hers. Each and every child who attended her classes was silently adopted. The children, too, felt the same way. Love and respect flourished as they passed from childhood to adults.

She looked around the playing field engulfed in the large pines, which seemed out of place. Then she looked out over the small lake and wondered where a good seat would be to see the fireworks. She knew she would be welcomed on any porch or blanket she chose, but she always found it in her heart to look for the Professor. She didn't know why she liked the cretin, but she did.

A few people in town had even thought at one time, when Monica and Chauncey were younger, perhaps, that they had had an affair. But, that was utter nonsense. It was his keen intelligence that she admired. Besides, he was pushing eighty-five and that would make him nineteen years older than she was. Generally when they were together, other teachers joined them, talking about the education system and how it was falling apart, the violence, drugs, and so on in schools was making teaching a much harder job than it should be. It was a mutual respect between her, the professor, and other teachers. "Birds of a feather," she often quoted to her husband, Harold.

Harold didn't mind. He liked Chauncey, even though he had mentioned repeatedly, in jest, that it was the English who had started slavery. Chauncey would just laugh and say, "Go ahead, and blame it all on me. The Irish already have."

She had hoped Harold would have returned from his business trip by now. The sales commission of a new mainframe computer would surely help their budget and put them closer to the nest egg they needed for their retirement, which was only months away for Harold and one school year for her.

She missed Harold dearly when he was away on business. They had promised themselves that they would visit Africa, the land of their ancestors. It wasn't something that they needed to do; it was just on their bucket list. She finally would have a chance to visit the lands that she had read so much about, maybe even take the time to find the so-called village where her ancestors were from. Now, that would be a thrill, more than the thrill when she saw the famous freedom march with Doctor Martin Luther King, Jr.; a milestone that went into every letter she could write and every phone call she could make. Oh, yes, that Dr. King was a promise...

The chatter of her babies soon brought her attention back from her daydreaming. She smiled. Oh, how she loved her babies.

She slapped at the mosquitoes that were feasting on her legs.

Gosh, the mosquitoes are horrible, she thought, and slapped away another one.

Little did she know that Harold and her surviving schoolchildren would miss her dearly. Her name would be placed upon a memorial that would be erected on that fateful corner where she stood to see Dr. King make his speech. That would have made her as proud of her accomplishments as she was when she saw Dr. King.

She loved her babies.

Chapter 10.

Amy leaned out from behind a shower curtain bearing a southwestern design. The lean body of a triathlete glistened as she reached for one of the two towels hanging on the wooden towel rack next to the bathtub. The towels matched the shower curtain as well as the southwestern mosaic-like rug that lay on top of the soft-pink and white tiles.

Travis quickly grabbed the towel and stepped into the tub with her. "Here, let me wipe your back," he said as he moved behind her. He kissed her neck and then began gently wiping the drops from her shoulders.

She smiled, turned, and whispered, "What about my front, mister?"

Warm sunbeams slipped through the frosted glass window and sparkled across her shoulders, arms, and breasts. Her eyes glistened with excitement, and her mouth had that devilish grin that he loved so much. She had used that grin the night he asked her out on their first date. At the time he had no idea what that grin meant but over time he learned it was special, used only during exceptional moments. Oh, how he loved that grin.

He lovingly wiped the towel down her back, caressing her. He kissed her neck making her nipples firm and then he seductively wiped the towel across her firm buttocks.

"In time. Let's not rush it. You know what a perfectionist I am," Travis said in an excited but faint exhale. She was everything he wanted. Everything he needed. He could not believe someone like Amy even looked at him, let alone loved him. He'd return to an empty shell with no meaning if she ever left him, the same empty shell that she had cracked open and climbed inside as she brought life into his existence.

What Travis didn't know was that Amy needed him as much as he needed her. She knew it was Travis who had pulled her out of the dreaming forlornly of what could never be, and pointed her on the road to achieving her dream. It had been Travis' idea to start training for marathons. It was also Travis' idea to run the Boston Marathon, to win as many medals as she could to capture the attention of the Olympic Committee. Travis knew she could win; Amy just needed to have the same faith in herself as he had in her. An undying faith that he held for her and for God, and he knew his prayers had been answered when God gave him Amy. He had faith in their love, their friendship, and companionship, and if it took every penny and every ounce of energy he had, Amy would compete in the Olympics.

"Such a gentle man," she murmured seconds before releasing a pleasurable moan.

He slowly turned her around and gingerly wiped the towel across her face, a face he loved the moment he had seen it from across Brett's backyard when he nearly knocked over the picnic table just to get over to Brett to plead for an introduction to Amy. Travis had grabbed Brett by the arm and dragged him to the corner of Brett's house, wanting every detail, everything he knew about her, and he had threated Brett with a life of hunting seasons alone if Brett left anything out.

After composing himself from sidesplitting laughter, Brett had told Travis that Amy was single and had not really been looking for anyone. She was tired of self-centered men, especially the immature idiots she had dated in the past. After several minutes of badgering, Brett had taken Travis over and introduced him to Amy. And that's when he first saw the grin. When Brett left, he knew they would be dating before long; Brett knew Amy's grin and knew she was interested.

He patted her neck, and then her breasts.

He kissed her. "You're so beautiful," Travis softly whispered, kissing her again, and then kissing her breasts, suckling each as he dried small droplets from her stomach, sides, and hips.

"And you need glasses," said Amy in the middle of a moan.

He knelt down and began kissing her stomach while seductively drying away the water from her firm legs and thighs.

The soft scent of perfumed soap flushed throughout the room.

She moaned again as she gently pushed his head down.

He dropped the towel and began kissing her thighs, feeling her firm legs tremble from excitement. His tongue caressed the nicely trimmed red pubic hair of her vagina searching for its soft, warm entrance. Its sweet scent caressed his olfactory sense while his tongue tenderly caressed it.

She moaned when his tongue entered her.

Her hands grasped the sides of his head as she lay back against the tiled wall, trembling with excitement. She pulled him tighter, deeper in her. She moaned his name. Her body tensed. The louder the moans, the gentler his touch became, and he stayed until she climaxed.

He kissed his way up as he stood and then cautiously stepped from the tub. He picked her up, and carried her to the bedroom and gently laid her down on their queen-sized bed. The Santa Fe bedspread matched their drapes, which cast soft rainbow colors across the sand-colored walls. Lithographic posters of old Santa Fe glimmered in its warmth. The silver frames shone brightly back as they cast their own halo effect.

Soft music flowed from the clock radio that sat atop the large oak chest and filled the room with a romantic quality.

Her damp red hair stuck to her forehead. Droplets glistened across her eyebrows. Her nipples were erect as chill bumps of passion raced across her breasts.

She softly called to him.

He quickly removed his wet shoes and soaked pants, and crawled toward her. He kissed her legs, stomach, breasts, and neck, as he found his way to her full lips. He stopped briefly as he inhaled the sweet spicy aroma, and then kissed her passionately.

She held his hardness in her soft hand and caressed it, releasing deep moans as their passion swelled. She then softly murmured his name when she felt him lie on top of her, and caught her breath as he entered her. Then she shrieked as she felt his hardness and she climaxed in sudden waves.

"Such a wonderful lover," she moaned as tears of ecstasy, from her climax, sprang to her eyes. "Such a wonderful, wonderful lover."

Chapter 11.

Marco stood in the back parking lot of Jennifer's Diner, listening to Jess gloat about his tour during the 'Desert Conflicts' which was what Jess called the wars in the Middle East, and how they kicked ass.

Marco's rounded cheeks forced his eyes into small slits as he laughed the laugh that typically made everyone else laugh. His thick black hair fell across his forehead every time he bent forward.

It didn't matter to him what Jess really did over there. It was the stories that he had grown to like, which made him really like Jess. To Marco, Jess was good people, especially the way Jess looked after Jennifer. He himself treated Jennifer as if she were his daughter and, because Jess looked at her as a sister, Jess could do no wrong.

Jennifer treated everyone who worked in the diner like family and Marco took that to heart. It wasn't very long after he considered Jennifer as his family that she had become a godmother to his first granddaughter. It did not escape Marco's notice that Jennifer and little Jasper had melded into his family and become more than just welcomed guests, more than his employer, and friend.

Marco watched as Jess ran his hand across his short military-stubbed hair, bellowing the orders that had been aimed at him at one time or another. Marco couldn't quite figure out what Jess liked the most; being in the service or being chastised by some gunny-sergeant barking out orders. Marco really enjoyed the stories though, and the passion that Jess had when he blabbed about them.

Yes, Jess and Winona were good friends, friends who spent a lot of time with Marco and his family. Friends Marco could trust. He knew Jess would always be there for him. But, he also knew there was something special about Jess that Marco couldn't quite put his finger on and often wondered if Jess would be around long, especially if things didn't go well between him and Winona. He wasn't really concerned about it, however; he had seen the way they secretly looked at each other when they thought no one would notice. He knew that the relationship would grow unless something out of their control took one of them. He then wondered who Jess would hurt in the process.

Marco knew Jess was much more than he appeared. Still waters that ran very deep. No, Marco knew Jess was not the simpleton that Jess wanted everyone to think... nothing bad, or so he wanted to believe... but something worth hiding.

Claude pulled a fifth of Macallan's—the world's most expensive scotch whiskey—out from under the driver's seat of his Peugeot and poured a large dram into a Maxima Decorated Burgundy

Spiral Goblet. He may have been a drunk, but at least not a cheap one; that dram was probably more like ten drams and it probably cost somewhere in the neighborhood of three thousand dollars, his goblet about forty-five. His whiskey, expensive, and his Peugeot, the top of the line and ordered over the telephone from France, brand new. Although he had hit rock bottom and was drinking scotch, his taste never wavered, nor had he run out of funds to support his taste. Not only was Claude a world renowned chef, he was also a master at hiding his money, especially from his ex-wife.

"Salud," said Claude as he lifted the Maxima to them.

"I thought you quit drinking," Marco said to Claude, ignoring Jess' punch line and actually stepping forward as if he was going to knock the goblet from Claude's hand. Had Marco not known about Claude's expensive liquor collection he might have.

Claude let out a loud pathetic laugh. "You're joking, right? I used to be goddamned famous. Cooking for people who wouldn't set a foot in this god-forsaken town." His expression bore a mask of anger, hate, and resentment. "Now I sling cheap hamburgers with you two. I need more than whiskey to get my mind out of here."

Claude took a drink and slovenly wiped his arm across his mouth. "I came to Dallas," he slurred, "and goddamned people waited in line for my cuisine... and then that, that jealous bastard didn't like someone out-shinning him and he fucked me over... now I'm here..."

"But you promised Jennifer you would stop drinking and throwing your life away," Marco snapped in near broken English and Spanish. "She opened her heart and home to you."

Claude leaned against the hood of his Peugeot and mumbled from intoxication, cursing the older man in French. Although incredibly rare, Claude's face was at this moment flushed with guilt. He hated his life. Once he had been famous but now he was in Quentin. Quentin. Even the goddamned name reeked of failure, because of some jealous bastard who spread lies about him, he lived in this god-forsaken town. This place was like hell on earth. He should have let the government deport him. He should have gone back to France where he could get his life together, if only his ex-wife would eat shit and die...

Jess froze as if what Marco had said was law. He ran his hands down the front of his tee with 'Dicks Last Resort' emblazoned on his chest as if drying the palms of his hands. "Marco's right. You did promise. Now put that shit away or I'll kick your ass."

Claude glanced at the two men, wondering how in the world he had ended up here. With a Mexican, who still believed Texas belonged to Mexico, and an arrogant little man who 'thought' he had won the Gulf war on his own. He drank the goblet dry, tossed it in the passenger seat, and slid the bottle back where he had found it.

He slapped at the sting on the back of his neck and groaned, "Okay-okay. I'm going home. Pitiful chiens—typical Americans—a pain in my derrière." His French and English blended into long syllables of disgust as he cursed both men.

Marco looked at Jess and said, "I'm going to clean up, would you drive him home?" Jess nodded. "Gracias. I'll see you later, tonight, amigo," Marco finished, and cursed while walking to the back-door entrance.

He stopped and shook his head as he watched Jess help Claude into the back seat.

"Merde!" Claude shouted.

Chapter 12.

July 4, 3:30 P. M.

Jasper cried out a horrifying scream when he fell from the swing and slammed down onto the hard-packed dirt with a loud, near-bone shattering whump. Blood ran from his nose in a thick stream while at the same time a bloody abrasive knot on his forehead swelled and turned an ugly purplish-blue. It took a few minutes for the scream to reach a high-pitched wail because the impact had knocked the wind out of him.

As soon as Jennifer heard the scream, she banged out through the back screen door of the bungalow and raced across the ragged lawn as fast as her legs could move her. She grabbed Jasper and pulled him tightly into her arms, wiping the blood from his nose with the tail of her shirt while running back to the bungalow.

"Poor baby," Jennifer crooned. "You're okay. Just a small bump," she lied with tears welling, and tried hard not to upset Jasper any more than he already was. She knew more than half the time he cried was because of her reaction and not because he was hurt. There were times he would trip, hit the ground, and look to see if she was watching. If not, he would climb up and scramble on. If he saw that she was watching, he would let out one of his screams. But, today he was hurt and hurt badly and, to Jennifer, his nose and head looked severe enough to get him to the hospital.

She hurried into the shadowy kitchen, ran cold water on a dishrag, and carefully wiped the blood and dirt from his nose and face. If his poor little eyes weren't filled with so many tears he'd scream in horror from Jennifer's expression. She bit her lip as she held back more tears. Jasper looked as if he had broken his nose.

Jasper screamed out when she ran the rag across the knot that was just above his left eye, and she was taken aback when saw more blood pool up instantly. New tears welled and cascaded across his inflamed cheeks.

Oh, God, he hurt his head and nose, Jennifer thought, and now worried if he might have a concussion.

Abruptly the refrigerator rumbled as loud as Jasper did, as if it could feel the small boy's pain, causing her to jump, and then settled into a soft hum.

"It's okay, honey," Jennifer whispered, kissing him on the cheek, glancing at the old stained and scarred refrigerator and wondering when it would collapse into a pile of plastic and rusted steel. Just like with the van, she couldn't afford too many extra expenses. She wiped the dishrag across his forehead, carefully avoiding too much pressure on the welt but then lightly kissed it as if that might heal this wound. She didn't believe so and wondered if he'd need stitches, she then hoped not: stitches would most likely leave a scar.

"Let's me and you go see Doctor Jay. Okay?" she continued, doing what she could to calm him.

Jasper sniffed and nodded. His lips quivered seconds before new tears found their way to his cheeks followed by a whine. At least he wasn't screaming which made her feel a little better, maybe it wasn't as bad as she thought.

Not remembering that she didn't have her van, she darted to the door. When she opened it, to her surprise there stood Cameron and Mindy, smiling.

When Cameron caught a glimpse of the crimson shade that lingered beneath the child's nose and the nasty contusion on his forehead, he quickly got down on his knees and examined him.

"Why don't you and Mindy head out to the truck," said Cameron in a calm professional manner, as he tossed his keys to Jennifer. He never took his eyes off Jasper and lightly moved Jasper's head from side to side.

"Lift your head a little, buddy boy, and let me look at that nose of yours," Cameron continued. Jasper lifted his head. "Ooooh, did Marlene catch you taking two ice cream cones from the cooler." Jasper chuckled, shaking his head no, and Cameron touched his nose with such gentleness, Jasper never flinched. "Well, I think Doctor Jay is gonna want to put a cast on that nose."

"They don't put castesses on noses," Jasper said in a nasal and near sobbing tone.

"Hmmm. Lean in a little, pal, and let me see that bump," Cameron continued. Out front, the truck roared to life a minute or so after Jennifer and Mindy climbed in. "Yeah, that little, teeny tiny bump will need a cast, too."

"They don't put castesses on heads," Jasper continued, sniffing.

"Well. I bet Doc Jay is going to run out of suckers by the time he's done with you. Come on, let's get outside, and let your mom know you're doing much better. Okay?"

Jasper nodded when Cameron picked him up.

"Whew, Jaz, you're getting heavy. In a day or so I won't be able to carry you."

Jasper wasn't laughing but he wasn't crying either. He then laid his head on Cameron's shoulder.

Cameron then hurried to the truck. He called out to Mindy and pointed to the passenger door.

Mindy quickly scooted across the battered and faded vinyl bench-seat, and pulled the handle. She then shouldered the door open and scooted back toward Jennifer.

When Cameron and Jasper climbed into the truck, Jasper let out another wail that brought new tears to Jennifer's eyes.

While backing the truck out of the driveway, Cameron asked, "What happened?"

"H-He fell from his swing. For the love of God, I didn't even know he had snuck out," Jennifer murmured near tears.

A faint grin appeared on Cameron's face as he noticed the serious expression Mindy had painted on hers. At her age, she was just as concerned about Jasper as the two adults were. This made him feel proud, as proud as a parent could be.

Chapter 13.

The pickup rumbled and backfired when Jennifer slowed. She swung onto Parker Street, fishtailed, and then sped toward the emergency room entrance of Quentin Central Hospital. Never once did Cameron think that old Betsy would let him down. It never did during a crisis, and this was as much of a crisis as he had seen since arriving in Quentin.

The pickup screeched to a halt at the entrance as Jennifer opened the door and quickly jumped out. She ran around the truck and grabbed Jasper from Cameron's arms, then bolted through the emergency room doors in tears of panic and screamed for help.

"How come you didn't help him, dad?" asked Mindy in one of her I'm almost an adult tone.

"Dr. Jay is a good doctor. Jasper will be fine," Cameron answered. He wondered why he hadn't done more... he could have, wanted to, and the pull was there, but he was also afraid that pull would grow stronger and, before you know it, he'd end up as an ER doctor in the middle of another gang war. He couldn't do that. The last time scared the hell out of him knowing Mindy might be without a father.

"Are you sure he's going to be okay?" Mindy asked. As usual, her manner was soft and caring. In a crisis she had the same attitude and calmness that Cameron had, which was probably the only thing she had inherited from him.

"I believe so. I don't think his nose is broken but he'll need a couple stiches on that hard head of his, but I believe that will be the worst of it... We might miss the fireworks," Cameron answered, nodding, as he found a parking space for Betsy

Mindy smiled a smile of relief and continued, "That's okay. We can see them from Miss Peterson's porch, if she still wants to."

Beaming with pride, Cameron watched her out of the corner of his eye to make sure she was okay. If he approached her head on, she would most likely blush with embarrassment and then clam up, not wanting to express her concern. "That's why I love you so much. You're always thinking about everybody but yourself, and if Jennifer and Jasper are not up to it, then we'll wander on over to the fair grounds and lose some money trying to win a stuffed animal."

She blushed anyway. She didn't think the statement was true, but she felt proud to hear it. In time, she would look at Jasper as her little brother, and Jennifer as her mother, forever appreciating what they had together.

"Bernie said he thinks you're in more danger as a deputy than as a doctor," Mindy said as she jumped to the ground from the open door. "He said you could walk into the mini-mart in the middle of a hold up and be shot."

"And that's why Bernard is a mechanic and not the mayor. In Quentin I have a better chance of catching the measles as a doctor than being shot as a deputy, know what I mean," Cameron said but Mindy didn't answer. "The hardest part about this job is putting up with Mahowee's complaints when I give him a ticket for speeding with his trash cart."

"Recycle cart, dad. Mr. M doesn't collect trash, he collects recyclables," Mindy defended, laughing. "He's saving the planet—"

And in unison, they both said, "—one can at a time," and howled in laughter. Maybe Mindy did take a little more after him than he had thought.

Cameron reached down and took Mindy's hand as they walked toward the hospital entrance. "I bet you were a better doctor than Dr. Jay is before you were shot..." Mindy continued. "Captain Z said you were one of the best DC General had ever had."

Cameron really didn't want to debate what was safer. All he cared about was Mindy and her future. If he had one ounce of handyman talent, he'd be working as laborer somewhere instead of as a cop. But his handyman talents was just enough to change a light bulb, and one of the reasons the truck ran so poorly is he was a lousy mechanic but he doesn't want to spend the money to have someone else repair it, and like Jennifer, he didn't want to take advantage of Bernard's generosity.

"Well, Captain Zoller is a good cop but a lousy detective—," said Cameron laughing, as he reached over and started tickling her, "—otherwise he'd be a detective and not a captain."

Chapter 14.

July 4, 5 P. M.

The area surrounding Crystal Lake Resort looked overrun by the entire town of sixteen hundred people and their friends from the rest of Quentin. There were farmers and ranchers with their entire families, who had not been in town for months, wandering the grounds. Blankets, lawn chairs, and picnic tables dotted the sides of the lake, and the chatter blended in with the music of the high school marching band. Their rendition of the National Anthem brought joyful tears to the band instructor's eyes. Surely, there would be an abundance of congratulations and handshakes before the night was over, the instructor thought, grinning from ear to ear. The marching was limited, but the music flowed in perfect harmony sending goose bumps up and down his arms.

The loud music from the carnival rides that sat across from the restaurant flowed in sharp notes of various rock groups, competing for the airwaves that the high school band had already taken over. It agitated many of the people wandering the fair ground or setting up their own private picnic areas, but added to the thrill of the stomach wrenching rides, drowning out the screams and laughter from the kids riding them.

The narrow midway housed the carnival games with barkers shouting out the possible wealth that could be won for the investment of one or two small quarters. And as they barked, the quarters fell until the stuffed animals were had or the players were defeated and shuffled away in slight embarrassment; more walked away empty-handed than those who won even the smallest of trinkets.

Bernard paced back and forth, as he fought off the line of men who waited at the kissing booth. Although Jennifer was pretty, he didn't believe a man should desert his wife or girlfriend for a friendly kiss and wondered how many women were at least a little jealous, but of course after the expenses were paid, the remaining money would be donated to the hospital, but still... Of course, he secretly had a few one-dollar bills tucked in his pocket and he planned to spend all of them.

He cared very deeply for Jennifer, but not so much to have his heart broken. He felt that one day Jennifer and Cameron would be married and he would be left with only her friendship. His heart skipped a beat. Amorous feelings swept over him. To have someone like Jennifer would make his life complete.

"I'm afraid you're not going to be able to open the booth," Dr. Alexander Jeanerette said as he, Monica, and Chauncey strolled toward Bernard.

"Little Jasper had an accident, three stitches on the forehead, and I recommended that she keep the boy home tonight."

"Come on, Dr. J. Say it ain't so?" Bernard said in panic and a high-pitched wail. His chins bounced as his head turned in confusion. "She can't miss tonight. Look at all these people. What am I going to do?"

"I'm afraid it is so, Bernie. Jasper wasn't hurt too badly, mostly frightened, stitches will do that to a little one, but he doesn't need this excitement, either," Dr. Jeanerette continued. He was near the point of laughing and it took all he had to keep a straight face. "I'm sure you'll find someone else, Bernie, Quentin is not only famous for our town actress, Sissy, bless her heart, but there are hundreds of beautiful women in this town who would be happy to help. I'll bet you a couple of one dollar bills that there are more beautiful women here than in all of Hollywood."

"I might disagree with you there, doctor," Chauncey broke in. "That Salma Hayek and Halle Berry are quite the lookers."

"Careful, Professor, you're edging closer to a heart attack than you think," Monica said, laughing. "And if you drop dead here I'm just going to keep walking, acting like I don't know you."

Chauncey looked at Monica, then to Dr. Jeanerette, and just when he started to say something, Dr. Jeanerette interrupted, "Don't look at me, I didn't say anything."

"Come on, guys, this is serious," said Bernard as he turned away, looking out over Crystal Lake. "Now who am I going to get? This is our best booth. It nearly pays for the entire fireworks show. Between Jennifer not showing up and those damned mosquitoes, tonight will be hell!" He was heart-broken as he strode around, searching for a stand-in, surely, someone attractive would be interested. "Damn... Damn!"

Chapter 15.

The flow of residents continued in thick lines as they walked the carnival midway. Some bumping into one another as they stopped at one of the kiosk games. The music from the rides nearly blocked the noise from State Highway 37 where at least a third of the high school teenagers cruised, looking for friends. Their outcries, cheers, and whistles percolated across the busy road to where another third of the high school kids were sitting and waiting for the main event.

Overhead, dusk began giving away to night.

The sweet aroma of mesquite from six barbecue pits tempted the hungry and enveloped the entire area. The aroma of cotton candy and popcorn could be found wedged between or on top of counters as kids of various ages waited in lines for the sweet or salty indulgence.

The humidity was thick. So were the insects, the Anopheles mosquitos more so.

The temperature, although high, didn't seem to affect the crowd. Soft drinks and beer flowed in rivers to quench the thirst of the attendees.

In the middle of the line, Travis and Amy walked hand in hand like newlyweds, and while heading toward the Funhouse they giggled like school kids, stealing a kiss and laughing when they caught someone looking at them, especially if that someone had a foul expression. They couldn't help it; the relationship was like that from their second date, and if Travis had his way it would stay like that until the day he died. He hoped he would pass on before she did because that meant he would be with her for the rest of his life. With the age difference, the odds were in his favor, at least tonight. Tomorrow would be different.

Travis handed the attendant their tickets, and they hurried inside the Funhouse and found themselves stumbling into a dark corner. Giggling, Amy pulled Travis deeper into the nook and wrapped her arms around him. "I love you so much," Amy said. "You really, really complete me, big guy. You really do."

"And you complete me," Travis said, then bent and kissed her. He pulled her into his arms and if he had had his way, he'd never let her go until the carnies needed to tear the Funhouse down before moving on to the next town.

The music inside the darkened rooms blared in horrible static feedback. The shabby speakers crackled and shrieked, but they blended awkwardly with the horrified screams of the Funhouse customers as they banged into the black walls.

The howling of ghosts reverberated throughout the plywood building drowning out the hum of mosquitoes. The floor bounced up and down as the line continued snaking through the darkness.

Amy slapped away the mosquitoes from her legs; she should have listened to Travis and worn jeans instead of her favorite khaki fatigues shorts.

Chapter 16.

Brett grew tired of searching for Travis and Amy and knew they were off somewhere doing something a kid would do, something he used to do until he discovered hunting, more specifically, shooting.

He stood in front of the shooting gallery and watched as the small wooden ducks swam lazily by. One behind the other, disappearing down the left side only to reappear from the right. A good ole shooting gallery, which he loved; it was something he liked to do to surprise the huckster when he came upon the booth like a country boy who had never seen a shooting gallery.

Dressed in a black tee that showed off his chest and arms, tight fitting jeans, and boots from Justin's, he looked like he just came ambling in from a long day herding cattle.

He cradled the small .22 caliber rifle in his arms and caressed the trigger with his fingertip as if the quarry that continued its circular task was a challenge. He slowly took aim at the target and quickly unloaded the entire rifle in one fell swoop, hitting a duck with each round.

He glanced at the attendant, who, as usual, was amazed, and quipped, "My daddy always told me, never waste a bullet." He then pointed to a weathered Teddy Bear that hung above the line of ducks, he was sure Amy would love it; she was cute that way. As the attendant handed him the token prize, he dropped another dollar and waited for a new load.

He moved a toothpick from the left side of his mouth to the middle, flicked his tongue, making the toothpick bounce, and then moved it back to the left and raised the rifle and smiled.

He pulled the trigger with a bang, ting, bang, ting, bang, ting, until the rifle was spent, all the while smiling; maybe he'd get that doll for Joan, if he could find her in this crowd. Nothing slipped by his eyes and observation; he saw the way she was looking at him.

Perhaps he did have the best eyesight in Quentin.

Perhaps he was the best sharpshooter Quentin had ever seen.

Perhaps he would be surprised at how much he truly loved his marksmanship and eyesight.

Chapter 17.

The music from the carnival made it to Jennifer's screened-in porch like background white noise. The A-frame looked out over Crystal Lake and sat deep in the pines. Its rustic facade radiated warmth and beauty.

She found the place the first day she drove through Quentin. A pickup truck carrying a Home for Sale sign pulled in front of her from Talbert's and she thought, Why not? She followed the truck until it stopped directly in front of this house. When the driver stepped out of the pickup she—without thinking—screamed, "Sold." Three weeks later, she and Jasper sat on the porch and watched as two men fished from their small bateau.

She knew this was home. It just felt too good not to be home.

Jasper lay in Mindy's lap as she drank a Dr. Pepper, and when Jennifer wasn't looking, Mindy would sneak Jasper a sip. She just knew he was going to be her little brother one day and she looked forward to it. She and Jasper became friends immediately. The short two-foot boy, who usually shied away from total strangers, fell gently into her arms the day they met and they were immediately inseparable.

She lightly thumbed the bandage over his left eye and kissed the top of his head as she stood from the couch and stretched. She knew he was hurt but she also knew a good doctor was on the porch with them, her dad.

"Did everyone have enough to eat?" Cameron asked, breaking the comfortable silence.

Jasper smiled.

Mindy nodded.

Jennifer thought, *this is nice, really nice.*

"Well, I guess this apple pie is all mine then," Cameron joked as he held the pie close to his chest. "Yum!"

Then, in unison, Jennifer and Mindy attacked him. Both pulled at his arms, fighting for the pie that he held high above their heads. The pie safely made it to the wooden picnic table that he had dragged onto the porch, but they all fell to the floor in a solid mass as they wrestled with Cameron.

Jasper excitedly hollered from the couch while they rolled around shrieking in sudden outbreaks of laughter. From Jasper's view, he knew Cameron was winning.

After the playful romp, Mindy sliced a small wedge of pie for herself and Jasper, while Jennifer, still lying next to Cameron, kissed him and whispered, "Thank you."

"I still have nineteen more dollars," Cameron said, smiling.

"And I have nineteen more kisses, sir. But you'll have to go back to the end of the line," Jennifer answered, then elbowing him.

Mindy and Jasper giggled in unison.

Jennifer kissed him again.

Chapter 18.

July 4, 8:35 P. M.

Over the tops of the tallest pine trees, they watched as a sudden burst of colors exploded, illuminating the sky, silhouetting thick full branches that cluttered the ground view. The surrounding area helped in creating a peaceful ambiance to the flowery explosion above them.

It was breathtaking.

Red, white, and blue starbursts, quickly followed by sudden loud pops, made Jasper nearly jump off the wicker couch and race inside. Their colors floated down and then disappeared, leaving thin contrails that Jasper seemed to enjoy more than the fireworks themselves. Pleasant sounds of "ooh's" and "ah's" made their way to the porch; at least that was what Cameron imagined. He noticed people in swollen clumps, looking up, and some pointing while others just sat close to their families.

Lee Greenwood belted out God Bless the USA from the various portable radios tuned to KSCS, which was simulcasting the event.

That, too, was breathtaking. A rare sight back in Washington. He loved Quentin. He loved the fourth of July. He loved Jennifer.

As Cameron stared out over the trees, swarms of mosquitoes clung to the screen around the porch as if craving to come in, but then pushed away by a warm breeze that swept across the porch and back toward the lake where they had come from. Back to feast on the large crowd sitting in various pockets around it. Back to where they had emerged.

Cameron felt very comfortable on the old wicker couch, almost like being at home. He sat back with Mindy on his right leg, Jasper on his left, and Jennifer sitting closely beside him. Her soft shoulder pressed against his side. Her head rested on his shoulder. Her perfume wafted past his nose and the scent drove him crazy as he breathed in a light floral fragrance.

He was in heaven. Although he did feel sorry for Jasper for getting hurt, Cameron was as close to heaven as he could possibly get and still be alive. He could not have asked for a better evening.

Both Mindy and Jasper lay back against his chest, nearly asleep, as the fireworks continued bursting high above the trees.

Jennifer brushed a kiss across his ear.

Now he knew he would never get her out of his mind.

A faint, "You're not too bad for a Yankee," sank in lightly through the grand finale. A gentle, but sensuous kiss quickly followed.

Now he was sure.

Chapter 19.

Jennifer sat sleepily in her favorite booth at the diner and stared out toward the courthouse, daydreaming and wondering what she was going to do. She hated to admit it, but she had had a wonderful time last night. She was relieved that Jasper was better today, but confusion ran rampant. She really did not need another man in her life. Everything was beginning to fall into place. A man would just crowd her goals, taking her attention away from what she felt she really wanted, and what she thought she really needed. That was the way relationships were, and the women were the ones who typically gave up on their dream. They were the ones who switched the radio station to the station that the man listened to, the women typically handed over the remote, and the women stayed home and had kids while the husband became the lord and master. At least that was how her marriage had been, a disaster fewer than six months after they said, "I do", and became the worst time in her life. Then to make matters even worse, Cameron was a doctor—an ER doctor—and had given that up to be a deputy in a backwater town that did not really need more than two deputies, max. She could not make herself accept the fact that he walked away from a career in medicine. What did that make him...?

She played with the salt and pepper shakers, thinking. She picked up her glass of iced tea and felt someone standing next to her.

"Missed you last night," Bernard hissed in disappointment. "I had to talk Shauna Munson into running the kissing booth."

"Well, you couldn't have picked a prettier woman," Jennifer replied, still half in thought. She knew Bernard would be a little upset. The concession stands were his responsibility, but she didn't think he would be angry at her. It wasn't like him.

"Well, she is pretty," Bernard continued in a near-whisper. "But she has arms like a man." Jennifer snickered as Bernard continued louder, "She French kissed a couple guys." Jennifer roared in laughter as Bernard grew even louder, "It ain't funny."

"Why? I thought you liked her?" Jennifer replied still laughing. She stood up and followed Bernard to his table, and poured him a cup of coffee while he stared at the menu he had long ago memorized.

"She's okay. Spends too much time in the gym," he grumbled, trying to be angry, but Jennifer wasn't a person he could stay angry with.

"You're upset because she didn't French kiss you, Bernie, admit it," Chauncey barked. Monica slapped Chauncey's arm while Travis and Brett snickered. Winona, who usually took advantage of a situation like this, stayed silent. She really liked

Bernard, and although she teased him quite frequently, she would never hurt his feelings, and from where she was standing, Bernard's feelings were hurt.

"Am not, and my name is Bernard, not Bernie," Bernard complained as Jennifer left. She stopped and visited with the other members of her extended family as she walked back to her favorite booth.

Relaxed, Jennifer glanced around the diner. The smoke from Chauncey's pipe drifted up to the ceiling in a thin stream where it joined a pool of cigarette smoke from a couple at another table. Outlawed in nearly every establishment she had been to, but not here, and as long as her family smoked, she would allow it.

The clatter of dishes rang out from the kitchen. Jess appeared to be having a hard time with Claude, who seemed to be in rare form. She knew he had been drinking; his eyes portrayed the worst hangover she had ever witnessed.

The normal crowd tended to their usual morning routine; Monica and Chauncey were discussing politics, the education system, and how Bernard felt hurt because Shauna didn't French kiss him. Travis and Brett were discussing Brett's keen eyesight, and how Brett had cleaned out the shooting gallery's entire inventory of stuffed animals. He found Joan but she looked very cozy on a blanket with one of the programmers for Quentin Telephone and gave the stuffed animals to a couple kids that were hovering around Monica. He commented on how he did enjoy French kissing Shauna. So much so, that they would be going on a date tonight. Travis silently reminisced about the wonderful loving moment with Amy in the Funhouse.

Jennifer watched Marco clean the grill while Claude acted as if he had just fallen off the wagon. She didn't really know what she was going to do with him. The once famous chef stumbled, and she just didn't know how to help him back up. But, more importantly, what was she going to do about Cameron? Why in the world had she agreed to the 'family date' last night? Why didn't she just tell him after they left the hospital that Jasper was hurt and that he and Mindy should go alone?

Cameron came in and sat next to Bernard. "Have fun last night?"

Bernard smiled and replied, "Yes, except for the mosquitoes—look at my arms." Large welts of mosquito bites dotted both arms and his neck.

"And the wet ground," Chauncey interrupted, somewhat agitated. "But it was probably the best Fourth of July celebration we've had." He, too, had large welts on his neck and arms.

"The music was fantastic. We missed you," Monica continued, stirring her coffee seconds after she dropped four packets full of sugar in it. She glanced at Cameron with a playful smirk.

Cameron smiled sheepishly and then glanced around the room and froze as he realized that he was looking directly into Jennifer's wonderful blue eyes. He felt a spark, wondered, and then cast a shy grin.

Suddenly Jess shouted, "Amy's coming, what's the time Trav, what's the time?"

Travis stood and as Amy passed the large windows he shouted, "The same as yesterday, damn she's good."

Everyone in the diner stood up and cheered and, as they did, Amy seemed to run faster. She quickly bolted out of sight.

Travis sat down staring at the stopwatch and thinking about how much he loved her. He proudly said, "She's going to do it. She is really going to do it..."

After repeatedly scratching his armpit, Brett slapped Travis on the back and said, "Another claim to fame that will put Quentin, Texas on the map. I can see it now. Amy's name right beneath Sissy's."

Words of pride streamed together like soft ribbons as they each slowly sat down. The newest pride of Quentin had long disappeared around the corner.

Chapter 20.

July 18, 7 A. M.

The eighteenth of July didn't appear to be any different than its predecessors of hot, humid, wet days and nights. It had rained another three days straight. The humidity hovered in the high nineties and the temperature did the same. The Dallas TV weather forecasters were predicting a cool front that would move into north Texas, from the northwest, but it wouldn't arrive in Quentin for another two or three days.

The clatter in the diner appeared to be less than usual. Bernard had not been in for two days. Chauncey didn't seem to be himself, and Monica, well, Monica just seemed disappointed about something. Perhaps it was her husband, who was away on another business trip.

All of a sudden, Jess tripped over a box Claude had left in the aisle and Jess dropped a hand full of plates. In his own defense, Claude nervously squalled out at the top of his lungs and stood as if ready for a fight. Marco raced from the counter to step in between the two. Jennifer honestly felt that soon, perhaps too soon, there would be a fight between them and Claude would lose. What most didn't know, Jess held a black belt in karate and knew hand-to-hand combat better than anyone she had ever seen, and according to Winona, he did cage fighting before coming to Quentin.

She could not put her finger on it, but the entire morning seemed to be difficult and different. So different that Jennifer could not quite understand what was happening.

It wasn't unusual for Bernard to miss a couple of days, however, this was the second week in a row that he had missed his morning coffee, three eggs, bacon, and pancakes. Jennifer was truly concerned. Not only because he hadn't shown up at the diner for breakfast and lunch, but because his station was closed as well.

"What's wrong?" Cameron asked, breaking Jennifer from her trance.

Startled, Jennifer blurted, "Huh, what?" She glanced up at Cameron and was surprised to see him standing there in a freshly pressed white shirt and khaki-colored slacks. She hadn't heard him come in. "Oh, nothing. Does everything seem okay to you?" She asked.

"I'm not sure what you mean?" Cameron replied. He sat across from her and waited.

"I don't know..." Her words faltered. "I mean, where's Bernard? What's with Chauncey? Claude is being a real butt. And where are Amy and

Travis? I haven't seen Amy racing past the front windows for the last couple of days..."

Cameron didn't reply. He just glanced around the very thin crowd, thinking that perhaps the heat and humidity were keeping everyone at home. "I don't know. Maybe it's just the weather."

"Would you take me to Bernard's?"

"Sure. What do you expect to find?" Cameron said in a manner of concern, and really meant it.

"I don't know," Jennifer answered, her voice clearly upset.

Cameron stood, waved at Marco, and followed Jennifer out to the unmarked police sedan.

Outside, the humidity felt thick and heavy. Thick beads of water cascaded down the back of the cruiser's window.

The pine tree boughs shook from a heavy wind. Their needles appeared to droop from the weight of the humidity.

Cameron opened the door and watched as Jennifer silently angled herself into the passenger seat, and then closed the door with a heavy heart. He rounded the car, opened the door, climbed in, and sat next to her. The silence was horrible, almost devastating. Jennifer hadn't spoken to him very much at all since the night of the Fourth and, now, she sat next to him with her arms crossed in that defensive gesture. It all but drove him insane.

Thick dark angry clouds hung overhead.

Cameron started the engine, looked around, and then as he put the car into gear he asked, "Was it really that bad?"

Jennifer glanced at him but then looked away, and then muttered, "No, it was really that good. Please. Let's just go see Bernard."

"Are you frightened of me?"

"No," Jennifer answered in a sullen tone.

"Then what is it? I thought we had a wonderful time. I thought you had a wonderful time. I know I did. Mindy did, too..."

Jennifer didn't reply. She sat and stared out of the front window.

"If it's something I did, I wish you would tell me," Cameron continued, his voice soft and gentle. "I mean, Jesus," he rambled. "Mindy and I had a wonderful time," he found himself repeating, rambling, just trying to get Jennifer to tell him what was on her mind.

Jennifer sarcastically groaned, "I don't want to talk about it, now is not the right time, damn it. You're usually pretty quiet, so please keep it that way today, okay? Let's go see Bernard."

She thought to herself, *why did I do it? Why did I have such a wonderful time?*

She wanted to scream how she felt, but she also wanted to give in. She just did not need a man in her life. She glared out of the side window in anger at herself. Angry because this man, this wonderful man, stepped into her life just when she felt she didn't need one, and a policeman of all things, just like her macho ex-husband, a Sulphur Springs policeman.

Soon the criminals and creeps would get to Cameron, just as they had gotten to her ex, and he would need someone else to take it out on. The job would affect his judgment, and who knows, maybe Jasper would feel the impact. No, she just did not need another man in her life.

However, in truth, she wasn't sure if she would feel any different if he had been a doctor. No, she just did not need another man in her life. Not now. Not ever. Damn it...

In silence, Cameron eased the sedan away from the curb, taken slightly aback from the lack of traffic. The more he thought about it, the more he realized that the morning traffic was unusually light. So were the shops, the courthouse, and the promenade; it wasn't just the diner, it was all of Quentin.

He stammered in an uncontrollable manner so unlike him and blurted out, "I love you... and..." He paused, searching for the right words and let loose, "And if you'll marry me, I'll make you happy." He paused again, still searching. "I know I will. I know I can..." His words faded and embarrassment quickly came. *What the hell?* he screamed to himself.

Jennifer's gaze remained forward. Her silence seemed to be her answer. The answer that he really did not want to hear. The brutal silence was crushing him.

He thought to himself how stupid that really was, and how he must have sounded like an idiot. *What in the hell are you thinking, Cameron? You don't just blurt it out that you want to get married, you get down on a knee, or at least in the right atmosphere, and propose,* he thought.

The sun peaked out from behind the threatening clouds, burning the side of his already embarrassed face.

In time, and very soon, being in love will take a holiday. All words uttered will become less important and the memory even more so.

Chapter 21.

They drove south on State Highway 37 for two miles until Bernard's house came into view just below the last crest. The grass was over twelve inches tall and old newspapers cluttered the walkway that led to his front door. Overflowing with mail, the rural mailbox door lay open with mail and advertisements feathering down in the occasional breeze. His Jeep Cherokee station wagon was in the driveway parked behind his Mercedes, with both front windows down. Streams of water cascaded down the large back window from the heavy humidity.

They stopped in front of his house and sat for a moment. The car's air-conditioner blew chilled air across their faces and chests, cooling their blotted shirts.

Other than the hum of the air-conditioner, silence filled the car with a deafening apprehension; even the usually busy State Highway that cut through Quentin was silent.

"You don't think he's upset with me, do you?" Jennifer finally whispered in a sorrowful timbre. Her gaze frozen on Bernard's front door.

"What?" Cameron asked, confused. "Why would he be upset? He knew Jasper was hurt. Besides, he hasn't been to work, either, for the last several days. I'm sure he'll be glad we stopped by—"

Jennifer interrupted by opening the door, getting out, and slamming it shut. She bolted up the littered sidewalk, and then bounded up the steps to the front door.

She rang the doorbell and waited.

Nothing.

She could clearly hear the bell, but she didn't hear movement in the house. The silence was driving her crazy. Thick nails of fear stabbed at her. She rang the bell again, glanced back at Cameron with a worried gaze, and then began banging on the door and calling out Bernard's name.

"It's locked," Cameron said as he tried opening the door. He jiggled the knob as if by magic the door would open.

"Well, are you going to break it in, or am I going to have to do it?" Jennifer complained impatiently. Tears quickly filled her eyes. "Come on, Cameron, help me out here!"

Cameron stepped back and shoved the door. Two. Three. Four times until the frame finally gave way with a loud crack. The wooden trim around the door splintered in deep piercing agony. It happened so fast that Cameron was somewhat surprised that the door opened so easily. It was then Cameron noticed that Bernard never bothered to install a deadbolt lock.

Jennifer shoved him aside and screamed out Bernard's name. She stepped inside the house as lifeless as a tomb, and tendrils of fear clutched at her spine from the eerie darkness. She slowly walked into the living room.

She snapped on the table lamp closest to the door, which lit a small portion of the living room that failed to add hope to a desolate gloominess.

Plastic plates of leftover microwave frozen dinners were stacked on top of the coffee table beside tall empty glasses, none of which were prepared by Claude. A lifeless fifty-two inch television stood in the center of the wall surrounded by large speakers. Sitting on top of a DVD player, a VCR blinked 12:00.

Other than the coffee table, the living room was immaculate. Nothing was out of place. Nothing appeared missing. Nothing other than Bernard, that is.

She stood in the living room catching her breath as she expected the worst. Cameron stood behind her as if he expected her to turn and run.

"Maybe he's out of town," Cameron whispered as if he didn't want to surprise her. He could almost imagine her jumping out of her skin. She was at her wits-end and the last thing he wanted to do was cause her more worry.

He glanced at the oil paintings handed down from his parents. Their beauty jumped out at him. Bernard did not match the expensive taste reflected in this wonderful decor. Cameron had been to three, maybe four parties at Bernard's house, and each visit reminded him of the Smithsonian Museum. The expensive paintings and rare pottery were breathtaking. He often thought that Bernard should have installed a security system. But, as Bernard always chided, this is Quentin, not Dallas or Fort Worth.

Jennifer left the living room and went to the master bedroom that was off to the right. Even in the darkness, she noticed the soiled clothing on an otherwise neatly made bed. Their stains screamed out that an odd sickness happened here, something she, nor he, had ever seen.

She left the bedroom, ignoring the other two bedrooms and office, and crept toward the kitchen in fear. A faint glow from the window above the sink illuminated a room that made even Claude envious. Water dripped irritatingly from the faucet into a sink filled with dirty dishes. A half-full coffee decanter stared back at her in loneliness. A thin white film floated at the top. It, too, appeared not to have been touched in days.

She wiped away a tear from her cheek with the heel of her palm. She knew something was terribly wrong, because Bernard was fastidiously neat.

The kitchen clock ticked in rhythm to the water faucet that blended with the beat of her heart. She wondered *where is he?*

Cameron, still in the bedroom, glanced around as if investigating the scene of a crime, looking for evidence of intruders. He almost felt like he was in violation; invading the private life of his friend. *What if Bernard was just out of town and had told no one? An emergency, perhaps?*

He opened the closet door and quickly peered inside. Green khaki pants that Bernard wore to the garage hung stiffly from hangers still in plastic from the 'A Plus' Laundry. To the right were his white shirts with Talbert's embroidered on the left side above the pocket, and his name on the right.

Fourteen to fifteen expensive suits hung silently in the far right corner next to at least seven or eight sets of matching casual and sports outfits that Cameron couldn't recall ever having seen Bernard wear. Sweaters lined the top shelf. Six pairs of shoes surrounded the boots that he wore to the garage. Flawless perfection lay hidden within the friendly mechanic's wardrobe; the work boots were neatly placed in a shoebox.

He closed the closet door and stood next to the dark mahogany nightstand that matched the elegant bedroom furniture, which all appeared to be as expensive as that in the living room.

The deep colors of the furniture seemed to pull Cameron into its own depth. His reflection escaped the dark wood and fled into the light that snuck through the drapes.

He opened the top drawer of the nightstand and smiled when he saw Miss July smiling back at him. He closed the drawer and looked around again. Everything was in place, nothing seemed disturbed. Actually, nothing seemed to have been disturbed in quite some time; a thin layer of dust was beginning to build on the long dresser. Abandoned, the room cried of loneliness.

He glanced down to the thick white carpeting and felt a nervous chill as he noticed a dark stain, which matched the one on the soiled clothing left on the bed. The color, although dark, did not appear to be blood.

"Coffee?" Cameron softly asked himself, but he didn't believe so. What he believed sent a chill down his back. He knew something was amiss—he had seen this in the ER with patients suffering from a serious virus or other intestinal illnesses that typically took their lives—and wondered if Bernard lay dead somewhere in the house, and knew it would be a matter of time before someone found Bernard lying in his own excretion of death. He only hoped Jennifer would not be the one.

He turned and walked toward the kitchen.

Chapter 22.

"Are you okay?" Jess asked as he placed a soft kiss on Winona's cheek.

She turned, smiled, and returned his kiss. "Yes." She glanced around the parking lot of Jennifer's Diner and then down at Bernard Talbert's garage. "Do you think he's okay?"

Jess turned and followed her gaze to the garage and replied, "Yeah. Wouldn't surprise me if he gave Marlene a couple of weeks off and then went to one of those weight farms. You know the kind you go to, to lose weight real fast." He chuckled and continued, "He's probably lying beneath the weight bar, working on those pecs and dreaming of his hot cakes and eggs."

"I don't think he's really the type, do you?" said Winona in the midst of laughing.

"The weights, no, the hot cakes, oh, yeah," Jess replied, laughing. He paused for a moment and then continued, "But on the other hand, you didn't think I was your type, either."

Laughing, Winona joked, "You're not kidding. You're the whitest white person I have ever met.

And I still can't believe what's going on between us." She giggled, and then shrieked when he started tickling her. Her voice softened when he wrapped his large arms around her. "But I'll be honest, I've never been happier... You are my knight in shining armor and I never believed in fairy tales, well, except for the big bad wolf."

Jess ran his thumb across her lips, then caressed her cheek and then leaned in and kissed her long and deeply. He held her tightly, but gently, against him in a tight warm embrace, and then gently kissed her cheek and ear. "My mother really, really likes you," Jess said as he pulled back and looked her in the eyes, almost wishing he could climb into those eyes to see if they were as deep as they appeared to be.

"What about your father?" asked Winona as her manner and tone did a subtle change that no one but Jess would be able to see, which was one of the reasons she loved him; he knew her better than anyone she knew. She also knew that his father was a bigot and although he was a bigot to all races, she took it more to heart because of her love for Jess. She didn't want his father to ruin the relationship; her mother, a bigot as well, was bad enough, she didn't need outside influences that she couldn't control to add more stress to an already stressed relationship, placed on them by living in a small town like Quentin.

"He'll get used to it," Jess grated in annoyance. He stared up at the thick clouds thinking that he should say something before the moment was lost. He didn't care what his father, or anyone else for that matter, said or thought. The only thing he knew was that he had fallen in love with a wonderful woman, and like Jennifer, race just did not matter. What mattered to him was the perfect partner and Winona was the perfect partner. He had never met a woman who cared for him and his well-being as much as she did. She was nothing like the gold digging loser his father wanted him to marry. In between missions, Jess would land at the nearest beach and was forever searching for love, but as the song and cliché goes, he was looking for love in all the wrong places. It wasn't until he moved to Quentin to care for his ailing mother that he found happiness. Therefore, his father and Quentin could all kiss his ass and go to hell, and take a long walk into the lake; Winona was the one.

She kissed him. "My mother thinks we're crazy... but after what happened between Sonny and me, well... she doesn't think this can be any worse. I told you, she doesn't really trust white people very much. She thinks you're just after what's between my legs."

"She might be right," Jess said with a mischievous chuckle and then softly squeezed her into one of his playful bear hugs.

Winona spun around and slapped him playfully on the shoulder, and started to say something when suddenly he removed a small jewelry felt bag from his pocket.

"Want to get married?"

Winona, wide eyed, could not believe what she was seeing, or hearing for that matter. She stepped back and, as joyful tears sprang to her dark eyes, she reached for that precious little bag laced with gold thread.

"Understand, it ain't much, but I promise you one day it will be."

She opened the bag and stared at its contents in deep silence. Joyful tears welled and cascaded down her cheeks and over a wide beautiful smile. She looked up at him with her warm dark eyes and stayed silent as he stepped closer and kissed her again.

"I love you... And I don't want to be like Cameron and race around town like a sick puppy. You're too good of a woman to let slip away."

She was still silent. Her gaze never left the small bag that she held above Jess' back.

"I know me. I'll go cotton-picking crazy if I lose you."

She glanced at him, then back to the bag and grinned. "I take that back. After that remark, you're whiter than white."

"I'll take that as a yes," Jess quipped.

She kissed him and laid her head on his shoulder. "The town is going to go crazy. You know that, don't you?" She mumbled more to herself than to Jess.

"I guess that was a definite yes," said Jess, laughing, ignoring her remark all the while thinking *who cares.*

She squeezed him and mumbled, "Yes. That was a definite yes. Jennifer is going to go absolutely bananas ..."

Chapter 23.

Jennifer and Cameron stood in Bernard's kitchen for what felt like an eternity. Between the ticking of the clock and the irritating drip of the faucet, she thought she was going to go insane. She wanted to go running through the house, screaming out Bernard's name in hopes he'd poke his head out of one of the rooms and yell boo!

Although not fully educated and experienced as a deputy, Cameron continued thinking of the house as a possible crime scene. He took note of everything: the butcher-block counter supported five sets of antique salt and pepper shakers; each had a matching napkin dispenser and was valued at more money than Cameron made as a Deputy Sheriff in a year.

"This guy is something else. I don't think he's missed collecting any rare thing of value," Cameron said, admiring the collection but more so trying to lighten the mood. He understood Jennifer's fear but he also wanted her to relax before she spontaneously combusted.

His effort wasn't working as Jennifer glared at him thinking, *God, why doesn't he do something? He just stands around like it's nothing.*

Cameron looked at the dishes in and around the sink and, although they appeared perfectly normal, he began to feel that this was potentially a biohazard area more so than a crime scene. It reminded him of when he had done volunteer work for the infirmed who could not make it to a doctor or a hospital except by an ambulance. The deathly ill lived in the same manner. Even the smell of Bernard's house now reminded him of the homes he had visited.

"Diet?" Cameron asked as he picked up a plastic dish. Something maybe from 'Weight Watchers', Cameron didn't know what it was, but he knew it didn't resemble any frozen food dish he'd ever seen or used.

Jennifer nodded before looking around the room. "One of Claude's dishes," she almost whispered.

Cameron opened the refrigerator and, after a brief scan, closed it. He opened the cabinet door above the sink, then the door to the large pantry. "Things look almost okay to me. What do you think?"

The silence was overwhelming. He hadn't shared his thoughts with Jennifer about biohazard rather than crime scene so, she was still focused on finding Bernard and perhaps a killer. Cameron, too, was thinking of a killer, but not in human form.

"Something is definitely wrong. Bernard wouldn't have left his place like this to go off voluntarily, even if a friend from out of town had called and needed him," Jennifer said.

"Nothing is missing. He has paintings worth thousands, with antique collectables and electronic equipment probably worth at least half that. Other than the clothes on his bed and dishes in his sink and in the living room, everything seems perfectly normal. No one, other than us, has even a suspicion that he is *missing*."

She shot him an angry glare and left the kitchen. She crept down the dark empty hall that led to the master bedroom suite. Her fear accompanied her.

As she approached the bathroom door, she stopped and looked back toward the kitchen and then ahead into the living room. She glanced at a painting that depicted Ajax, the Mighty Greek Warrior committing suicide by falling onto his sword. The sorrowful face in the painting sent an unfamiliar chill through her. Although she had seen the painting numerous times, for the life of her, she couldn't remember its name. She could remember that it was a painting of a Greek warrior who had fought in the Trojan War. He had committed suicide because he was disappointed that he did not receive the credit he felt he deserved. She knew that it was worth more money than she would make in the next fifteen years. It hung conspicuously in full view of the living area. No alarms or security cameras. Cameron was right. With these priceless paintings, and expensive furniture and collectibles, a burglar could easily retire.

She pushed against the bathroom door, stopped and glanced back at Cameron, who seemed to be doing nothing. She almost wished he cared as much about Bernard as she did. This was her extended family, damn it. At least have the decency to care.

She pushed again on the door and finally pushed it completely open as she unleashed a horrifying scream that sounded throughout the house, and probably all the way out to the highway.

Cameron rounded the corner with his police issued Glock G22 drawn and then he froze as he saw Bernard lying on the floor. Quickly holstering the pistol, he carefully pushed the wide-eyed, mouth-agape, mute Jennifer aside as he stepped cautiously inside the bathroom.

Cameron knelt down next to Bernard and yelled back at Jennifer who was standing only a few feet behind them, "I've got a pulse. Call 911." As Jennifer raced for the telephone, Cameron lifted Bernard's torso off the floor and rested him against the tub.

"How's it going, Bud?" Cameron whispered sympathetically as he began scanning both Bernard and the small room for clues so he could reach back and slam the door to keep Jennifer out if it was, in fact, a biohazard area.

"I don't feel so good," Bernard whimpered, his greasy hair, which now appeared to be fully gray, stuck to his pale cheeks. His body shivered. He looked as though he had lost over a hundred and fifty pounds in nearly two weeks!

Cameron looked at Bernard's sagging face, disheveled body, and quivering blue lips, and asked, "How long have you been like this?"

"I don't know. Since Monday, I think. What day is it?" Bernard asked weakly. His chest rose and fell in faint gasps. Perspiration trickled down his sagging cheeks as he let loose deep heavy coughs wet with mucus. His eyes cast a faint ruddiness of death as they sat behind dark circles. His chest, stomach, and legs were marked with horrible bruise-like lesions.

The bathroom smelled of intestinal gas and feces. Cameron recalled the same stench from people found dying in their homes, most dying before they made it to his ER. He knew that Bernard, too, was dying.

Dark stains laced the rim of the toilet. Soiled magazines lay on both sides.

Jennifer came around the corner, sobbing. She grabbed Bernard's robe from the hook on the door and gently placed it over him. She then pulled a washcloth from the shelf, ran cold water from the sink and placed the wet cloth on Bernard's forehead.

"I knew you would be here," Bernard mumbled in a raspy voice as he looked up at Jennifer. His voice faltered in heavy gasps and weak coughs as he strained for air. "If anyone would—" He coughed again. "—it would be Jennifer." He began trembling, tears welled as he sobbed, "I'm scared, Cam... I'm really scared."

"You'll be okay," Jennifer cooed. For an instant, she felt as if she were talking to Jasper. "I missed you... We've missed you..."

Sirens blared faintly in the background.

Bernard glanced at Cameron. "Take good care of her. Will you?" He coughed. "S-She's the best friend I've ever had."

"Bernard!" Jennifer screamed out in dismay. "Don't talk like that!"

His breath came in wet heavy gasps. His entire body shivered in horrible trembles. He began coughing in uncontrollable, painful wails as he spat mucus between each hack.

"And just where do you think you're going?" Cameron tried to joke as he bit his lip. Tears formed at the corners of his eyes as he stared down at Bernard.

Bernard was too exhausted to laugh. He held his stomach and cried out in a sudden burst of pain.

Jennifer wiped the damp cloth across his forehead again, whispering to Cameron, "Do something, damn it".

Bernard shuttered as if chilled.

Cameron surveyed the room. A dark ring circled the bathtub. The shower curtain lay crumpled near the drain. Watery feces had collected in a dank puddle in front of the drain. He looked at Jennifer, sighed, and shook his head in an almost imperceptible nod.

"Come on, Bud. You hang in there. Help is on the way," Cameron said as he tried to make Bernard a little more comfortable.

Jennifer trembled as she silently wept.

Cameron dry-washed his face, the same gesture as when he had seen a patient die on his watch at DC General hospital. The memory of the gunfight slammed into him and he sat back on his haunches.

The warble of sirens sounded closer.

Heavy gasps escaped Bernard's lungs as he fought to hang on to every word that Cameron said, "Stay with me, Bernie, stay with me..."

Bernard collapsed and his limp body fell into Cameron's arms.

Cameron wept as he thought, *this is surely one of God's darkest moments.*

Chapter 24.

Blue and crimson lights blinked through the window shades and cast a macabre glow against the immaculate walls of Bernard's living room. The large paintings adorning the living room looked bloody and bruised as if they, too, were dying.

Deputy Anderson alternately wrote in his notebook and chewed his fingernails as Cameron described what he and Jennifer had found. Nausea crept through his thin frame as he watched the EMS medics tend to a man who had been his friend since elementary school.

He looked at Bernard lying on the stretcher, barely breathing, as the EMS medics placed an oxygen mask over his pale-blue lips. He watched as a thick stream of mucus and saliva spilled down the sides of Bernard's cheeks as his eyes rolled back.

He's going to die, Anderson thought. *He's going to die.*

Jennifer wept and tears sprang to Anderson's eyes mere seconds before he wiped them away with the fingers of his right hand.

She couldn't handle watching Bernard suffer like this. What happened? How could someone get so sick so fast and lose so much weight? What was going on? How could he be healthy one minute, then be in a near-death condition, the next?

Chapter 25.

The ride to Quentin Central Hospital was unbelievably tense. Jennifer could not stop thinking about the way Bernard looked, his complexion pale, and his body weak and sprawled across the bathroom floor. A foul discharge lay between his legs. The whites of his eyes gazed up at them.

"He's lost at least one-hundred pounds in two weeks," Jennifer mumbled. She wiped her eyes with a tissue, then blew her nose. "What's wrong with him?" She continued, more so to herself.

Cameron glanced at her and then at the EMS van in front of them. He was just as concerned as Jennifer was but he had no answers. He didn't know what to say. He wanted to say something, anything, just to see if he could ease her pain and her mind, maybe comfort her at least a little, but he knew no matter what he said it wouldn't help, especially if things go the way he thought they were about to with Bernard.

The ambulance quickly whipped into the circle driveway in front of the emergency room entrance. Cameron did the same. They darted from the cruiser and made it to Bernard's side in time to enter the emergency room with him.

Cameron and Jennifer suddenly stopped in unison, bumping into each other, completely surprised by what they were witnessing. The small, twelve-chaired emergency waiting room was packed with people. Every chair taken, and a line had formed from the emergency admittance desk to the door. Cameron had never seen the waiting room so full; he had never seen the hospital so busy. The most he had ever seen at one time were the families of two kids who had nearly drowned. They had been in the middle of Lake Quentin when their boat capsized.

In the background, an admittance clerk spoke quietly but frantically to a young couple whose baby was as sick as Bernard. The small hospital had reached its annual limit of pro bono cases yesterday and now needed proof of insurance or the baby would have to be seen in Dallas.

Their cries of poverty claimed that they had insurance and were sure it would cover this sickness, but the clerk only continued to defend that the hospital could not afford another charity case.

Moans echoed eerily in the halls, the sources not seen. The squeaks of rubber soles rushed here and there in an otherwise cold, but hurried environment. Then the horror of a mother's scream dwarfed everything and filled the emergency room with sheer terror.

As Jennifer looked in disbelief around the emergency entrance, she saw the fresh stains of blood and stool on the antique-white walls. She realized there was a foul odor so strong Cameron had to cover his mouth and nose.

Cameron looked over to Jennifer and winced, she looked pale as if she were going to faint. He moved close and put his arm around her, trying to steady her when she fell against him as if exhausted, as if she were going to collapse. Every muscle in her body was tense as her tired and shocked mind processed the scene. Fight or flight? Was this contagious? Airborne? Could it find its way to her house and into Jasper? New tears sprang to her eyes as panic set in.

The EMS medics rolled Bernard into the small three-bed emergency room as Dr. Jeanerette hurried in behind them.

When Jennifer rushed to the glass wall, she watched the EMS team lift Bernard onto another bed, jerking the gurney from under him and sending it out into the center of the room. The gurney slammed into a wall as if announcing the foul discharge released from Bernard's bowels in a dark watery stream. The discharged splattered across the room. Bile rose to her throat and she gagged as if getting sick.

New screams echoed the halls.

Sickly moans quickly followed and they drowned the cry that escaped from Bernard's parched throat.

Jennifer stood by the window while Dr. Jeanerette and a nurse examined Bernard; muted behind the glass and beneath the screams, their murmurs confirmed her fears. Their mood exemplified the loss of a good friend.

Chapter 26.

July 20, 7 A. M.

Jennifer paced in front of the emergency entrance, trembling. It seemed like forever since Dr. Jeanerette examined Bernard. She shrank as Cameron wrapped his arms around her, gently hugging her. She fell into his arms again as if he could protect her from this or any other horrible event.

"I'm sure he'll be okay," Cameron whispered the lie, wanting so much to tell her the truth; that Bernard was dying. "From what I hear, Jeanerette is one of the best," he lied again, because he knew there wasn't a doctor good enough to save Bernard in this late stage.

Off in the distance, the roar of traffic released a ghostly rumble.

A thick, cloudy shadow crept along the sidewalk. Ripples of heat jumped from the black tarmac.

The small town seemed even smaller now.

"He's dying," Jennifer whimpered. "Bernard is dying."

Their pacing came to a halt as the doctor walked out, his blue scrub gown covered in Bernard's discharge. Had he known what he was dealing with he would have burned the gown the moment he left the ER.

He shook his head sorrowfully and they knew that Bernard had died.

Jennifer dropped against Cameron's shoulder, sobbing, as the doctor spoke to Cameron.

"We need help," Jeanerette said directly to Cameron. "We started seeing this yesterday and now, well you see what's going on in there," Dr. Jeanerette confided. "With what I can tell from the blood work, they're dying from Cryptosporidiosis—"

"Crypto—what?" Jennifer blurted.

"It's an intestinal disease caused by a protozoan," Cameron answered." It's usually found in livestock, farm animals. Dogs. Cats. Just about any animal, I believe." He paused as if he could not believe what he was saying. "Generally from their feces. It causes cholera-like symptoms."

"Basically, he died from severe dehydration and diarrhea," Dr. Jeanerette interjected. He paused as if he had more to say, but then waited for Cameron or Jennifer to say something. He knew there would be a thousand questions, none of which he'd be able to answer but at least he could let them express their pain before darting back inside to the next patient.

"Animals? The only way he could possibly come into contact with an animal would be if a customer had brought it to his garage. He was allergic to dogs and never owned a cat," Jennifer rambled, her expression showing a world of confusion.

Dr. Jeanerette shrugged and shook his head.

Jennifer looked up through red eyes. "How?"

He shrugged as he searched for words that would comfort her, she was like a daughter, one he never had, but couldn't bring himself to hurt her and finally said, "I'm so sorry... I'll know more when the autopsy is complete..." He paused and cleared his throat. "I, uh, I called his mother in Dallas, she's on her way. The poor woman was devastated."

Jennifer leaned against Cameron while the doctor came to an awkward close as if this were his first day out of med school. He then turned and left for the emergency room. What was happening to her friends, her extended family? Everyone she knew was acting strangely. Everyone.

They walked back to the car in silence. The death of Bernard weighed heavy on Jennifer's shoulders. The fear of what might happen to Jasper terrified her.

Although not even remotely close to being insensitive or selfish, the heavier weight on Cameron's mind at this moment was the potential death of his relationship with Jennifer.

Chapter 27.

Cameron's entire body hid beneath the hood of his Ford F150 pickup truck, something he learned watching Bernard. He jiggled the spark plug wires and then toyed with the carburetor. Finally, he waved his hand around the side of the hood and waited for Mindy to key the ignition.

The truck sputtered. Then backfired. Thick black smoke billowed from the engine. He jumped away from the truck, and with timid steps, went forward again only when he was sure the engine or anything beneath it wasn't on fire or about to explode

Cameron arched his eyebrow in disbelief as the engine rumbled for a minute or two then idled calmly. To him, the damned thing was close to purring.

Mindy stepped out of the truck, and for one brief moment, looked exactly like her mother. Her thick auburn hair rolled down her shoulders and fell across her soft green eyes. If Mindy grew up to be as enchanting as her mother had been, she would be lovelier than most women Cameron had ever seen, and that thought scared the hell out of him. It wouldn't be long before the boys would be hanging around, and if any of them were like he had been at that age, he'd have to make sure they knew he carried a gun.

Mindy asked, "Tell me again why you're saving all your money?" She had already inherited her mother's attitude and wit.

"To send you to college. Why?" Cameron answered with one of his silly smiles, his face black from the smoke, and his clothes soaked from the burst of rain.

She giggled from the corny smile and then laughed as drops from his hair cascaded in a sooty trail across his nose. "Because I think you should buy a new truck."

Cameron slammed the hood closed and then wiped the rag across his face. "No can do, little lady. Your education is much more important than a vehicle—"

"Not if I can't get there," Mindy chided, quickly turning into a human ball when Cameron began tickling her. She was growing more like her mother every day.

He picked her up, kissed her on the cheek, and then ran his greasy hand across her face. She screamed out as he tossed her onto his shoulder, tickling her as he ran inside, jumping up and down before bolting up the steps. He put her down and she fell to the floor laughing. He then he went to the bathroom and turned on the faucet. In a burst, he howled in laughter when he saw his reflection in the mirror above the sink.

She stood by the door giggling, watching while he wiped his face. Clearly, Mindy adored her father and she worried that he was passing up an opportunity to, again, have a family. "What happened between you and Miss Peterson?" Mindy asked after she caught her breath.

"I'm not really sure," Cameron answered. He knew this was going to be one of those adult conversations that he had had many times with Mindy and that saying nothing was going to aggravate her. He loved her dearly, but sometimes she just seemed to be a little older than she should be. "I think she just doesn't want to get serious."

"Why not?" Mindy continued, trying her best to prod him along. She was definitely like her mother.

Cameron paused, thinking in earnest. "Well... I don't really know for sure. The only thing I know is that everything was going just great until I told her I loved her," he answered in honesty. "I suppose she doesn't want to get married and, well..."

"And well, what?" Mindy continued as a slight grin emerged.

"And, well, it's time for you to take a shower. We're already late."

"Please?"

"I take it you don't want to go to camp today, huh?"

"It's not that. I'm just worried about you."

"You're much too young to be worrying about me, young lady. Now hit the shower."

Mindy turned and walked toward her bedroom. She stopped at the door, turned back, and asked, "Does she love you?"

"That, you'll have to ask her one day," Cameron answered in an exhausted manner as if he were too tired to broach the subject with Jennifer. Who knows, maybe she liked dating Cameron but didn't love him, especially enough to want to marry him.

Mindy looked back at him and blurted, "How can I? You keep sending me to that stupid camp," then quickly shut the door.

On the other side of the door, Cameron heard Mindy laughing and laughed along with her. He shook his head and then walked into the kitchen. He willed the telephone to ring as he poured himself a cup of coffee and sat at the small kitchen table, wondering if Jennifer was sitting in her booth. He could visualize her sitting there, smiling. The sun is peaking through the window, highlighting her freckles. Damn, he loved those freckles.

He looked around the kitchen, thinking about the ugly rental furniture in the ugly rented house and he sighed. He hated it. Rental houses and rental furniture were two things in his life that he didn't think he would ever resort to again. He and Amanda had started their marriage together in a furnished apartment when he had graduated from med school and into his residency; however, now he believed that saving his money was the best thing he could do for Mindy's future. If something ever happened to him, he wanted to make sure Mindy was well taken care of. When he was in the hospital, near death, the only one he thought about was Mindy. What would happen to her if he died? Who would take care of her? His parents, bless their hearts, were really too old. His brother had four children of his own, and he hadn't spoken with his sister in over five years. Actually, he really didn't even know where his sister lived these days. Somewhere in France, he believed. The French hated Americans and he knew Mindy would hate it there.

He looked around the sparse kitchen, and mumbled as if trying to convince himself, "It's not really that bad." Without realizing it, he was fingering the scars on his chest. "Pretty nice actually. Comfortable."

The image of the social worker who had visited him twice in the hospital and then every week at home for three months came to mind. An otherwise sweet woman who wanted to take his little girl away, as she repeatedly said in a shrill voice, *it is for her own good, Dr. Nickels. What happens if you get upset and everything concerning the shooting comes rushing back, and you murder the poor child?*

He could see her too-large nose and dark-black eyes, watching him like a raven over her steno pad, as if he were a criminal and she ready to devour him. She constantly scribbled notes into her pad as if she were his biographer or maybe his stenographer.

He loathed that woman.

I'm going to keep a close eye on you, Dr. Nickels. The first time you get angry, upset, or belligerent, I'm taking her away. It is for her own good, she echoed. Those words sent chills down his back and he remembered them as if the bitch had said them yesterday. In his dreams, he saw his hands around her throat, watching as the racing pulse slowed and slowed until it nearly stopped. He'd then let her go, just long enough to do it again. In the morning he'd sit with his coffee trying to analyze that dream and came to the same conclusion – he hated the bitch.

The sound of the shower brought him back from the frightening memories and, for the first time, he realized how lucky he was to have moved away from Washington. Sure, things weren't going well with Jennifer, but at least he still had Mindy. She was healthy, her grades were good and, like her mother, she had spunk and ambition.

He smiled at the thought and then poured himself another cup of coffee.

His baby girl was growing into a young woman, *and she was healthy.*

Chapter 28.

Monica looked up at Chauncey with puzzlement. "I don't think I'm voting Democrat this year," she blurted unexpectedly. Chauncey didn't reply. Her statement was confusing. "I sure ain't voting for that no good Ronnie Reagan."

Chauncey, through the shuttering tic, starred at Monica for almost a solid minute, trying to understand what she was saying. *What is wrong with her*, he thought. Her diction, typically perfect, as an example for her students, was suddenly gone and she had resorted to slang.

"Monica," Chauncey whispered in a thick English accent. "Reagan wasn't a Democrat and he is not running for office."

Monica swatted at him in jest. "I don't care. I ain't voting for him. Look what he had gone and done to welfare."

"Monica," Chauncey blurted in a loud panicky whisper, then, "Jennifer!" Chauncey called out, turning toward Jennifer's booth.

Across the room, Jennifer and Winona glanced up but then went back to their conversation, talking, wondering aloud what each would do once the bank took the diner, but then Jennifer looked back at Chauncey and slowly angled herself from the booth. Close behind her, Winona stood as well.

Monica looked around the room in confusion. "I'll sure be glad when summer finally gets here. This cold weather bout got on my nerves, you know what I'm saying. I'm jus chilled to the bone..." She rubbed her arms, warming herself. Chills ran the length of both of them. She then sipped her coffee and ran her arm across her lips before putting the cup down. "Them democrats don't like black folks, just ask Martin Luther what them Kennedy brothers did for us. They ain't done shit but chased after all that Hollywood pussy as though that was the only thing that mattered in this country. Damn rich white folks."

Chauncey jumped up from the table like he was going to run away, then he stumbled back and knocked over the chair in which he had been sitting. He grabbed the table, catching himself, this time screaming out Jennifer's name in a volume that expressed sheer terror.

In a panic, Jennifer and Winona bolted toward the table.

"What is it?" Winona called out, "What's wrong?" Jennifer shouted, as though they were rehearsing a part for a movie. They moved in unison across the room, coming up on Chauncey as if he were the one in trouble.

Chauncey looked down at Monica, who by now looked lost and confused. She glanced around the room as though it finally dawned on her where she was, and said, "Dr. Martin Luther King should be coming by shortly. I better go home and get ready."

Jennifer and Winona stood next to Chauncey. Chills raced across Jennifer's forehead as Winona covered her mouth, stifling a scream. Neither woman could speak.

"What?" Monica asked, looking at Jennifer and Winona's expressions.

Chauncey, his eyes shimmering with tears, stammered in heartfelt concern and worry, "A-Are you okay?" His arthritic hands trembled uncontrollably as he tried to reach out and touch his dear friend.

Monica looked at Chauncey for a long few seconds, then over to Jennifer, and then finally to Winona, and shrugged as if she didn't have any idea what they were asking. "I've never felt better—well, my health is okay—it's—what's his name—Bernard that I am worrying about. His heart you know. He weighs too much. He'll have a heart attack before he's thirty-five."

She took another sip of her coffee and grimaced. She looked around the room, then at her wrist as if she were wearing a watch; "You old coot, you better get that narrow ass of yours home before Jocelyn thinks you're up to something," Monica said laughing, looking at Chauncey as if looking at a bad boy.

She kept laughing as she picked up her purse and slipped it up to her shoulder. "I just can't believe them Kennedy boys..." she said, shaking her head, and continued with a "tisk, tisk, tisk..."

She left the table in silence and walked to the cash register. At the counter, she dug through her purse, exhuming her change purse and then one quarter from inside. She gently placed the quarter on the counter and waited for a moment without saying a word as though she were expecting change.

Winona silently stared at her, perplexed, and before she could speak, Monica said, "You can keep the change, sweetie."

Stunned, Winona didn't know what to say, she could only stare at Monica and the quarter, hoping someone would come to the counter and rescue her.

"It won't be long before Dr. Martin Luther King gets here, sweetie—are you going to the march?—I better go home and get ready. I sure don't want such a good looking man seeing me in my pajamas," and without waiting for an answer she turned and left.

Silence followed as everyone stared at their favorite teacher.

Chapter 29.

The ride to summer camp was not without a blistering conversation. Whenever Cameron tried to avoid talking about something, Mindy was relentless in getting him to open up. A dentist with a terrified patient needing a painful extraction would be in awe of her tactics.

Cameron tried his best to answer each and every question in detail as Mindy threw them at him, knowing that if she wasn't happy with his answer she'd dog him until he caved. He often wondered if she had inherited all of her mother's genes and almost none of his; even as a doctor and then a deputy he had never interrogated anyone as hard as Mindy did him, of course being a deputy in Quentin he not once had the opportunity to interrogate anyone and wondered if he could. Mindy looked, acted, and often spoke like her mother, and even carried her mother's middle name, so it didn't surprise him that she was growing up and turning into the woman he had hoped she would. The only thing he continued to hope for, and often spoke to *God* about, was that Mindy would stay on course. It would kill him if she veered off.

He glanced at his wristwatch and mumbled, "Late again."

"Well?" Mindy blurted.

"Well, what?" Cameron sheepishly replied.

Startled, Mindy jumped when the truck backfired, then laughed at her own reaction. She could never get used to the noises the old truck made. Every day she expected him to pick her up in his police sedan with an explanation that the truck had died and it was in Bernard's wrecking yard.

A large mosquito splattered against the windshield. Its greasy remains made her jump the moment it hit. Her stomach churned slightly from the grotesque color as her face contorted into disgust.

Cameron looked at her, the remains, and then turned on the windshield wipers. He wanted to laugh, but was afraid that if he did, she would start drilling him again.

"What did she say when you asked her to marry you?" Mindy asked as she gave him one of her infamous *I'm the adult here* glares.

"Nothing," Cameron answered without hesitation, remembering Jennifer turning and looking out the window as though Cameron had never asked.

"Nothing? What do you mean nothing?" Mindy continued.

He grinned, but replied in honesty, "She had a lot on her mind. She knew something was wrong with Bernard. And..." He paused, thinking, looking at that moment in his life that he was now embarrassed about, "and, I guess, it was just plain bad timing…" His words faltered as he remembered how he felt: embarrassed, lost, and just downright defeated. *It wasn't bad timing*, he thought, *it was just plain stupid.* "She was worried about Bernard, and justifiably so," Cameron reminisced aloud. Cameron could recall in detail how she had looked and acted as they were driving to Bernard's house. How she had chewed on her nails, which was something he had never seen her do, and how she had fought back tears. "She and Bernard were close, best friends if I didn't know better, and he was missing… she was worried."

Cameron glanced around the small town as they drove past the courthouse. He looked over to the diner, taken aback by the emptiness of the parking lot. There were only two cars parked in the front, and none across the street. He looked at his wristwatch again and noticed that it had stopped. He slapped it, held it to his ear, and mumbled, "Time for another watch."

"I can stay home, you know. You could be spending the money on a new truck or a watch." Mindy continued in one of her *I got you tones.*

"No, you're too young to be staying home by yourself," Cameron said, grinning.

"Dad!" Mindy shouted in her own defense. "I'm eleven, almost twelve. Most kids my age stay by themselves."

Cameron nearly gave in, but then replied, "Next year when you're thirteen, okay? Besides, it's good for you to be with kids your own age. Oh, my God, next year you'll be a teenager."

Mindy shot a quick look at him, but after the kids your own age remark, said nothing. She looked around the quiet streets and then waved as they drove past Mahowee's.

Cameron thought about Mahowee and his warning the morning of the Fourth.

The cleansing.

It had been predicted by so many and insofar the end had not occurred.

However, a cleansing is the not the end but a beginning.

A chill, for some odd reason, ran down his spine and he became frightened. He pulled the truck over to the shoulder of the road and dry washed his face and then sighed.

"Are you okay?" Mindy asked. She was no longer upset, she was now worried.

"I think you're old enough to stay home by yourself," said Cameron, acquiescing, as he made a U-turn. "But promise me you'll stay inside until I figure out what's going on."

For some unknown reason, Mindy became frightened.

Chapter 30.

July 20, 12 P. M.

Twelve-noon crept up quickly. It was beginning to dawn on Jennifer that the diner was as close to empty as she had ever seen it. First Bernard. Now Monica. Something was happening. She sensed it, felt it, but she didn't know what, and it was something that was nagging at her in that faraway sick sensation that told her this was just the beginning, that something worse was coming. The tsunami after the quake.

As usual when she wanted to think, Jennifer merely looked out the window and dove headfirst into whatever problem she needed to solve. However, this time when she looked out she saw Travis walking by with his head down and his hands shoved deep into his pockets. The postal truck parked in front of Bernard's garage, but Travis was walking away from it. That postal truck meant more to him than his own truck, and he loved his truck. As Amy used to joke, Travis is madly in love with me, but that postal truck of his is a close second.

"Oh, my God, not Travis, too!" Jennifer shouted out to Winona and Jess. She bolted from the booth and then banged out the front door.

Winona and Jess watched while Jennifer called out to Travis, but he kept walking as though he didn't hear her, as if he were in a world of his own. She ran to his side, grabbed his arm, and froze when she saw the ashen expression on his face. Worry. Fear. Pain. All separate masks rolled into one miserable expression.

"Travis," Jennifer gently said, her voice was soft, filled with compassion.

Travis looked up and then away.

"What's wrong, Travis?" Jennifer asked her voice still soft. "Please tell me."

"Amy is sick," Travis said with quivering lips. "She hasn't been able to run for the past week. Yesterday she collapsed. She's having trouble breathing."

An EMS van screamed by. Crimson and blue lights whirled in time with the warbling siren. A Quentin Sheriff's cruiser followed immediately behind it. Its blue letters were blurred as it sped by.

"Did you take her to the hospital?"

"Yes," Travis answered. "I took her last night." He began sobbing. "They, they don't know what's wrong with her."

"Maybe it's just exhaustion, Travis. She's been training really hard for a long time now," Jennifer replied. Somehow, she knew that wasn't the case.

That faraway sickening sensation came closer. Chill bumps covered both arms as nausea filled her belly.

"What will I do if something happens to her?" Travis continued.

Jennifer stood speechless. *Please, not her, too,* Jennifer thought, *if something happens to her it will kill him.*

"Tell me, damn it! What the fuck am I going to do without her?" Travis shouted, jerking his arm from Jennifer's grasp. He starred at Jennifer with the expression of a crazed man for a long moment as if she had the answer and just wouldn't give it to him. His nostrils flared as his breathing came in huffs. He then violently shoved his hands into his pockets, and with his head slumped down began walking toward the hospital.

The postal truck, with its engine running, remained alone in front of Bernard's abandoned garage.

Chapter 31.

Jennifer followed Travis as he gradually shuffled over to Quentin Central Hospital. The short walk was dreadful, like that of a dead man walking to his own execution and each step brought Travis closer to an end he feared to reach.

A bead of perspiration trickled down her temple; the heat and humidity an unwelcome blanket, and the dreadful situation added to the claustrophobic feeling she had while trying unsuccessfully to comfort Travis.

It occurred to her that she had been spending more time at the hospital in the past two weeks than she had in the entire time she lived in Quentin.

The streets were empty. Deserted.

The small housing project two blocks east on Goode Road was silent. Where were the children? Where were the parents or grandparents who usually sat on the front stoops watching over them? Where was everybody? On days like today, there were usually ten to fifteen children playing in front of the project. Today it was as if they did not exist.

She watched the stillness on the elementary school playground a few blocks farther down the street. The swings hung limp as if waiting.

A pickup truck pulling a U-Haul trailer sped quickly by. She knew the driver but he didn't bother to turn and acknowledge her as if the effort would delay him, as though acknowledging her would put him and his family in jeopardy.

When she entered the hospital through the sliding glass doors of the emergency room, new chills streaked her forehead. The emergency room was crowded and smelled of sickness, even more so than during her last visit. Parents huddled together and comforted each other as their children lay against the walls, surrounded in their watery feces.

While they waited at the admittance desk, she heard complaints of people having trouble breathing. Others were complaining of constant diarrhea. Worried mothers and fathers were checking their children's necks for swollen lymph nodes. It was like seeing Bernard again, only now it appeared to have affected sixty or seventy people and most of them were young, some of them she recognized as Jasper's and Mindy's friends.

A young woman, around twenty maybe, sat on the floor in the corner, coughing. Coughs followed by horrible sounds of suffocating breaths. She gasped for air and flinched from the sharp pains in her chest. Jennifer guessed that, judging from her sickly complexion and bluish lips, she would die soon.

People stumbled through the entrance in never ending waves.

The small town hospital could not handle the epidemic. Its beds, filled to capacity, as were the hallways. The Admittance clerk cried as she tried to find nurses, or doctors, or anyone to help manage the flow of sick humanity in her lobby. She then took it upon herself to turn away anyone who could not pay or didn't have insurance as if she were paying the fee out of her own purse.

Jennifer left Travis in his catatonic state and searched for Dr. Jeanerette's office. She wandered down a narrow corridor filled with gurneys occupied by people who were dying. Some reached out to her in a zombie state, looking for help, which made her run even faster.

She came to a set of stainless-steel double doors, which were bolted on the outside with a large padlock, but the screened glass window was broken. She looked through the opening and froze as she witnessed the worst scene in her worst nightmare: stretchers piled with two and three bodies cluttered what had been the operating room. Each body covered with a sheet or in a plastic bag. Their faces were covered. Their identities hidden.

After turning away from the operating room, she darted down the hall to the admitting office. Her footsteps echoed against the aging yellow-white linoleum, now covered with dried blood, feces, and vomit.

She pushed open the door to the administrative corridor and was struck by the eerie silence. Mimicking the surroundings, she crept up to the intersection as silent as she could and peered around the corner. After several panic filled heartbeats, she quickly stepped through the door. She was shocked to see two doctors and a nurse dressed in blue surgical gowns and masks, whispering while they looked at a printed computer report. Chills ran up her arms. What was happening to her home? Her friends? Her family? Her town?

Feeling awkward, she hesitated, took a deep breath, and then walked toward a small reception counter.

A woman dressed in a surgical gown, sat in front of a computer monitor typing in sudden bursts. She appeared to be searching for some kind of information. The woman glanced up in surprise. "Can I help you?" Jennifer stammered, but failed to answer. "You really shouldn't be in here. I'll have to call security," the woman continued, reaching for the telephone.

As the woman picked up the phone, Jennifer replied, "I am looking for Dr. Jeanerette's office. He's expecting me." She lied, but she also knew that that would be the only way she avoided eviction.

As Jennifer had done earlier, the woman hesitated for a moment, took a deep breath as exhaustion caught up with her, and returned the receiver to its cradle. She pointed down the hall. "Through those doors." Jennifer nodded. "He's very busy. I doubt he'll have time for—"

"I can see that," Jennifer interrupted, her voice quavering. "But this is urgent."

The woman looked down at the computer monitor, continuing her search, and absently said, "Make it fast. Security has been ordered not to let anyone in this corridor."

Jennifer smiled nervously, and then rushed down the brightly lit hall, through the double doors, and into Dr. Jeanerette's office. She opened the door and stood in silence and surprise as she saw the darkness creep toward her. The blinds where tightly drawn and the lights were off. The glow from the hallway painted odd shadows across Dr. Jeanerette's ashen face.

"Alex," Jennifer whispered.

He turned toward her with only his face lit from the outer hallway. Fear was set deep in his gray eyes. "I know Jen. I know. I've called the County Health Department and CDC..." His words trailed off as he turned toward the darkened windows. "We have an outbreak... A goddamned outbreak and I don't have a clue what's causing it."

Jennifer froze as she watched his head, like a frightened child, drop to his desk and begin to sob.

Chapter 32.

July 20, 3 P. M.

Monica stood in front of the courthouse dressed in a rich, light-tan cotton suit. Her gloved hands held a silk handkerchief, which her husband, Harry, had given her for her birthday last year. Her hands, folded gently together, rested peacefully against her bosom. Her hair, neatly pinned into a bun, sat beneath a soft tan hat, which matched the suit perfectly. It had a sheer tan veil that draped lightly across her forehead and rested just above her nose.

She looked lovely. Surely, she would catch the eye of anyone who saw her.

She was excited.

She was waiting for Dr. Martin Luther King, Jr. His parade was going to pass the courthouse in five minutes. From there, it would proceed down Lincoln Memorial Circle, SW 23rd St in Northwest, Washington, DC, and stop in front of the Lincoln Memorial. There Dr. King would rise above the crowd on his pedestal and render his historical speech.

She wasn't going to join in the march, of course, but the thought of seeing the charismatic leader sent shivers of excitement through her.

The streets were empty, but she waited. Perhaps she had the wrong time.

She moved the top of her glove away and glanced at her hidden wristwatch. The diamonds that circled the face sparkled. It was 3:15, August 28, 1963. The speech was to be at 3:00, she was sure of it. She knew the speech would be for only 17 minutes surely she hadn't missed it. She was certain that the parade started at three, so it would be a few more minutes before they passed in front of her. She was so sure.

Excitement filled her heart as she gazed around the small town. Then tears filled her eyes. The Washington Monument was missing! Surely, it wasn't hidden behind the thick pines. She knew she should be able to see the towering building, the landmark that had always impressed her, high above the trees. She had seen hundreds, maybe even thousands of pictures of it as a small child, and then the real magnificence of it as a young woman. Where was it now? Did they remove the impressive building for a government housing project that she had seen during her summer trips to Washington D.C.? Where was the mall, or the water that stretched the distance between the monument and memorial? *Oh, my God, was poverty taking over the capital city,* she thought almost aloud.

A humid breeze fluttered past her. Her skirt clung to her clammy thighs. A sheen of perspiration formed on her forehead.

A clap of thunder roared in the distance.

She looked at her wristwatch again and felt somewhat dizzy. Surely, it was her allergies.

3:20. *Where was he?*

She removed a compact from her purse and opened it. She stared into the small round mirror. Her lips, although painted a soft pink, appeared dry and chapped from the horrible cold weather. She shuddered and felt the temperature growing colder by the minute. If the parade didn't get here soon, she knew she would have to leave.

Where is everybody?

Her mouth was unusually dry. She opened her mouth and saw an odd white film on her swollen tongue and the inside of her cheeks. She stuck her gloved finger into her mouth and the film stuck to it like glue. She withdrew her finger, looked at it and flinched; she couldn't imagine what this horrible tasting goop was.

She then thought of Bernard and began to cry. She thought of Dr. Martin Luther King, Jr. and sobbed even harder.

Where is he? She thought again.

She just couldn't miss the moment of listening to his speech. The one she remembered so clearly and so well. However, how could she remember it, if she had not heard it yet?

She was disoriented as this thought passed through her mind in concentric circles.

"How... how could I know the speech?" She mumbled. She stopped and regarded her confusing comment. "He hasn't spoken yet," she said aloud it as though she had to hear it to believe.

Anxiety overwhelmed her as she struggled between then and now.

Her hands shook and her knees trembled.

She dropped the compact, and when she bent over to get it, she shrieked as she saw dark lesions on her left leg in the reflection of the shattered mirror. She couldn't recall hitting her leg on anything.

She carefully touched the lesions as if it were a bruise, taken aback that the bruise did not hurt.

Slowly standing and through thick tears, she looked toward the courthouse, believing she heard someone call her, and mumbled, "Yes, Lord. Yes, Dear Lord, I am ready."

She fell to the hard concrete sidewalk and lay on her back.

"I have a dream... I am ready Lord," said Monica as tears streamed down the sides of her face.

She exhaled.

"I am ready, dear Lord... I am ready... "

Seconds before she closed her eyes, she saw the Washington Monument, beaming in an iridescent glow, standing in front of her. The clear blue sky filled with soft white clouds draped ever so beautifully above it, just as she remembered.

She heard the chants.

She heard his speech.

She heard his dream.

She smiled.

Jennifer raced across the street with her hands clasped over her mouth as she held back another scream.

She came upon Monica just as she closed her eyes, and listened as Monica's last breath escaped within a faint sigh.

Chapter 33.

July 20, 6 P. M.

Cameron sat on Mahowee's front porch drinking down the last of a glass of bittersweet iced tea. Sweat beaded around the sides of the tall glass, cascading in shallow drops, and then dripping onto his shirt as he lowered it from his lips. Two paper plates scattered with toasted breadcrumbs sat on the wooden table between them.

Mahowee glanced toward the dark slate-gray sky in silence. He leaned back and yawned as if the snack they had just consumed was a feast fit for a king.

"People are still getting sick, Mahowee." Cameron spoke softly. Perhaps that was why he visited Mahowee so often these days. He was searching for inner peace, some kind of understanding. "Jeanerette thinks we're in the middle of an outbreak, an HIV outbreak, if that's even possible... I've never heard of anything like this." He paused, then, as if he put on his medical coat, he continued, "Even during the eighties when HIV was first being recognized, the hot zones, although frightening, were not considered *outbreaks*. It certainly raised eyebrows and in some, prejudice and fear, but not an outbreak by any means..."

Mahowee glanced at him and then back to the slate-gray sky filled with thick gray cotton-like plumes. He nodded his head in agreement. "Mother Earth is angry."

"I know," Cameron morosely whispered. "You have been saying that. Now, for heaven sakes, can you tell me why? We have an outbreak, Mahowee, and somebody has to do something..."

Mahowee shrugged, but said nothing. He stared out past the yard in deep thought.

Vague ripples of heat and humidity rose from the empty macadam road. The shadow of an angry cloud crept across the lawn, gnawing away the light. A faint rumble followed the cloud, which had not yet produced even a sprinkle of rain.

"You know what's wrong, don't you?" Cameron asked.

Mahowee shrugged again but remained quiet. He wiped his hand across his forehead, dabbing away the beads of perspiration with his neatly folded napkin. "Yes, I'm hot and out of iced tea".

Cameron shot him a confused, but uncompromising glance, and then looked back out across the yard. "Are you going to tell me what you *think* is going on, or are you just going to keep jerking me around?"

Mahowee put his ice-filled glass down on the wooden table, stood, and looked out over the thick green Bermuda grass to his most cherished shrubs, the Azaleas. They had lost their blooms to the hot summer months, but they remained thick and hardy, and rich green from the constant rain.

Silence crept by, until Mahowee said, "Man travels to foreign lands."

"So?" Cameron interrupted with a low, almost whispered tone, not wanting to disturb him, but afraid Mahowee might stop if he said nothing. He wanted to make him angry, but not angry enough to cut off the conversation.

"He returns with treasures that belong only to that foreign land and sometimes with things that he doesn't even realize he is carrying. Things hidden inside other things."

Mahowee went inside the dimly lit house, but quickly returned to the porch and stood in a near silent, statue-like stance. He finally handed Cameron a newspaper article from the 'Dallas Morning News'. Its frayed edges already faded and slowly turning a yellowish-brown.

Cameron glanced at the article.

"What am I supposed to do with this?" Cameron said, looking up at Mahowee more confused now than when he had sat down beside him for the bacon, lettuce and tomato sandwich, and sweet tea.

Mahowee's insistent scowl cut through Cameron. "Sometimes things are hidden in other things. Those things are then hidden in other things, and so on."

Cameron barked, totally frustrated, "Yeah. Smaller fleas on top of larger fleas or some bull crap like that. I've heard the story before, Mahowee. Now tell me what the hell you think is going on.”

“Go home and read the article, you moron, and after you read it, check out the other article that's on their web page...” He paused. Wiped the back of his hand across his mouth. “I don't have the means to fully articulate the meaning of that article but the message scares me.”

Agitated with the mystery and the sarcastic remark, Cameron replied, “I'm not quite sure I understand. Are you telling me that this article is going to explain to me what is happening around here?”

Mahowee let go a harsh grumble, “I like you, Cameron, but sometimes you are just plain brain dead—”

Cameron complained to himself as he gripped the handles of the chair, fuming, holding back what he really wanted to say.

A blackbird shrieked off in the distance.

“You stretch my patience. Now, go home. Read the article. Get on Mindy's computer and read the other one about South Africa. Put on your white coat and best bedside manner, perhaps you can make people listen. To everyone in this town, I am just a crazy old man who collects garbage.” His words trailed off before he blurted, “Even I believe them, sometimes.” He looked down at his feet, gazing at the top of his socks above his construction boots. “Brown and black.” He shook his head in disbelief. “I can't even pick out the same color socks anymore, and you want me to explain what's happening?”

Cameron shook his head as Mahowee replaced and lit two incense sticks attached to the frame of his front door. Then, without a word, Mahowee stepped inside, shut and locked the door, leaving Cameron sitting on his porch, alone.

He glanced around Mahowee's yard and for the first time realized that the incense sticks were all around him. Their faint glow glittered like faraway stars. Their streams of smoke flowed through the bushes and occasionally jetted toward the house like soft contrails in a breeze.

'What the?" Cameron silently counted each faint glow, noticing that each window had at least two. The front door frame held four; two positioned at the top and two at the bottom.

Stunned, Cameron stood and wandered down the steps to the unmarked sedan. He glanced back every few seconds in hopes that Mahowee would come back out and tell him what he knew. When he didn't, Cameron opened the car door, angled himself in and sat down.

Jess' forest green Toyota 4-Runner with a camouflage canoe atop its roof swept by, breaking the silence and frightening away the blackbird. Jess didn't notice Cameron, nor Cameron him.

A slow darkness fell as thick rain clouds began creeping around him, swirling above his head gathering the blistering winds and conditions of a tornado.

He left the car door open and stared up in confusion. What was happening to Quentin?

Thunder rumbled in the distance, from two or three miles west of town. Cameron knew that it wouldn't be long before the rain started again.

He glanced at the article, and then thoughtlessly tossed it in the passenger seat; he wasn't even sure Mindy's computer still worked. Looking back toward the house, he wondered just what the hell the old man was trying to tell him. Or not to tell him. Perhaps the old man really was crazy. *What did he mean that Mother Earth was angry? What did he mean there was going to be a cleansing?* Damn ancient cultures and riddles—a bunch of bull crap—were starting to give him a headache. Why didn't he just tell him what hell was going on and then let him do whatever needed to be done?

He chuckled at Mahowee's brown and black socks remark, and then, with a grin, looked down at his own, hoping they matched, chuckling when they did.

He started the cruiser, but continued to stare toward the house.

Damned ancient cultures... Nothing but bull crap...

Chapter 34.

Without reading the article, Cameron parked in the hospital parking lot and stared at the emergency room entrance in stunned silence. The number of patients appeared to have tripled since he had been there earlier. A line of people stumbled through the glass doors to what now looked like hell. The line then stretched the length of the building and around the corner.

Cameron felt paralyzed. He had spent many hours in an ER during one of Washington's worst snowstorm that created a pileup on Interstate 495 but he had never seen anything like this. Quentin's ER was small compared to the ones he had worked, but the crowd dwarfed any busy night he had ever seen in his life.

He really did not want to go in, but something in the back of his mind forced him to push open the door of the cruiser and step out.

A starless evening was quickly upon him, and he had only a few minutes before he needed to be home with Mindy—he hoped she listened and stayed in the house—but he wanted to look around and see if the disease was spreading.

His shoes felt as if they were dissolving into the heated tarmac as he walked aimlessly across the parking lot to the emergency room entrance. At the door, he stopped in awe and disgust: people sat on the floors in agony while waiting for someone or something to help them. Some already appeared to be dead, their bodies limp against the walls or across their loved ones' legs, yet others were sprawled in the middle of the floor. He knew there was no hope for them.

Horror was evident in the eyes of those still alive.

Changing his mind, and to avoid the sinking feeling that this was only the beginning, Cameron went around the building to the front entrance and darted inside. He also knew that the more he stood there, the more he'd want to help, and he fought that urge, trying to forget the dreams of the social worker. The moment he stepped in to help, he knew he'd be up to his elbows in whatever was happening, and although he knew it was selfish of him, he had Mindy to think about.

While creeping down the hallway, he noticed a man standing next to Tommy Johnson's bed. He had a warm smile and his soft words appeared to put Tommy at ease, but his face wasn't familiar to Cameron; he couldn't recall ever having seen him before.

The stranger was tall, maybe around six feet two inches, and somewhat thin. Perfectly kept sandy-blond hair draped across his forehead—as if a stylist had groomed him when he stepped into the hospital—nearly touching a pair of tortoise-shell glasses. The tinted lens hid the color of his eyes. Draped across his left arm at the elbow lay an impeccable blue suit coat like the suits worn by the sales representatives he had met as they peddled pharmaceutical meds to the doctors around DC. The stranger's tie was dark red with thin blue stripes and it hung about a half inch beneath his belt.

His wide smile exposed near-perfect teeth. So perfect that Cameron immediately thought they were dentures.

When Cameron came to the door, he noticed the off-white curtains were open. Thick clouds hung angrily outside the window. He thought of Mindy home alone with a storm coming.

One get-well card stood on the bed stand next to a plastic water bottle and two cups. A fishing magazine lay on the floor next to the bed, partially hiding two Almond Joy candy bar wrappers.

Cameron knew that Tommy's wife, Arlene, had been by. Arlene was addicted to Almond Joy as much as Tommy was to Coors beer.

Tommy's leg cast was elevated on two pillows and the autographed cast on his arm lay heavily across his stomach. A new bandage had replaced the older one wrapped around his head. His pate now had sutures where the lacerations had been. Purple bruises tattooed his left cheek and both swollen eyes. The left one, nearly closed, hid a dark crimson eye.

"Evening, Tommy," said Cameron as he stepped into the room, smiling.

Tommy looked at Cameron and grinned a nearly toothless grin; he had lost four of his front top teeth in the accident. Cameron had found them on the passenger seat. "Howdy, Cam. What brings you here?" said Tommy with a subtle lisp.

Cameron glanced at the man next to Tommy's bed and returned his smile. "I was just in the neighborhood and stopped in to see if there was anything you needed."

He handed Tommy an issue of the Fish and Wildlife magazine.

Tommy grinned. "Thanks, Cam. Looks like the new issue."

Returning Tommy's grin, Cameron held out his hand toward the stranger. "Evening. I'm Cameron Nickels. Have we met?"

"No. I don't believe so. Damien, Damien Butterfield."

An odd, mousey intonation, Cameron quickly thought. Making mental notes, Cameron decided the man was handsome but quite frail; his grip was loose and clammy as they shook hands.

"Cameron is one of Quentin's finest," Tommy interjected with a stronger lisp, having some difficulty with the f in finest. "Stops by just about every day to see how I'm doing. Brings me something to read or munch on just so's I can hurry and get well, right, Cam?"

Cameron nodded with a smile all the while thinking about the next steps for Tommy and the possible Driving While Intoxicated charge.

Damien smiled along with Cameron and Tommy. A natural chameleon, he was forever blending in, being what he wanted people to believe instead of who he really was.

"Well, I think I have all the information I need, Mr. Johnson. I'll get back to you as soon as I can." He turned to Cameron. "Nice to have met you."

"A pleasure," said Cameron with a subtle nod, something Cameron did when he wasn't sure to whom he was talking. He often used that subtle nod moments before he gave bad news of a patient to a waiting loved one. He then wondered why he had even remembered that. Was there something about Damien Butterfield that he did not like? He didn't know, but when he had these thoughts, he was usually right. Bad news.

Moments after Damien Butterfield left, Cameron looked back down at Tommy and asked, "Who is he?"

"Insurance agent... I think," said Tommy with a shrug. "Fanciest damned dresser I've ever seen for an insurance agent." He stopped and exhaled a rugged sigh. "He asked a bunch of questions about the accident... I guess they're just trying to see who was at fault. Probably gonna screw me out of something or other."

Cameron sighed, trying to show Tommy some sympathy, but seriously knew that Tommy was in more trouble than Tommy cared to admit. Cameron was waiting to arrest him for DWI, and this would be number three. Even his brother-in-law, the mayor, would not get Tommy out of this mess, no matter what judge presided over the case. Tommy had run out of favors with the authorities in Quentin.

"He wanted to know who pulled me out of the car." Tommy continued. "How much I had had to drink. Did I even see the truck? Same stuff you guys asked—and I don't care, I was not drunk—and it ain't my fault the man was kilt. I hear tell he was speeding anyways," Tommy defended with a louder lisp that showered his chest with spittle.

Ignoring the defense, Cameron remarked, "I don't recall you telling me someone pulled you out."

Tommy shot a nervous glance around the room as if he was trying to remember what he had said and to whom. Nervously, he began picking away dried blood from his sutures.

"Do you know who it was?" Cameron continued.

"No. Not really, but if I was a betting man, I'd have to say it was that crazy Indian."

"Mahowee?"

"Yeah. You know how he goes around picking up trash, collecting cans, bottles and paper, trying to save the planet from the garbage and whatnot. I really couldn't say for sure—I didn't see his modified shopping cart—but he's usually walking the streets in the middle of the dang night with that blessed thing clanging and clacking all over the blessed sidewalk and the road in front of my house. Saw him a few times myself just before summer. And..." He exhaled another defeated sigh and continued, "Hell, Cam, I must've heard him a thousand times, that's fer sure." Although the lisp had become unbearable, Tommy's words faltered as he tried to envision the dark figure that eased him from his car. His only witness that said the trucker driver was guilty. Nevertheless, the only thing he could really recall was the large raindrops that slashed against his broken face before he finally blacked out.

Cameron looked at his wristwatch—it stopped again—and then at Tommy. "I'll try to stop by tomorrow. If you need anything before I get here, call the office and have them radio me." He then patted Tommy on the shoulder. "Get some rest and get well."

Tommy gave a nervous smile that said again that it wasn't his fault. That he did not mean for that man to die.

"It was a gall-darn accident, Cam. A gall-darn accident." His cries of innocence grew louder. "That's all. It weren't my fault I'm telling you... It weren't my fault the man was kilt." He began to sob as he continued, "It was a gall-darn accident, that's all. A gall-darn accident."

Cameron heard Tommy's whiney protestations as he walked down the hall toward the front entrance until, finally, his words foiled beneath sickly moans from the dying.

At least you're not sick, Tommy, Cameron thought. *That accident might have just saved your life.* He shook his head, *you certainly are one lucky drunk.*

Chapter 35.

July 20, 8 P.M.

The clanging of free weights and the whirling of exercise bikes clamored throughout the room. Coupled with the clanging was the pounding of feet slapping against the moving rubber track of six treadmills, and a chorus of heavy breathing that came and went in tired gasps. Each machine faced an eight-foot tall mirror so that its occupant could stare at themselves as they brutalized their body for that healthy, sculpted look.

The small athletic club housed in half of a prefabricated warehouse, sat two blocks west of State Highway 37 and was a recent addition to Quentin. The owner was proud the day he opened the doors, but later felt it had been a huge mistake. The population of Quentin consisted mostly of farmers and ranchers who put in so many backbreaking hours of hard labor that most thought going to a gym would have been a waste of time even if they had time to spare. Consequently, few residents needed the facility. Besides that, the automotive garage, which shared a wall with the gym, was gradually expanding and inching the health spa into nonexistence.

Tonight, however, the club was nearly full. Of men. And Shauna Munson of recent 'French Kissing' fame, with a body that needed little sculpting.

Stretched out on the weight bench as she did three nights a week, Shauna maneuvered the weights like a professional. Perspiration glistened in a thin sheen from her forehead, neck, arms and legs. Her short blond hair lay pasted to her forehead in thick, dark sandy-blond strips. Her body slid across the padded bench as she pushed up. "Come on, damn you," she groaned, pushing the weight above her head, and then letting out a huff as she cleared her lungs.

She could feel the perspiration beneath her as she pumped the weights as fast as she could. The sweat felt good, a sign that she was getting everything out of what she was putting into the workout. Her audience couldn't have agreed more.

"Come on. One more. You can do it," Chet joked. He watched Shauna strain at the hundred and thirty-pound bar of free weights.

She set the weights back on their stand as her chest rose and fell in heavy breaths. Sweat cascaded profusely into salty beads that stung at her eyes before streaming down her neck and onto the weight bench. Her back and ass were soaked. What a beautiful sight.

While sitting up, she wiped her face with her towel and joked, "Your turn, big mouth." She looked at his crotch and laughed, "Your cup grew an inch, didn't it?"

Chet grinned sheepishly trying to ignore the comment and boasted, "Get out of the way. Let a man show you how to bench press some real weight." He lay back on the padded bench, slid beneath the weights, smiled and rallied, "I just love laying in your sweat."

"That's the only way you're going to get the chance," Shauna answered, her chest rising and falling with each deep breath. Her arms hung limp at her sides, radiating the burning sensation that she had worked so hard to achieve.

He pushed the weight bar up, then brought it down to his chest and continued thrusting it up and down. His sweat began dripping down to the bench and mixing with Shauna's. The bench darkened and squealed as he edged back and forth in the perspiration.

As he strained for the last time, he put the bar up on the stirrups, sat up and smiled. "Want to get a beer?"

"I can't. I'm meeting Brett Jackson," Shauna answered with a smirk.

He looked at her for a few seconds, trying to hide the disappointment in his expression and voice. "Oh, really? When did you two start seeing each other?" Chet asked after he was sure the frog that lodged itself in his throat had gone on down.

"The Fourth of July celebration that you skipped out on," Shauna answered. "See what happens when you stand me up, Mister Macho?"

Chet stood closely beside her, took a deep breath, mumbled an apology, and then kissed her on the cheek. "I love the smell of your sweat.

Think I'll just go on home and wait a couple hours before I shower."

She slapped him on the ass and darted to the women's locker room, laughing.

Shauna's spectators began filing out now that the show was over. Although one or two lingered for the chance to catch another glimpse on her way out.

In the disappointment of the closing show, Chet lay back down on the bench and stared at the ceiling with an image of her firm breast tattooed in his mind. He still felt the warmth of her body radiating from the bench. He could still smell her. Her perspiration seemed to flow and mix with his, clinging to his shirt, shorts, and pores.

This was one time he wished he hadn't stood her up. This was one of those days that he wished he hadn't stopped seeing her. This should have been one of those days that he didn't see her and lay down in her perspiration.

Chapter 36.

Cameron steered his beat-up pickup down the rutted pine needle and gravel road toward Jennifer's house. The front left headlight winked at each rock and pothole, but stayed out for most of the drive. The right headlight cast just enough light to see the graveled road that extended in front of them, and he watched as its edges disappeared into the thick pine trees, almost expecting the entire road to disappear and he'd end up running into one of those trees.

Mindy moaned as the truck slammed hard against a deep furrow only seconds before the truck shimmied and swayed right, then weaved left, taking Cameron a full five seconds before he had it under control and back on the gravel road. It was worse than trying to maneuver a rowboat in a choppy lake.

"I think you need a new truck, Dad," Mindy moaned. "This thing is going to kill us. I mean, at least buy something that works and is safe, for crying out loud, sheesh."

"When we hit the lottery, my dear daughter, when we hit the lottery." Cameron joked but knew she was right. The pick-up was a death trap and he was amazed it had passed inspection last year but, then again, Bernard was the last person who inspected it along with a word about how newer models get better gas mileage, which was Bernard's way of saying the truck had a place in his wrecking yard. Nevertheless, Bernard had slapped the inspection sticker on the windshield and waved as Cameron bounced out of the garage. A new set of shocks and springs were on both of their minds, but Bernard knew Cameron's passion for saving his money in case something ever happened to him again. A couple of shots to the chest force you to focus only on the important things.

Mindy laughed causing Cameron to laugh along with her as the truck hit another rut and bounced, swayed, weaved, and shimmied like a rowboat trying to jump across angry waves.

"Well," Cameron continued. "Let's give her another week or two."

Mindy rolled her eyes and looked up at the ceiling, mumbling, "As soon as I'm old enough, I'm buying a car..."

Cameron didn't usually stop at Jennifer's unannounced but Mindy felt that, if they just stopped by for a friendly visit, perhaps they could talk. Perhaps they could work things out in conversation instead of simply avoiding each other. He was amazed at how fast she was growing up. He knew that before long he would be talking to her about the birds and the bees and that thought truly frightened him. What frightened him even more was that someday, some bonehead would appear at his door with impure thoughts about his daughter. Cameron knew that was just a few short years away, too.

She was growing up too fast. She was turning into a young woman right before his eyes. His baby, although young in his heart, was maturing a little too fast. He just wasn't ready.

When they stopped in front of Jennifer's, they looked in and watched as she sat in the darkness holding Jasper tightly in her lap. Clouded moonlight swept across her soft face. Her hair shone as she looked down at her sleeping child.

Mindy jumped out of the pickup and raced to the screen door, hesitating as she noticed trickles of tears cascading down Jennifer's face.

"He, he's not sick, is he?" Mindy whispered, feeling Cameron standing behind her and taking his hand all the while thinking that would be the end of everything. She was attached to Jasper and dreaded the thought of him becoming sick.

"He's asleep." Jennifer whispered while shaking her head. She then motioned for them to come in. "Come in ..."

Mindy opened the door, tiptoed across the porch, and then sat next to Jennifer. She looked down at Jasper and then at Jennifer and whispered, "I would die if something ever happened to him."

Jennifer bared a sorrowful smile and kissed her lightly on the cheek. "Me, too, if something ever happened to either one of you."

Cameron sat in the lawn chair next to an old rusting ornamental table that Bernard had given her the day after the Independence Day celebration. The day he brought her mini-van home. At first, she wanted to have Cameron refinish it, but now, it was a fond memory of her dear friend just the way it was.

Cameron pulled the article that Mahowee had given him and placed it on the table. "A gift from Mahowee," Cameron said as he nodded to the article and tapped it with his finger as if to add emphasis.

Jennifer glanced at the faded newsprint. "This has something to do with the celebration, doesn't it?" Her voice was trembling. The wonderful melody that usually accompanied her intonation had vanished, disappeared due to deep-rooted fear.

Cameron shrugged, but didn't reply. He didn't know what to say, and if he did, he didn't know what was true and what was conjecture.

He began reading the article, searching for something, anything that would explain what was happening.

"Monica died today," Jennifer murmured. "Right in front of the courthouse." A tear fell from her eyes. "She was waiting for Dr. Martin Luther King. She thought she was in Washington." Jennifer took in a deep ragged breath, hesitating, and fighting back more tears. "Something called Candidiasis. Thrush, or some crazy name like that. Her mouth looked horrible." Jennifer coughed away the pain. "And she also had pneumonia and Cryptosporidiosis." Jennifer dropped her head and whispered, "Just... Just like Bernard."

Cameron didn't reply. He just cast a sorrowful gaze in her direction.

"Amy is really sick, too," Jennifer continued. "Dr. Jeanerette thinks she has pneumonia—Pneumocystis Carini Pneumonia to be more precise—whatever the hell that is. She collapsed. I saw her, she looks horrible, Cameron, really horrible. She has the same lesions that Bernard and Monica had all over their bodies..." Her words faded into a sobbing whisper. "I, I just can't get her out of my mind."

"Did he say how or why?" Cameron asked while looking at Jennifer. Her face was somewhat hidden in the darkness, but it still showed the deep-rooted fear and pain that had overcome her.

"No."

"How's Travis? Is he sick?" Cameron asked in a manner that said he didn't want to know the answer.

"No. But if she dies, I just don't know what he'll do to himself..." Jennifer's words faltered. The stories of suicide were running as rampant as the horrible sickness. "Fifteen new people came to the hospital just this afternoon. Dr. Jeanerette said that tomorrow there will be twice that."

Cameron looked back down at the newspaper. Chills streaked his arms as he read about a ship quarantined in Virginia after transporting tires from Africa. The article mentioned that the tires had been infested with Mosquitoes—Anopheles—that carry Malaria. Authorities were concerned at the time that a malaria outbreak could occur in the US; however, there had not been an outbreak, and all concerns have dissipated. The article also mentioned that the tires were en route to Dallas and Fort Worth via truck along the Interstate 30 corridor. The shipping company didn't mention whether they retrieved the entire shipment.

"Oh my, God!" Cameron blurted, chills streaked his forehead before rushing down his back.

"What?" Jennifer asked. She saw something in his eyes.

"Mahowee's article is about a load of tires from Africa."

"I don't understand?" Jennifer and Mindy blurted in unison as if they were thinking the exact thing.

"The tires were carrying mosquitoes."

There was a heavy confusion of silence on the porch as Cameron read the article aloud. He finally looked up. "The truck that went through Crystal Lake Resort was carrying tires. It took the trucking company nearly three days to clean the place up."

"You don't think it was the same one, do you?" Jennifer asked.

He hesitated for a moment, thinking, wondering if it were possible. Were the mosquitoes spreading a mutated West Nile or mutated Malaria virus? He knew neither would cause the exact same symptoms but he also knew an unknown mutated virus was capable of just about anything.

"I don't know, but if it was, then we could have an even bigger problem and an answer to what is happening."

Silence replaced the confusion. It swallowed the music of Mother Nature as they sat in the darkness, immobilized.

Cameron felt he knew what was on that truck and it wasn't malaria or West Nile. He had studied the effects of the viruses along the Mosquito Coast and that thought began to frighten the hell out of him.

Chapter 37.

July 21, 9 A. M.

An unmarked solid-white Chevrolet panel van stopped in front of Quentin Central Hospital. While the engine rumbled softly, its driver stayed hidden in the shadow of the van's obsidian windows and the large sun visor attached above the windshield.

After a few moments, the side door rumbled open and two figures, clad in yellowish-orange biohazard safety suits that resembled space suits, appeared and then stepped out. Like the driver, their faces hid behind glass that sparkled from the bright sun. An odd battery powered apparatus hung at their sides allowing them to breathe fresh air inside their helmets. Their bulky arms moved awkwardly as the rubber-like material slowed them when they picked up various silvery metal attaché-like cases.

A third biohazard suit stepped out carrying a box that resembled a hatbox. Its sides displayed the red trefoil biological hazard symbol.

Cameron stood in the shadow of a dark cloud and stared at the three figures as if he had just entered the Twilight Zone.

"Excuse me," Cameron called out when the three figures made their slow, cautious walk toward the emergency entrance. "Can I have a word with you?"

One figure stopped and turned toward Cameron while the others disappeared into the hospital. "Yes."

Holding his badge in front of the strange figure, Cameron asked, "You are?"

The Biohazard suited creature hesitated then replied in a muffled voice, "Dr. Adam McCormack, Atlanta Centers for Disease Control. I was under the impression that all official personnel had been informed."

"Can you tell me what's going on?" Cameron said, stepping closer to the doctor.

As though the question had not been posed, the silent figure quickly turned and hurried for the entrance, leaving Cameron alone and totally out of sorts. Why was the CDC here? What had Dr. Jeanerette discovered that he wasn't sharing with the Department of Public Safety?

Chapter 38.

Chauncey sat in the far corner with wide eyes that glanced oddly around the bright, but charmingly lit diner. His eyes darted toward the door, the tables that surrounded him, the floor, the corner where Jennifer kept the coffee pot and mugs, his own table, and then to the floor on his right. He mumbled. He cursed. He trembled.

Winona watched him with her soft, dark eyes. Her usual pleasant expression portrayed bewilderment. For the life of her, she could not fathom what was going on, or what was happening to Chauncey. He looked nervous, anxious. He looked lost, maybe even afraid.

Chauncey eyed two men sitting across from him and frowned as he listened in on their conversation. The one closest to him wore a dark navy blue baseball cap with Quentin Telephone written across the front in white letters. The other man wore a solid black western style hat. Both were unaware of their surroundings and neither paid any attention to the elderly man who glared at them in an angry, almost hateful manner.

More curious than ever, Winona picked up the coffee pot and made her way toward Chauncey but stopped at the table where the two men were locked in a whispered conversation and, although she smiled at them, her eyes never left Chauncey.

"Good afternoon, gorgeous," the younger man in the baseball cap spoke up in a soft, flirting manner, a manner that Winona had seen many times before and through which she could spot the phony charm coming from miles away. The man who had left her for dead at Lake Quentin had spoken in that same soft manner when he wanted something but, Lord help her if she caught him on a bad day.

Winona smiled as she looked at Chauncey, trying to get his attention. Something was definitely wrong, even uncharacteristic, with the way Chauncey was acting. His usual smile and soft-spoken antics were missing. Where was his jocular mood? Usually when he sat at a table for more than five minutes without getting someone's undivided attention, he'd lose what little patience he had, and he'd tap the table with his knife and fork like the prisoners do in the movies. He wasn't doing that today. Today, he appeared nervous and somewhat aloof to everything around him except for the two telephone technicians dressed in dark blue pullovers and jeans.

A soft Mozart filled the room in the form of white noise.

Chauncey's temperamental gaze again darted to the door, the kitchen, and the two men. He turned his head and whispered to an invisible figure crouching next to his table on his right.

Winona watched as Chauncey appeared to be having a conversation with no one. Not only was he speaking to this invisible being, but he seemed to be arguing with it.

The man in the baseball cap caressed Winona's arm. "Anyone special in your life, Darlin', or have you been waitin' for me?"

Winona smiled, but kept looking at Chauncey.

"Got a phone number you want to give out?" The young man boldly continued, winking at the older guy who sat across from him.

Winona didn't hear the question. Her mind was on Chauncey.

Pockets of conversation from a booth behind her echoed past her.

Mozart swayed.

Chauncey argued with the invisible figure, negotiating with it, trying to reach a mutually agreeable solution to a problem of some sort. His arthritic hands angrily moved across his face, then his chest, and finally his stomach. It appeared that he was swatting at something that was buzzing around his head and crawling across his chest, which reminded her of when her grandfather had dried out and suffered from the DT's.

"No, 'fraid not," Winona finally answered with the smile she saved for customers she was uncertain of, "I'm engaged."

"Well, dang, sugar, such a big loss for a man like me. But I have to say, you're the prettiest little thing I have ever seen in this one horse town," came a gentle reply that led into pleasant, but deceiving laughter.

Winona laughed uncomfortably and wished he'd just shut up. "Thank you. That's very kind." She then looked back at Chauncey. Something was not right with him. To her, Chauncey seemed to be sick, and that thought hurt her as much as the death of Monica had.

With trembling hands, Chauncey reached inside his right coat pocket, frowning and shaking his head back and forth as if saying, "No, no, no."

Chapter 39.

Cameron followed the three Biohazard suits into Quentin Central only to be stopped by the Chief of Police and the Mayor of Quentin.

"Morning, Cameron," the Chief uttered.

"Buster," said Cameron with a nod.

"You might want to step outside," the Mayor interjected, his pate shone from the overhead lights. The sides glistened with thick hair oil. His rubbery neck bounced as he spoke.

"Might not," Cameron grated. "At least not until someone tells me who these people are and what the hell is going on!"

"It's none of your concern," the Mayor uttered in one of his infamous mayoral tones used to instill shock and awe whenever he was in a conflict with one of his minions.

Cameron ran his hand through his own hair, and then massaged the back of his neck as he watched the three Biohazards disappear down the corridor that led to the administrative offices. He glanced at the Mayor, then to the Chief. "I think it is."

The Mayor nodded to Buster who then gently took Cameron by the arm and led him outside.

"Look here, Cam. Things are pretty strange around here, you know it and I know it," Buster said with a thick Texas accent.

Buster spat a long stream of tobacco juice toward a perfectly trimmed Florida Anise tree. He pulled his hat off, removed a neatly folded handkerchief from his back pocket and dried his forehead. He carefully put the handkerchief back into his pocket and ran his hand through his thick mane of gray hair before putting his hat back on.

"Really strange," Buster continued in a sigh.

"You're telling me!" Cameron snapped. "People are dying around here, Buster! I want to know who those Biohazard people are!" Cameron continued, motioning toward the three rapidly receding figures in the odd space suits.

Buster cleared his throat, straightened his tie, and then looked at Cameron in compunction and drawled, "Centers for Disease Control, CDC. They're here to find out what the hell is happening to our little town."

Cameron glanced at the van then back to Buster. "Why the secrecy?"

"Don't want people in a panic."

"Come on, Buster! People are dying. We're way past panic!"

Buster spat again, wiped his chin with the tips of his fingers, and then wiped his fingers across his thigh. "Just stay out here until we know what's going on. Okay? Can you do that for me, partner?"

"No!" Cameron spat.

Taken aback and surprised, Buster looked at Cameron and then at Cameron's clenched, white-knuckled, fists. He moved the tobacco to his left cheek and softly pleaded, "Please?"

Cameron's eyes looked down to the ground as he tried to relax. After a couple of seconds, he sighed and looked up. "Let me know as soon as I can speak with them, but let me tell you, Buster, if something happens to Mindy, Jennifer, or Jasper, and I find out you could have done something about this, you will wish you had died first."

Chief Givens nodded, spat another thick stream of tobacco juice, turned and strolled back into the emergency room as though everything was under control, but with the image of Cameron's anger firmly etched in his mind. He knew Cameron well enough to trust him with his life, but not well enough to know the limits of his anger, and the blatant threat did not go unnoticed. The threat settled in the back of his mind like a smoldering ember waiting to ignite.

As Cameron watched Chief Givens pass through the entrance, Damien Butterfield joined them. The three stood in silence, looking down the hall toward the administrative offices.

Chapter 40.

Winona poured the two men another cup of coffee and kept a steady gaze on Chauncey. It was obvious that he was having an argument with someone who wasn't there. He was acting exactly as Monica had before she died.

Oh, my God, she thought to herself. *Not Chauncey, too.*

The two men appeared to be absorbed in their conversation with her, with the younger one still trying to coax a telephone number.

She gave them a cursory smile as she moved away from the table and, as she started to turn back to the counter, she saw Chauncey spring up from the table.

"Goddamn Nazi sons of bitches!" Chauncey screamed. "You killed my wife!" He drew a Smith and Wesson 9-millimeter pistol from his coat pocket and pulled the trigger.

The blast rang throughout the diner and deafened them all.

A baseball cap flew across the room through the smoke of the gunpowder.

Blood from the young man's head splattered in Winona's eyes.

Thinking she'd been shot, she screamed and instinctively flung the coffee pot as she fell to the floor.

The older man jumped and Chauncey pulled the trigger again, hitting him in the face. The second blast added another, higher pitched ringing in their ears.

Winona cried out, "Oh, my God, I've been hit! I've been hit!"

Another shot rang out. Winona saw it rather than heard it beneath her screams.

The stench of nitro compound filled the room.

Another blast of white and orange flashed from the barrel of Chauncey's gun.

Then another.

The older man fell back against the table in slow motion as Marco and Jennifer darted from the kitchen with Jess quickly following. As Marco rounded the counter, Chauncey's mouth opened wide as if screaming but no one could hear as he pointed the pistol at Marco. In the instant before the trigger could move again, Jess leaped across the counter and wrestled Chauncey to the ground. The gun flashed again as it fired a final shot, shattering a window. The last piece of glass holding on to the window frame fell like a guillotine blade to the bottom of the window, shattering into pieces as it toppled into Jennifer's favorite booth.

"Run, Jocelyn, run! We're surrounded!" Chauncey screamed as he and Jess rolled on the floor.

Jennifer stood looking down at the frail man, watching as he sobbed. How long would it be before the rest of them were reduced to this?

Little did she know, almost everyone she knew would be doing the same thing.

Chapter 41.

The EMS team arrived shortly after the call. Winona was lying in Jess's lap, crying. The bodies of the two men lay between two tables. Glass was strewn everywhere, fresh brewed coffee poured down the walls into puddles on the floor, large bullet holes gawked at everyone; the humidity poured in through what used to be a window. Smoke slowly dissipated. Sound was slowly returning to their ears.

Chauncey was sitting in a chair in panic and confusion. He didn't realize that he had pulled the trigger, nor did he realize that he was even at the diner. He thought he was still in that god-awful basement, the same basement that he had hidden in for weeks and watched his Jocelyn. He could still hear and feel the bombing. He could still see Jocelyn's lovely face stricken with fear, shimmering with thick tears.

His Jocelyn was gone.

The man hiding behind his table had told him that the two men sitting across from him had murdered her. They were Nazis sent by Hitler to murder them. They had already murdered his parents, and it was just a matter of time before they murdered him and Jocelyn.

"Run Jocelyn... Run..." Chauncey mumbled as his head bobbed like that of a very old and weak man.

"You're going to be okay," Jess whispered as he hugged Winona tightly. "You were not hit. It was just spray."

Winona sobbed. Tied in knots, her hands trembled. Her legs kept moving as if she were trying to run.

"Nothing can hurt that pretty face of yours," the EMS medic said softly as he bathed pieces of scalp and blood from her face and eyes and examined her for injuries. "You're going to be fine."

She sat up, looked at Chauncey, and fell silent as she saw him being handcuffed and taken outside. Her throat froze when she saw the two men, their bodies cold, lying on the floor. She looked at Jennifer and Jess and murmured, "He's going to die. H-He sounded just like Monica..." Her voice trailed as she began sobbing. "He's going to die, just like Monica—" Then she screamed, "What is happening?"

Jennifer, her hair mussed across her forehead, stared at her. Jess stared at the ceiling. Both felt defeated.

Chapter 42.

Moments after the call had belched from the radio, Cameron raced to Jennifer's Diner. He couldn't believe his eyes. Two police cruisers and an ambulance sat in front of the diner. Chauncey was sitting in the back of one of the cruisers. His frail body leaned forward. His hands cuffed behind his back. His head drooped as he cried out to Jocelyn.

"You don't have to cuff him!" Cameron snapped. "He's an old man for Christ sakes!"

"Tell that to the two bodies inside lying dead in their own blood!" Deputy Anderson screamed in uncontrollable anger. His Texas Ranger style hat sat skewed, exhaustion, pain, and fear sat on his slumping shoulders. "I don't like this any more than you—but, for the love of Pete, Cam—he just murdered two of my friends!"

Confusion spilled out from the diner's doorway.

Cameron leaned against the hood of the cruiser, squinting as the crimson and blue lights blinked across his face. His head pounded. He pinched the bridge of his nose and wondered what was happening; wondering who was going to be next. Suddenly, he heard whispers. Whispers that baffled him almost as much as everything else that was happening around him.

"I love you," strained unconscientiously through an open window of the cruiser.

Cameron peered inside and felt goose bumps race up his arms. Chauncey was speaking to Jocelyn, whispering. Chauncey continued in his hushed tone. "You look wonderful. Even more beautiful than the day we met." Tears of affection brimmed in Chauncey's eyes. "Your skin is so soft." He was moving his head up and down against the back of the headrest of the front seat as if he was leaning against her and caressing her shoulder and arm.

"What the hell? ..." Cameron mumbled.

In his mind, Chauncey was sitting next to his deceased wife, Jocelyn. Cameron listened as Chauncey lovingly commented on her milky complexion, velvety skin, and the smell of her shampoo and how it made her dark brown hair feel like silk. The brightness of her lipstick and the moisture that clung to them each time she licked them. Her large blue eyes, which sparkled as he peered into them. The firmness of her petite, but perfectly rounded breasts, at least to him. And finally, her perfume, which befits her perfectly, and as always, she was breathtakingly beautiful. She was sixteen, again.

"I love you more today than I ever have..."

A foul taste lunged up from Cameron's stomach and burned his throat. He had never witnessed anything like this in his entire career. His entire life.

Stunned, Cameron stood in amazement and looked over to Talbert's garage, then to the courthouse, and then to Jennifer's Diner, wondering why this had happened. Could Mahowee have been right? Could this be some sort of cleansing or whatever? Mahowee says it is a known fact that the earth will cleanse itself in preparation for renewal. It is simply the way of nature, itself. Every so often, humanity comes up against something that is a force of nature that they are unprepared for: the Black Plague of the Middle Ages. Modern day estimates suggest that the plague wiped out as much as—or more than—half of Europe's entire population. It took around 150 years for that continent's population to recover.

The plague was thought to have originated in China but was carried by Oriental rat fleas making their residence on the rats of the merchant ships of the day. No one started the plague. It was nature. Is that what was happening now? What's to say that this is not a simple, effective cleansing of Quentin, then maybe Dallas, then maybe all of Texas, and with the rapidly mobile society that we now live in, the entire US.

Some believe an apocalypse–or, Ragnarok, or whatever other name one might call it–will be dealt by the hand of God. Some believe that humanity will simply run its course and a massive die-off will occur. Some believe it will be by a meteor. And some even believe another plague like the Black Plague that may be manmade or made by nature, and these thoughts sent horrible shivers through Cameron's body. Shivers that made him afraid. Very, very afraid.

While he waited for a coroner to arrive so the police could have a look at the bodies, he paced back and forth in front of the diner, cursing to himself.

He had to figure out something. A typical man, he had to fix this.

He had to stop this madness—somehow.

He had to do something. He just had to.

The thought of Mindy, Jennifer, and Jasper entered his mind with a bang and he actually turned to run, but to where he didn't have a clue, home to get Mindy, and then to Jennifer's? Crowd all of them into the piece of junk he calls a pickup and race out of town like some of the cars and trucks he had seen today. But, that was the cowardly way out and he didn't have that flight instinct in him, he'd always been a stand and fight type of man when confronted with a situation such as this. He couldn't run but Jennifer with Jasper and Mindy could. She could take them and flee to Arizona where he would meet them when the incident was over.

"Cameron," a woman's voice whispered, breaking Cameron from his tornado of thoughts.

Startled, he rebounded toward the voice and saw Marlene. He didn't recognize her at first; she wasn't wearing the apron that had Talbert's Mini Mart written across the front, but he felt relieved that a voice could actually pull him from the depths of fear he had never known.

"Marlene?"

"What happened?" she whispered again. "What's going on?"

Cameron stood next to her. "Chauncey murdered two people. They said he was talking to himself. Suddenly he began screaming and shooting—ah, hell if I know..." His words faltered. He looked past her to her car. "Where are you going?"

Marlene hesitated. "Since, since Bernard passed on, I'm out of work. I have to leave. So many people dying, there's no work here." She began sobbing. "I'm so ashamed, but I have to feed my babies, Cameron. I'm really scared for my babies."

If anything, Cameron not only understood but also was relieved again that someone else felt the same and openly admitted it. He held her in a tight embrace while she sobbed.

"I know how you feel," Cameron whispered. "I know exactly how you feel and I don't blame you."

"Run, Cameron. Take your girl, and Jennifer if she'll go, and run as fast as you can and don't stop until you're out of this miserable county."

Cameron wanted to, but he just wasn't born with the flight instinct.

The town reeked of death and confusion. The cleansing had begun.

Chapter 43.

July 21, 1 P. M.

Jennifer and Cameron paced the front of Quentin Central Hospital, waiting. Jennifer knew Winona was more frightened than injured, and the medics, as a precaution, and to relieve her of her anxieties, wanted her to see a doctor.

"I called my father," Jennifer shrieked nervously as if finally releasing a deep, dark secret. "He's on his way. He should be showing up any time now."

Cameron didn't reply.

"He's bringing an epidemiologist, a captain that he has known for years, a friend of his. It appears the CDC hasn't released anything yet," Jennifer continued, squinting from the bright haze.

Cameron looked up at the clear, cloudless sky and sighed in a long breath of air, clearing his lungs of frustration and strain. He removed his sunglasses and armed the beads of perspiration from his forehead, and then finger-swiped sweat from his eyes before putting his sunglasses back on. "Don't you think it's a little too soon? I mean... I'm sure they haven't had the time to find out what's going on yet."

Two old men, somewhere between seventy and eighty, stood across the street eyeing them. Both were clad in western style clothing as though they had just stepped out of the 1800's. The one on the left lit a cigarette and placed it between his deep, wrinkled lips like a cowboy Cameron had seen in the movies when he was a kid, and a few of the recent comebacks. If Cameron didn't know better, he would have sworn that the old man rolled his own; it had that hand-rolled wrinkled look.

Sunbeams baked the dark tarmac in front of the two men. The ripples of heat created an eerie illusion that made it appear that the two men were melting right in front of his eyes.

Frigging hotter than hell, Cameron thought as he armed more beads of perspiration.

"Dr. Jeanerette said it is an HIV outbreak. Every patient who has died has been diagnosed with full blown AIDS..." Jennifer's words nervously faded into the sweltering heat.

"I don't understand how," said Cameron, more so in afterthought. He cursed himself for not learning more about viruses that were more deadly than the common cold.

"It's the mosquitoes, damn it. You said so yourself."

"I'm no expert," Cameron answered. "I'm merely guessing."

"You're a cop, damn it. Read a book. Investigate! Jesus, Cameron, you're smarter than that, but you just stand there and do nothing. Don't you even care?"

Cameron stepped back as if her words had struck him between the eyes.

She wrapped her arms around herself in a tight embrace, shivering. The back of her white sleeveless blouse had a swarthy patch that disappeared into her faded blue jeans.

She couldn't see his eyes behind the dark glasses, but she just knew he was laughing at her.

Tears brimmed.

Damn him.

Cameron removed a pack of Winston Lights from his breast pocket, shook one out and lit it.

"I thought you quit?" Jennifer snapped, and then glared at him with an expression he had never seen her use. An expression, a mask where fear, anger, and pain are all the same and he wasn't sure which mask she was wearing. He hoped it was fear and not real anger toward him.

Cameron removed his sunglasses, looked at her, then to the ER entrance, and mumbled, "I don't think it matters anymore." He then threw the cigarette down and crushed it beneath his shoe.

She glared at him. Angry. Hurt. Defeated. He wasn't sure.

From over the roof, the roar of two United States Army helicopters broke the silence that was building like a thick wall between Jennifer and Cameron. The first helicopter was a Loach. The second was a Huey with its gunner hanging partially out of the opened side door. The whirling thop—thop—thop brought a few residents out of their houses and some from the few shops that remained open.

The old cowboy tossed his cigarette and glared at the helicopter astonished.

Cameron put his sunglasses on to cover his eyes as the first beastly resemblance of a dragonfly drifted back and forth before settling its feet-like rungs down on the melting tarmac. Its whirling blades threw ripples of heated wind across the thick Bermuda grass of Quentin Central.

Small pieces of paper fluttered endlessly in the whirling airstream, slapping the ground while whipping across the parking lot and into the street. The two old men held their hats with rough, sun-beaten hands. Jennifer's hair slapped her cheeks while Cameron's fluttered on the top of his head. Both were bending forward, trying to dodge the blast of heated air.

Jennifer darted toward the Loach when she saw her father, Colonel Orion Peterson, step out onto the asphalt parking lot.

When the two met, they embraced in a warm hug. She kissed him on the cheek, then urgently took his hand before he could walk away, and led him over to Cameron.

"You must be Cameron," Colonel Peterson said in a rigid tone. It was obvious whose features

Jennifer had inherited, certainly, not her father's, because she didn't look anything like him. Although his hair was light, it wasn't blond. His face was scarred with deep pockmarks. His eyes were dark, almost black. However, it did seem that she had inherited his strict and forceful personality.

"Yes, sir," Cameron answered as he removed his sunglasses. He didn't know if he should shake hands or salute. He extended his hand. "I'm happy to meet you, sir, and pleased that you could come here."

Ignoring Cameron's hand, Colonel Peterson's eyes darted around the hospital grounds. His rugged visage seemed to be looking for snipers or other enemies that he wanted to conquer. However, Cameron knew that this was one enemy that couldn't be seen with the naked eye. It was one-billionth the size of a man, and it was killing man faster than anything he had ever witnessed.

"Nothing, and I mean nothing, will ever hurt my baby again." Colonel Peterson replied harshly looking directly into Cameron's eyes with one of his commanding officer expressions that he used on his troops.

Cameron didn't reply, only nodded. He couldn't agree more. Living and working in DC, he had met his share of Colonel Peterson's in his life. The difference here was this one was Jennifer's father.

Colonel Peterson turned to Jennifer and kissed her. "Got work to do, baby. You know how I feel about my work." He then marched toward Quentin Central. His back straight, his arms at his sides, just like a toy soldier; a man marching into the battle without a weapon or shield. Little did Colonel Peterson know, but he was a small fish in a small pond and that Ridged attitude would soon be squashed.

Jennifer knew her father well enough to know that when it came to his work, little could stand in his way. Although she needed him at the moment, as always, his work came before his family.

Cameron turned to Jennifer and watched as she turned away, walking toward the diner. Nothing. Not a good bye nor a so long was said. She seemed to be sulking, blaming him for the outbreak.

He took in the view of her walking away thinking that he might never see her again. He took a mental snapshot of the woman he loved, walking away from him, possibly forever.

Slowly and methodically the two epidemiologists from the United States Army Medical Research Institute of Infectious Diseases (pronounced "You SAM Rid"), who had arrived with Colonel Peterson, left the helicopter. They, too, like the previous CDC virologists before them, wore biohazard suits.

Trying to keep the government entities straight, Cameron nearly thought aloud, *USAMRIID is one of two organizations that investigates and studies infectious diseases. USAMRIID generally concentrates on chemical warfare and the effect that it could have on army personnel, but they also become involved in outbreaks, if there are threats to the United States.*

Angry at what was happening, Cameron put his sunglasses back on and walked toward the entrance grumbling aloud, "Enough of this nice guy bullshit, it's not getting me anywhere."

Cameron hated what was happening to this town and what was happening between him and Jennifer. He felt stranded. He also hated being tough. It had never been part of his personality. Both friends and family members were amazed when he left his medical practice and had become a deputy. He just didn't fit the image. A social worker perhaps, but not an officer of the law. But as he explained, a deputy in Quentin, a small town in the middle of nowhere, was as close to peace as he could get and still make some sort of difference. A social worker's life was filled with too much drama.

He also heard the nagging utterance of the social worker in the back of his mind and instantly tried to calm down. *You will lose it and kill someone, someone close to you*, resounded, as if the ruthless bitch was standing behind him.

He pulled the door open, stepped in, and stopped beside Chief Buster Givens.

Buster turned. "I thought—".

Cameron leaned close to Buster's ear, grumbled, and then shot a stern look.

Buster, remembering Cameron's earlier flash of anger, swallowed his tobacco juice, glanced down to the floor, and let him pass.

The Mayor turned and as he started to speak, Buster gestured no as Cameron grumbled, "I'll hurt you like you have never been hurt before if you stand in my way."

Astounded, and frightened, the Mayor stepped aside as Cameron hurried past the two men to catch up with Colonel Peterson and his entourage.

Chapter 44.

July 21, 11:30 P. M.

The rental house, near total darkness, lit only by a forty-watt light bulb attached to a golden metal ginger-jar style lamp. Cluttered with books and Mahowee's newspaper article, the surface of the wooden desk mirrored the soft, golden glow. A lone cigarette butt lay in a small imitation crystal ashtray. A glass, impotent and dry, sat next to the ashtray, marred by smudged fingerprints. Despair, the only host to the inanimate items, lay over the house, suffocating Cameron and Mindy.

Breaking the silence, Cameron read aloud from an aging book, "When a mosquito takes a meal of blood from an infected person..." His words trailed off as he squinted his eyes and lost his place. He looked around the room, taken aback by the utter silence.

"The parasite that causes Malaria enters the mosquito's salivary glands, where it multiplies." He stopped, shuddered at the words, but continued, "When the mosquito feeds, it subsequently injects an anticoagulant, along with the malarial parasites, to keep the blood flowing."

He leaned back, surprised. He wiped the chill from his arms. It was ninety-two degrees, but still the chills engulfed him. Although innocent, it sounded gruesome. He almost imagined he was reading a horror story.

"But unlike the organism that causes Malaria, HIV is unable to replicate in the cells of insects." He quickly glanced around the room, studying the windows, scrutinizing each to be sure that all open windows held a screen to shield his home from the pesky insects.

"Jesus, Mary, and Joseph. Is this eerie or what?" he mumbled to himself, rubbing his arms, forcing the goose bumps down. Then, unknowingly, he tapped his fingers on the desk and then twisted a yellow number two pencil in his perspiring hands as if he was wringing out a towel.

Suddenly he felt something drone past his ear. He bolted from the chair, nearly falling as his foot caught the leg of the desk. He cursed, and swatted at the invisible insect.

"God, this is driving me fricken crazy!"

He went into the kitchen, opened the refrigerator, blinked from the brightness of its inside light, and removed a cold Pepsi-Cola. He twisted the cap off, tossed it in the paper bag that stood next to the door, and drank the entire bottle.

He tossed the bottle in the bag, wishing that it had been stronger. *A stiff shot of Jim Beam or Jack Daniel's would have gone well with the soft drink,* he thought. A couple of shots would have helped him go to sleep, which was something he wasn't doing very much of lately. His demons went to bed with him, woke up with him, and stayed until he finished his morning coffee.

"I am out of my fricken mind." He paused, trying to suppress the anger. "I used to own a house much larger than this one. What the hell am I doing here? What am I doing to Mindy? She should be going to the finest schools and wearing the finest clothing. I've failed as a husband, as a father, as a boyfriend, as a doctor, and if I'm not careful, as a cop."

He angrily strolled back into the living room, dodging the scant pieces of rental furniture, and sat down. He then continued reading, "If HIV cannot survive in the mosquito, the only other way in which such a blood-sucking insect could theoretically—oh, for Christ's sake, give me a break—theoretically transmit the virus, is mechanically. The insect's tiny mouthparts would have to act as a hypodermic syringe. Researchers have explained why transmission is very unlikely." Unlikely—unlikely! It's doing it, damn it. Everything is hypothetical or theoretical, or unlikely. Either they don't know for sure, or they're not telling us. Why can't people just be honest with us for once? Why in the hell would they want to cover up something like this?"

He stood up, ranting aloud to himself, and picked up the pack of Winston Lights, shook one out, and lit it. Then he thought about Jennifer. He looked at the cigarette, pathetically shook his head as he walked to the front door and peered out into the darkness.

The night was thick and still.

Perspiration from his nervous fingertips blotted the sides of the cigarette in dark patches.

A car sat across from the rental house. Its occupant sat in darkness. His gaze settled on Cameron.

Chapter 45.

"How is your headache?" Shauna whispered.

Brett glanced around the darkened room as his head pounded. His eyes burned. The pain stabbed at them so fiercely that he thought that they would explode.

"Almost gone. I think those aspirins did the trick," he pinched the bridge of his nose as he lied.

"Are you sure it wasn't me?" she said joking.

She moved closer to him. He could feel the warmth of her naked body lying next to him on the damp sheet. Her soft hand caressed him.

He chuckled but the chuckle faded when the pounding started again.

She kissed his ear. "Maybe if we do it again, it will make that nasty, old headache go completely away. I've read that sex is great for headaches, relieves the tension."

He didn't reply. The pain rushed behind his eyes in forceful bursts and then illuminated in sharp sparks that seemed to set his eyes into a roaring blaze. He just knew they would explode.

Shauna kissed his chest, his stomach, his thighs.

The pain was excruciating, but her soft lips caressed him into near arousal. He had to stop her but didn't want to hurt her.

She slowly moved back to his chest; her legs straddled his.

Again, sharp pain exploded behind his eyes. He could barely see her expression. Her face seemed to disappear for a brief moment, and then it reappeared as a contorted image and flickered, as if the reception inside his head was all wrong.

She sat high up on top of him.

Their naked bodies moved rhythmically as one. She lightly moaned as her head tilted back, disappearing into a blurry darkness.

Then she disappeared from his eyesight altogether in a sharp explosion. The pain hammered at him in forceful thumps.

Her passion filled the room as thick as the humidity.

A bead of perspiration trickled down the center of her back.

Sharp snaps of pain exploded again and burned his eyes. His eyelids felt like sandpaper and scratched his eyes each time he blinked or closed them. He tried to push her away but didn't even have the strength to lift his arms.

Crickets chirped. Their song played lazily through the open windows, serenading in rhythm to her lovemaking.

He stared up at her and cupped each of her firm breasts in his large hands. Gently massaging them, he raised up and kissed them, and then murmured, "They're so soft, and so deliciously wonderful. So firm."

He murmured, almost breathlessly, between warm soft kisses. Then he feathered his tongue across her pebble-sized nipple, before abandoning one for the other.

Kenny G began a clarinet solo. His soft music blended with the outside serenade.

Shauna giggled and moaned simultaneously. His words seemed to increase the arousal that she was already trapped in.

There was another, more painful, explosion.

Her pace quickened as she raised herself up and then quickly let herself back down. He lay motionless as her movement propelled her in a deep passionate, near-grinding rhythm.

She released a loud moan as she leaned forward and squeezed his shoulders.

His eyes were pinched tightly together in pain.

She looked down at him and breathed with a slight smirk. "What's wrong?"

Brett didn't reply.

"Brett? ..."

A single tear spilled down the side of his temple.

"Brett!" Shauna shouted, no longer seductive, no longer tempting her orgasm. "What's wrong?"

Her brows knitted together as worry overcame her. She began to tremble.

"I... I can't see," Brett answered in a dull emotionless manner, as though he were teasing her, although in truth his words were thick with fear and pain.

"What do you mean? You have the best eyesight in the world," she continued as worry and fear engulfed her. She knew he had been complaining about pounding headaches behind his eyes for the past two days, but the thought had never occurred to her that it was this serious.

She rolled from atop him and sat up. She gazed down at the man that she was falling in love with and couldn't believe it. He was crying like a small, frightened child. "What do you mean?" she continued, hysterically. "What do you mean?" she screamed.

She leaped off the bed, scrambling for her cell phone, and dialed 911.

Chapter 46.

July 23, 2 A. M.

July twenty-third was the longest day in Cameron's life. People were dying, and there was absolutely nothing he could do to help them. He was afraid that today would be the same as yesterday had been and that no one would believe him.

He spent nearly every waking moment reading about viruses, particularly the HIV virus. He tried to grasp the lifecycle: how it originated, how it reproduced, how, and if, it mutated. He studied the conditions under which it could survive and how it was transmitted. What frightened him most was one book that he had read explained how the body sheds the virus, excreting it through various bodily secretions. He had never understood why his optometrist wore rubber gloves when he had his eyes examined, but now it made sense. HIV had been found in tears.

He also discovered that the virus passed in saliva, that it could survive as long as seven days in saliva without a host, and even longer under ideal conditions. A few other books alluded to the possibility of exchange in perspiration, but only mentioned it with strong reservations. He wasn't sure, and he knew the Centers for Disease Control would never admit it, if they knew.

He did know there was documented evidence that proved HIV could be transmitted in saliva, and of course, in blood through open wounds. What he found most shocking, though, was what he had read about the virus passing through intact skin. He knew of the Langerhans cell, which has long finger-like extensions and is found in the mucous membranes in our nose and mouth, and distributed across our skin. It can attach itself to the HIV virus from the outside surface and transport it down to the lower layers where the white blood cells (T-cells), would then attack the virus pulling it deeper into the circulatory system. HIV then attaches itself to the T-cell and begins to infect it by fusing with the membrane of the cell. This action releases a viral RNA into the cell, along with enzymes to tell the cell to make DNA from the RNA of the virus. The viral DNA enters the nucleus of the cell and integrates itself into the DNA. The viral proteins migrate to the surface and then, by a process known as bubbling, attack other cells, destroying each as it repeats its replicating process.

He read documented proof, which stated that an affected child had bitten his younger brother and, although the skin was never broken, the saliva from the bite passed the virus through the skin.

He had learned that blood, semen, tears, saliva, breast milk, vaginal secretions, urine, amniotic fluid, cerebrospinal fluid and possibly perspiration were some of the many ways the virus could be spread. It was also believed that microscopic droplets could become airborne and transmitted as far as twenty feet through coughing or sneezing.

Perspiration trickled down his arms in large drops.

Then came the showstopper: the virus had been documented passing through surgical gloves and condoms. The size of the virus was small enough to pass through the micron holes in the latex material. Their size was so microscopic that if they were joined together in a number that equaled the population of New York they would fit on the point of a needle. Had he still been in the ER, he would most certainly double-gloved when working around bodily fluids.

Now he understood why this information wasn't made public. It was as frightening as hell! It frightened him enough that he wanted to stay inside and let the virus run its course, dying when it ran out of hosts. He also cursed himself for not studying viruses when in medical school, and knew he was lucky to have never contracted something while aiding the intravenous drug addicts.

In yet another book he read about mosquito transmission in heterosexuals in Africa along the mosquito belt. It stated that the human retroviruses could be transmitted by mosquitoes or within the parasite itself. The book implied that HIV might genetically incorporate itself into the insects at risk so that their offspring would carry the virus. Therefore, insect transmission of the virus may not necessitate mechanical transmission from person to person as had been thought. The proof, although ignored, was the large number of documented Kaposi's Sarcoma cases in that area.

This was what was happening in Quentin. Not in a distant country on the other side of the world, but in his own backyard. He believed these were the mosquitoes that had inherited the virus and were now passing it on to humans.

After further reading, he also learned its various stages. Stage one infiltrates the eyes, lungs, liver, spleen and various other organs. It could cross over into the brain, which made him think of Chauncey and Monica.

He felt crippled.

His friends died of full-blown AIDS and, in the process, one of them was so demented that he had murdered two strangers.

The second stage is even worse. The infected individual begins to manifest HIV symptoms. Although singularly they may be harmless, together they are a sign. They consist of sudden unexplained weight loss, diarrhea, night sweats, and swollen lymph nodes in the groin and armpits. The list went on and, as it did, Cameron became increasingly horrified.

Finally, stage three. Full-blown AIDS. This is when a complete breakdown of the immune system occurs, leaving the body defenseless and vulnerable to diseases, many of which could ordinarily be fought off. Some of the more common end stage diseases are Pneumocystic Carini Pneumonia, Candidiasis, and Kaposi Sarcoma. Pneumonia was Bernard's final attacker, and it would most certainly take Amy's life.

Candidiasis, otherwise known as thrush, is a fungal infection of the mouth, tongue, and lymph nodes. Candidiasis and dementia were the diseases that had afflicted Monica.

Kaposi's sarcoma was the cancer that had finally brought Brett to the hospital. The initial sudden blindness caused by Cytomegalovirus (CMV) was as frightening as the lesions that now laced his legs and torso.

It was incredible.

It was incurable.

It was certain death.

From what he had read and discovered, his friends had died or were dying of an HIV-like AIDS virus.

Still it made no sense. How? Why? Could this virus mutate? Could it leap from humans to an insect, and then back?

After all, it was suspected that it had leaped from an endangered subspecies of chimpanzee in West Central Africa to a human. It was believed to have been a long sought after source of the AIDS epidemic for quite some time.

Was it then passed on to the mosquito's offspring from a human or a chimpanzee as he had read? Was that even possible?

Or did the mosquito contain enough of the HIV virus and feasted rapidly enough so that the virus survived until it had a new host? Possible, but that meant that the mosquitoes had to feast on someone already infected.

During his research, he discovered that Lyme disease was suspected to also be spread by the mosquito. So why not the HIV virus?

The only thing that did not make total sense was the sudden deaths. HIV generally took years to turn into full-blown AIDS, if at all. This mutated version was taking weeks—some, depending on the health of the host, took only a matter of days.

It didn't make sense. Unless manufactured, it just did not make sense. He knew there were over seventeen different AIDS viruses, but still, it did not make sense. Could this be a new virus not yet identified in Africa or could the DNA of the HIV virus have been inserted into a mosquito as an experiment and later released?

The telephone rang.

Cameron jumped, startled when the lone silence came to an abrupt end. He stared at the telephone as if it was a beacon of bad news. He had been reading the books for three days and nights, solid. Even during the crisis that was occurring around him, he stole time to read, learning more about HIV and other deadly viruses: how they spread, their cures, if any, and what could cause an outbreak of this magnitude. No, it wasn't in Dallas or any other large city, but it could happen.

He also read, but could not comprehend, that over sixteen million people across the world would die of AIDS. Sixteen MILLION. Was humanity going to lose to this one virus? Or would another one find its way from the darkness to overshadow this one, which was quickly killing his friends?

The telephone rang again.

He glanced at the plastic imitation antique wall clock and frowned. "Now who's calling at two in the morning?" He quickly picked up the telephone receiver before the next ring could wake Mindy and quietly said, "This better be important."

"I knew you would be awake," Jennifer whispered.

Cameron hesitated, embarrassed, then softly replied, "Can't sleep." Her voice was like music to his ears. Soft, almost warm. "Is everything okay?"

"Yes. Considering." Cameron could now hear and feel the tension in her voice, but as usual, he didn't know how to reply. "I just wanted to call and apologize."

"An apology is not needed," Cameron answered in a near whisper. "I know this is not the proper time, nor what you want to hear, but just remember that I really do love you and miss you terribly. And... and if there is anything I can do, please tell me."

There. I said it, Cameron quickly thought.

The silence on the other end felt heavy, almost heart breaking.

He started to speak when. "I know," was barely heard through the telephone line. "And I've been treating you like this is all your fault."

Crickets chirped. Something droned past the window. Off in the far distance a faint clap of thunder sounded out. Yet another night of rain, followed by more heat, and humidity.

"Well, I guess I could have been doing more than I was. At least now, I've read a book, a couple of them to be honest with you. I have checked out every book on viruses, HIV, and mosquitoes that the library had." There was a faint nervous laugh on the other end. "I'm not completely sure they're the cause of it, but I called the CDC and told them what I thought. They had a good laugh."

More silence.

The chirping seemed to be louder than Cameron could ever recall. Or was it that his ears were straining to hear her breathe? Her voice, although sullen, sounded wonderful. He could visualize her wonderful smile, if there was one, which he knew there wasn't.

"I'm sending Jasper to Fort Hood. He's going to be staying with my mother."

"Good."

"I want Mindy to go with him. I would die if something happened to either of them."

"Okay."

Suddenly she whispered, "I love them so much. And..., well, good night."

She hung up.

He stared at the telephone wondering how she would have ended that sentence. And, what?

He placed the receiver down on its cradle and made his way to the window. As he peered out into the darkness, the lone vehicle peered back.

A dog barked in the distance.

Chapter 47.

July 24, 9 A. M.

Dr. McCormack sat at the head of the large mahogany conference table. He silently counted the chairs. Eighteen, counting the one he occupied. He counted the ceiling tiles, then the windows hidden behind thick, white drapes, and finally the portraits of the founding virologists adorning the walls of the conference room. He was trying just about anything to get his mind off what he'd just witnessed on film, and what replayed repeatedly in his mind's eye.

The tape noisily clicked as it finally rewound to the beginning and began playing again. There wasn't music, nor the thrill of credits that normally accompanied a film or a major Hollywood production.

A large flat screen television hung on the wall at the front of the room. It recaptured his attention as he stared at a virus that he thought he would never stumble across in a Biological Safety Level 4 lab.

It was HIV. He was sure of it. Somewhat different from the strains with which he was already familiar, but it was definitely HIV.

He had filmed the virus in action while using an electronic microscope, and although he had already witnessed it earlier, watching the film sent shivers down his spine. He watched the bubbling of the virus as it escaped the living cell that it had infected. He watched as it, and others like it, abandoned the dead cells and attacked its healthy neighbors.

It attacked more ferociously than any strain he had seen, and its speed of replication was at least ten times faster than normal.

Could it really be a new, more virulent strain? Or was it simply the type O strain—which at one time was basically restricted to west-central Africa—that had mutated.

He sat back in the large leather chair, paged through the reports that had been given to him only minutes earlier and shuddered. It was airborne. HIV. Aerosol.

The testing was complete.

His colleagues had performed various tests producing indisputable, conclusive proof. Some of the tests were as rudimentary as using a rotating bone drill, with a twenty-four inch piece of IV tubing attached to it. This test had been done repeatedly by other doctors not affiliated with the CDC. Infected blood was dropped on the spinning drill bit and the resulting air that traveled through the tubing was infected with HIV. The same test had been performed with lung tissue taken from Bernard. It, too, was found to be aerosol.

The calculated distance of travel was twenty-feet, maybe more. They did not feel the need to continue with the calculation. The CDC already knew the AIDS virus was aerosol, but they needed to prove that this new strain was too.

And, they had done so. This HIV was airborne.

The other tests proved that the virus remained alive and active in saliva. Placed in a petri dish without a host and tested every day, HIV was shown active and transmittable.

Dr. McCormack rubbed his eyes. The political pressure was beginning to get to him. How was he to explain that a new strain of HIV had been discovered? That its lifecycle was shorter, much faster and more deadly, than previously reported strains. That it was aerosol and was active in saliva testing. Think of the panic in densely populated areas, in daycares, elementary schools, grocery stores, trains, airplanes, and subways.

How was he going to put a politically correct spin on this? The Executive Branch of the government, the people at 1600 Pennsylvania Avenue, would be none too happy with this and would start the spin machines immediately. But, they weren't being called, hounded, and threatened by Joe Citizen, Mr. Cameron Nickels. Nickels and his harangue to convince the CDC that the mosquito was the basis for the outbreak? Surely, he didn't believe such nonsense.

Dr. McCormack stared at the ceiling and thought about Cameron. He loathed that man and his telephone calls. His incessant remarks and accusations. Who did he think he was? He's no scholar. He is nothing more than a second-class citizen, a police officer in a small town. Barney Fife. Cameron Nickels was the reason he was stuck in this conference room, rather than with his wife who was now on a cruise ship, possibly taking pictures of glaciers as large as Mount Rainier.

Cameron was the reason he was sitting here glaring at the walls of the Centers for Disease Control.

He picked up the telephone receiver and punched in a number, sat back, and waited. The information that he was about to give his superiors would make Quentin, Texas a Hot Zone for HIV.

It was ridiculous, but true.

"Yes. Dr. McCormack, here. We have an outbreak... Yes, sir... HIV... Yes, sir, I am sure... Yes, I am aware that the military is involved, but... Yes, sir... Yes, sir, I am sure that Mr. Nickels has called again, he calls every few hours. Yes, sir, we will trap the mosquitoes and test them ... Yes, sir— what's that, Mr. Nickels is—was a doctor. No sir. I wasn't aware... ER? Yes, sir... I will treat him as such... Thank you."

Dr. McCormack placed the receiver on the telephone cradle and cursed Cameron Nickels. "Quentin, Texas is a Hot Zone, Dr. Nickels." He rubbed his eyes again and uttered, "And chaos is about to hit the fan. Try as you may, Dr. Cameron Nickels, there is nothing you can do about it."

He counted the ceiling tiles again before letting his eyes return to the television screen.

HIV.

A silent and deadly killer.

He picked up the telephone again and punched a new number. "Dr. McCormack, here. We need to prepare for a new visit to Quentin. We need equipment for a normal sweep. Yes. Insects, birds, rodents, you know the procedure." He listened for a moment, then continued, "Yes. The military. You-SAM-Rid is involved... Yes, I am sure they will be collecting samples themselves, but we must follow our procedures as set forth until the military has been given complete control." He placed the receiver down again. "And chaos has begun."

He watched as the tape stopped and automatically rewound. He was going to watch it one more time before he left for his office. Even though the meeting had been cancelled, he was going to use the conference room to its fullest. Perhaps to escape the reality of what had already been known and proven, but ignored. Or, perhaps to escape Cameron Nickels.

"Hunh. A doctor turned deputy..." he mumbled. "Everybody used to be something..."

Chapter 48.

July 25, 9 A. M.

Four days had disappeared into a silent abyss. Quentin, the home of the World's Largest Big Mouth Bass would not be written about. Not one history book in our lifetime would depict the terror that was slowly murdering the residents of the once quiet, peaceful little town. The war on drugs and the final months of the presidential election dominated the networks, and the event in Quentin was lost in the glory of a potential new leader. Terrorism continued attempts to strike at the United States from both home and abroad. People were becoming confused as to who was friend and who was foe. Sporadic religious persecution lashed out at the United States while horrible wars abroad continued to divert the nation's attention. The rich were getting richer, the poor were getting poorer, and the middle class was still carrying the national debt on their shoulders, as if it were their responsibility to see things through. Unlike the Ebola or the Marburg viruses, which could be quarantined and its victims inoculated with the blood of another recovered victim, the spread of this horrible virus was still growing. Exponentially.

The breakfast club had disappeared. The extended family that Jennifer once knew was now a memory in her heart. The unexplained virus was still crippling those she cared for, only to later release them from their pain and horror.

Four days had come and gone since the CDC, USAMRIID, and Colonel Peterson had made their grand entrance and then disappeared with blood samples.

The CDC had interviewed at least two-dozen people, USAMRIID twice that number. Each had taken blood from at least four times as many, as well as blood from the recently deceased.

Obviously, it wasn't as critical as it seemed, Jennifer thought, or surely, they would have been out before now.

She sat and stared out the window of the diner at the lone courthouse and at the deserted shops that encircled it. Every shop in the little downtown area she had cherished so much was now abandoned. Talbert's would never open again, at least not with Bernard as the owner.

The town itself was dying. It would soon reflect the poverty caused by a decimated population. It would also suffer the high cost for those who were left behind, but did not have medical insurance. They were now the responsibility of the town, the county, the state, and in the end, the country. Those who survived would be the walking wounded, living in a class of their own, forever wondering why they had survived when their friends and loved ones were taken away with such suffering that it would still frighten them fifty years from now.

The virus pained the entire town with horror and was leaving it abandoned as the homes and shops were being boarded up. Greenery was left to die or to grow into a twisted weedy patch. It wasn't fair. It wasn't supposed to be here. It was supposed to be in the jungles of a distant land.

Jennifer slumped down.

This was just too much for her to handle. Her lips quivered as tears cascaded down her cheeks. A foreclosure notice from the bank lay in front of her. Since the outbreak, she had had two, maybe three customers. She was devastated. There wasn't enough money in her savings or checking accounts to give to the bank to prevent the foreclosure for one more day, let alone one more month. Her friends were dying around her and the banks still hungered for their money. Life goes on for some, but at the same time, it ends for others. Either figuratively or literally.

She looked over to the kitchen and watched Claude. He looked ashen, sickly. He had been coughing and sneezing for the past two days. He claimed it was his allergies, otherwise, he felt great.

The warm, loving Marco was silent as he ate a breakfast burrito that Claude had prepared for him between his allergy attacks. Marco had sent his family to stay with friends an hour away. She knew it wouldn't be very long before he joined them. He only stayed behind to help her, because he felt he should. Jennifer had always been there for him and his family, so this was just a small favor in return.

Jess, well, other than losing the childish sense of humor, was just Jess. His thoughts and concerns were with Winona. Shortly after the shooting, she developed an infection in her eyes. Jess had taken her to Dallas to an eye specialist. He wanted to stay by her side, but he could not force himself to abandon his parents. He chose to drive there each evening and then back to Quentin the following morning. A small sacrifice in his mind, but a lovingly generous act in hers.

His father had become infected by the virus and died. Now his mother was sick too, and he didn't want to leave her alone for very long. The doctor had assured him that Winona was okay. There was no sign of a virus, particularly HIV.

Jennifer kept trying to make sense of it all. Suddenly she sat bolt upright and shouted, "Marco! Did you go to the celebration?"

"No. I didn't want to say, but we went to Garland," Marco replied while walking out of the kitchen, toweling his face and hands. As he rounded the counter he continued, "We went to Caroline's parents then to downtown Garland."

Jennifer stood. "Jess! Did you go?"

Jess stuck his head out of the door and answered, "Nope. I went with Marco. When we finished cleaning up, we took off—"

"Claude!"

"Yes," Claude answered as he left the kitchen. His eyes were burning red with deep, dark circles.

His face, pale. His lips, blue. His hair, slowly turning gray.

Then it hit her. How could she have been so blind? Everyone who went to the celebration was sick. Everyone who went to the celebration was dying. She glanced around the empty room, mumbling to herself. "Winona?"

"She was my date," Jess answered. "We were afraid to say anything. We've been dating for about seven, eight months now."

Jennifer froze.

"Claude! Out of the kitchen. Get out of the diner! Get out now!"

As Claude ran from the diner like a frightened child, Cameron's words echoed in her mind. *Coughing. Sneezing. Airborne up to twenty feet. Look what happened to Winona. She got blood in her eyes, for Christ sakes. I don't care what the doctors are telling Jess-she is infected. I am telling you, no I am begging and pleading, please, please be careful.* She had hoped to God that it wasn't too late. Could it be true? Could he have already passed the deadly virus through the food, infecting the very few people who took the time to visit?

"Please, God. Please, no," Jennifer murmured.

Marco and Jess stood perplexed, staring at her in silence while she stared back.

At Marco.

At the breakfast burrito.

Chapter 49.

July 25, 3 P.M.

Cordoned off from the entire world.

At 2:45 P.M., an outer security ring completely encircled the small town of Quentin. Per orders of Colonel Orion Peterson, no one was allowed to leave and the only personnel permitted to enter were in the vehicles from the United States Army.

Two gunboats patrolled Lake Fork and one in Lake Quentin. An M1 Tank stood hidden near each major byway leading to downtown Quentin.

News of a natural gas leak left the reporters and surrounding population unconcerned. Surely, there wasn't anything new in something that had happened a hundred times before. Perhaps a five-minute mention shortly before the end of the broadcast would be sufficient. The event and its horror passed off nonchalantly and went unnoticed.

Mahowee sat on the front porch shaking his head as he watched the Army rumble by. The constant rumble of the trucks was now nerve shattering for the Quentin residents. He had known it was coming. Now, he waited for it to end. His only thought was how many innocent, non-infected lives would be wasted in the confusion, which was about to ensue.

Mother Nature had shown her ugly side to the residents of Quentin. The cleansing had begun. It was in full force.

The town's people had taken to darting in and out of their homes, trying to understand what was happening. Confusion hung over Quentin in a thick shroud. People were demanding to know what was happening but there was nothing on the news and they suddenly had lost telephone and Internet service. What was going to happen next?

The second wave of the invasion had come in the way of the high-ranking Army personnel. They had arrived with the thop—thopping sound of various Army helicopters, which roared louder than the vehicles, loaded with infantry personnel from Fort Hood. The droning swept across the courthouse toward Quentin Central Hospital.

Colonel Peterson stepped from his Loach and the USAMRIID personnel from their heavily guarded Huey. Four other helicopters landed around them with troops guarding their superior officers.

The sky came alive with AS 565 Panther and RAH-66 Comanche gunships. Their guns mounted on both sides of the helicopters conveyed fear and death to the citizens who stared at the small wing-like crafts with their massive cannons. Their thunder roared louder than the storms approaching from the west.

The third wave was even more horrendous than its predecessors. Monstrous Sikorsky S-70 Black Hawk transport helicopters were bounding over the courthouse carrying heavy equipment and portions of prefabricated sections of a biohazard lab. Although not discussed aloud, fear wracked the nerves of the CDC personnel.

It was an outbreak, and it was spreading faster than anyone in the United States had ever witnessed.

Cameron stood in the middle of the chaos like a statue. He angrily watched as the last wave of helicopters appeared over the horizon. A Bell 212 helicopter used by the CDC landed in the parking lot of Quentin Central Hospital.

Behind Cameron, a sergeant barked orders as soldiers, in field dress, unloaded the heavy machinery and equipment.

Three Humvees roared by, loaded with soldiers in chemware gear. Two Red Cross Jeeps quickly followed in tow.

Other soldiers sped through the town as if they knew what they were doing, their faces covered with chemware masks. Their uniforms and equipment clattered as they ran from building to building and house to house in search of Quentin residents. They quickly took inventory, making note of those missing.

The first virologist on scene, Dr. McCormack, the one who Cameron had come to know well, departed from the Bell 212 and walked toward Cameron and the entrance of Quentin Central Hospital.

"It's not airborne," Cameron shouted angrily over the conflict.

"It very well is," came a sarcastic reply. "Actually, up to twenty feet or so."

An evil chill raced Cameron's arms as he recalled holding Bernard. His suspicion of the virus being aerosol was just confirmed by someone of authority. "A new strain—right? It mutated and leaped from monkey to man to insect and then back to man. Now it's being spread by the Anopheles mosquito."

"That, Dr. Nickels, we don't know. And your phone calls and harassment are preventing us from getting our job done," the virologist replied in a muffled, but harsh tone. "You have no proof that is the case. We have no proof that is the case—"

"Well, just raise my rent, city boy. I guess the whole damned town has been doing drugs and being promiscuous. And, I bet every one of them has received tainted blood, too. You stupid, son of a b—"

Dr. McCormack raised his hand in front of Cameron's face, then in a sudden rage grabbed the collar of his shirt and blurted, "You have no proof. We have no proof. And frankly, I don't give a fuck what you think!"

Spittle collected on the inside of his facemask.

The thought of his wife alone on the cruise ship raced through his mind.

Cameron slowly removed his Glock, smiled, and tapped the man's facemask.

Chief Givens darted toward them, followed by two armed soldiers.

Stepping back, shocked, the virologist let go of Cameron's shirt as Cameron continued in a very low, soft tone, "Perhaps this will make you give a fuck. If you lie to me, if someone else dies because of a mosquito that hypothetically cannot spread the HIV virus, I will blow your fucking ass apart."

The cruise ship thoughts were quickly replaced by fear. Fear of the man and his promise.

Chief Givens stopped behind Dr. McCormack and watched while Cameron pointed the massive pistol toward the man's legs and continued, "First the left knee, and then the right knee when another one dies. And so on, until you tell me the truth. An official or unofficial denial will not work with me—understood?"

The faceplate sparkled as Dr. McCormack nervously nodded. A bead of sweat fell from his colorless chin. His hands trembled slightly through the rubber-like gloves. His eyes widened in fear.

"That's enough, Cameron!" Chief Givens barked with his hand resting somewhat casually on his own pistol. He did not want a confrontation, because he believed that he would lose.

Ignoring Chief Givens's command, Cameron continued, "They're from the African mosquito belt, I've already checked it out. Give the County and State Health Departments orders to spray! Attack those bastards like you did the white tail deer mice in Arizona, or I promise you this, this country will be too fucking small for you to hide in."

Dr. McCormack nodded, then quickly darted behind Chief Givens until they reached the entrance of Quentin Central.

Colonel Peterson stood behind Cameron in amazement. He nearly laughed as he thought, *this cowboy thinks he's tough. He hasn't seen what tough really is. Wait until I get my hands around his neck.*

Cameron quickly turned to the Colonel and unconsciously blurted, "You better start spraying this place or we'll all die! Including you and your men!" He then stormed off to the emergency room entrance.

Colonel Peterson laughed. "What a pathetic little man." He laughed again. "My daughter sure knows how to pick a loser when she sees one."

Once at the door, Cameron was amazed at what he saw and wondered why he had not noticed it before. On the other side of the sliding glass doors were thick sheets of clear plastic suspended from the ceiling, each piece overlapping the next.

He froze as he strained to peer through the haze. He could not tell who was who. The entire hospital staff, as well as the virologist and epidemiologist, wore field biohazard safety suits. Each was busily darting around the room in panic, taking blood and administering medication, trying to comfort those who were there.

Behind the emergency room desk stood two nurses, their faces covered with surgical masks. Their fearful eyes peered through thick plastic surgical glasses. They were the only two who resembled medical personnel.

Two RAH-66 Comanche helicopter gunships roared overhead in unison, flying toward Lake Quentin.

A large Armored Personnel Carrier rumbled down Parker street toward Winnsboro street.

Soldiers raced around inside the building while Level 4 biohazard lab walls were quickly being erected.

Stunned, Cameron walked to the front entrance of the hospital in a catatonic state. Winnsboro street was flooded with Army personnel. Goode street resembled a war zone. Although HIV was considered a Level 2 virus, which meant that blood could be handled without biohazard precautions, the entire hospital was now considered a Biohazard Level 4 (Hot Zone) and a Level 4 Lab was being constructed in the middle of the aging building.

In front of both entrances, odd rooms were being constructed. Each room bore the red trefoil Biohazard Symbol with its proper number displayed in black. A Level 0 (Gray Zone) was constructed much like a changing room. Biohazard equipment was unpacked, tagged, and neatly placed into position for use. A Level 2 biohazard area, which usually meant that the virus was not airborne, was now air-locked. After entering this area, the door would close and lock, and contaminated air would quickly be replaced with fresh air before the inner door was opened. Between the level 2 area and the hospital was a level 3 room. Its Decon showers resembled skeletons with their skulls drooped forward. The hospital itself was designated a Level 4 area. Hot Zone. Cameron could not believe his eyes. Walls were being constructed around the entire hospital faster than he ever could have imagined.

Two tents, across from the hospital, presumably for the infected, contained rows of army-green cots, while massive rows of barbed wire encircled the chaos.

The pandemonium was unbearable. Rampant.

Other soldiers, directed by the CDC, began laying traps of all types. All rodents and insects were to be captured and tested for the virus. The search for the carrier, if there was one, was in full force.

While Cameron stood staring, Jess stood behind him and shouted in a tone that did not fit his normal, thick Texas intonation and country boy style. "It's one hell of a sight, Cam."

Cameron turned and nodded before he looked back at the maddening scene.

"They have the whole area cordoned-off," Jess continued, his voice growing more serious. "I really have to tell you, Cameron, I am not very happy about this. No, sir, I am not very happy at all."

Cameron let his gaze follow the soldiers and then replied "Me neither, Jess, me neither."

"You do realize that we're all going to die."

"I am very afraid that that thought has already occurred to me, Jess."

A helicopter roared overhead.

"I'm not going to die here, Cam. Just as you did not die in that hospital" He dry-washed his face, but never taking his eyes off Cameron. "You may have given up your life and pride of being a doctor after being shot, but I'm here to tell you, I will not give up my life and love for Winona…"

As Jess walked away, Cameron wondered how Jess knew so much. How did he know something that only Mindy knew? Everyone knew he had been a doctor back east, however, no one knew about the shooting.

Chapter 50.

The troops began a house to house search while Travis paced around the small bathroom of his and Amy's house. The remembrance of their happiness flashed in his mind as he stopped and stared at the bathtub. He tried to recall how many times he had held her just in this small room. How he had stood at the door and watched as she brushed her teeth or maybe run a brush through her hair. He swiped the tears from his eyes with his fingertips and ran his arm under his nose. He could not recall loving someone as much as he loved her.

The turmoil melted through the walls and reverberated throughout the empty rooms. Its impact was lost once it entered the dense shadows of the otherwise warm, comfortable house.

Travis cursed when he thought of how Amy looked only minutes before she had died. Her once strawberry-red hair had faded to a very dull red with thick gray patches. It clung to her in thick, sweaty strands. The muscles in her arms and legs sagged horribly. It was as if she had never exercised a day in her life. She seemed to have aged seventy years in only a month.

Muffled voices raced through the streets, soon overshadowed by the roar of helicopters, the screams of women and children, and the cursing of men.

Explosions echoed in the midst of the chaos, quickly followed by rapid firing gunshots.

Unison marching drummed along the center of Rosemary Lane toward the cottage that Travis and Amy had shared. The place that had quickly become their home the moment he carried her across the threshold.

He exhaled a slight chuckle as he recalled her arms tightly around his neck. *Oh, God, how he loved her*, he thought as he tapped his forehead against the doorjamb.

A loud roar rumbled above him from multiple directions, shaking the shelf that held her favorite trinkets and whatnots.

The windows vibrated until the roar disappeared.

More gunshots echoed from outside, some in retaliation to the rapid fire.

A war ensued outside as he left the bathroom and paced their bedroom. He really, really loved her. More than life itself. He knew there would never be another Amy.

Soldiers pounded on doors, one by one, taking inventory and queueing up the inhabitants for a quick scan with a hand-held, laser thermometer. They took those who appeared to be sickly including anyone with a temperature above 99.3, keeping note of those who appeared to be well. All missing persons were to be located, lasered and contained. A map of their trail would be created, investigated, and pursued. One missing person meant the outbreak could devastate the southwest, or the entire country.

Amy's smile sprung to Travis' moist eyes. Her laughter echoed in his mind. The warm feeling that he had lost earlier, swept over him seconds before disappearing again forever.

The unison marching drew closer to the house.

Travis sat down on the couch and looked around the small living room. He looked at the pictures he and Amy had taken down at the sandy beach in Corpus Christi. She was so beautiful in her red skimpy bikini, so perfectly sculptured. He in cut-off jeans and a baggy shirt.

Tears spilled.

Scuffles outside his door appeared just seconds before the banging began. Another irritation added to all the others since Amy had passed away; an irritation that no longer meant anything to him.

"I could give a rat's ass," Travis muttered. "What the hell..." Travis continued as he removed his shoes, then his socks. He tossed them across the room where they fell in disarray.

He looked at the television and then his eyes focused on the wedding picture that sat atop it. The left side of the silver and gold frame sparkled as a sun ray found a sliver of an opening in the tightly drawn drapes.

I have to pull those tighter, he thought. He coughed, clearing his throat. "Amy doesn't like the afternoon sun coming... fades the fabric... cracks the plastic..."

He was the luckiest man alive.

"Was," he mumbled to himself and then sobbed. "Ah, hell..."

The doorknob turned, then stopped. A muffled child-like voice demanded that he open the door or it would be broken down. Forceful pounding quickly followed. "Open the fucking door!" said the boy-voice in a hurried and frantic manner.

Travis picked up the shotgun that lay on the couch beside him and placed the wooden-stock on the floor next to his naked feet.

More pounding that sounded like African drums from an old Safari movie followed louder demands.

"I love you so much," Travis muttered between sobs, ignoring the pounding that had grown even more forceful. "I miss you so much," he continued, sobbing harder now.

"Come on, man! Open the fucking door!" The soldier barked out as he tried peering through the sheer curtains that decorated the front door, desperately trying to see the man who sat only a few feet away.

Travis placed the barrel of the shotgun in his mouth.

"No!" The young enlisted man screamed out in horror. He pounded on the door one final time before breaking out the windowpane closest to the lock.

Glass flew across the wooden foyer in agony as an arm clad in Army camouflage followed it.

Travis gently stuck his toe on the trigger, closed his eyes, and muttered, "I love you, Amy, like nothing else in this world."

Beads of torment trickled down his cheeks, blending in with his tears before streaming down his neck.

The door flew open and slammed against the wall shattering the remaining glass panes. The soldier raced toward Travis.

The blast reverberated throughout the house. The crimson splatter dripped silently down the wall behind him.

A gruesome silence fell over the room as the soldier dropped to his knees. He slumped his head and sobbed. If only he could have moved a little faster. If only he could have been there five minutes earlier. If only he could have been back in Fort Hood looking at the pictures of his wife in Virginia.

Chapter 51.

Chet couldn't get Shauna off his mind. The memory of perspiration clinging to her when they were exercising in the gym sent a chill through him. The scent that she left behind when she went to shower and change clothes nearly drove him crazy. He could still smell her. The soft aroma of her perfume blended in with the scent of her glistening body. Damn, it was driving him crazy. He shouldn't have stood her up. It was a simple festival that would have been over in an hour, maybe two at the most.

He should have met her like she asked. He traded that night for a few beers with a couple of his buddies at a deserted bowling alley.

If only he could stay out of the bathroom long enough to call her. His stomach had been acting funny lately. Diarrhea had kept him close to the bathroom for two days in a row. Instead of getting better, he felt he was getting worse. Maybe Irritable Bowel Syndrome from too much liquor, he thought; drinking was known to cause IBS.

"I'll go see the doctor in a day or two," he mumbled to himself as he leisurely read the sports page. Or maybe it was the bad catfish that he had for dinner the other night.

Chapter 52.

July 28, 3 A. M.

The sky was cloudless. The moon burned so brightly that Jess noticed his own shadow as it stretched across State Highway 154 in a long, dark patch.

Two days had slipped by since Quentin had been separated from the outside world. Two days since he had had a chance to see Winona. Two very long days.

He had spoken to Winona's doctor earlier. Her condition was getting worse. She had lost all vision in her right eye and the left eye had only about thirty percent remaining. She was growing worse by the day. She was going blind.

Her physical condition had worsened, too. They were running tests but, so far, they had not been able to determine what was wrong with her. If they couldn't diagnose her condition soon, they were giving her only about a month to live, maybe

two, because her condition was declining so rapidly.

There was no hope.

He leaned against the steering wheel of his
Toyota 4-Runner and tried to think of a way to get
out. He had driven to Mineola earlier, but was
forced to turn back. He later had tried Alba, but
State Highway 182 was blocked. State Highway
154 had been no better. They had the bridge that
spanned Lake Fork closed. No one in. No one out.

He sighed as he ran his hand across his face
and mumbled in defeat.

An AS 565 Panther roared overhead heading
back toward the center of town. Its spotlight
shone eerily across the hood of his Toyota before it
slunk across the top and then appeared in his
back window.

He glanced into the rearview mirror. His eyes
were red and moistened. "Got to find a way," he
mumbled. "It had to be the gun shot spray," Jess
mumbled to himself. "I'm not sick, and Winona
wasn't either, before Chauncey..." His words faded
in a sorrowful gloom. He shook his head thinking
about Chauncey; mixed emotions ran through his
veins as he thought of how he died and what he
did to Winona.

Jess started the Toyota and drove northwest
on State Highway 154 toward Lake Fork. There
wasn't a wind, perhaps he could canoe across it.
He had done it three times before. He did have
everything with him. Of course, at that time, determined armed guards weren't patrolling it.

But he was determined, too, and he felt he had no other options.

He had swum it once also, on a bet. It wasn't the widest part of the lake, but it wasn't a picnic either. Echoes of martial law followed him. *This was goddamned America. You don't treat Americans like this,* he thought. "Especially a damn Vet," he groused aloud, slapping the steering wheel.

He piloted the Toyota 4-Runner off 154 just southeast of the fishing lodge. He turned the Toyota's headlights off and drifted down between two deserted cabins, coasting to a stop. He turned off the engine and the dome light, then opened the door and stepped out into the darkness.

An unusual fetid odor crept through the dense pines from the lake. *The smell of dead bodies,* Jess wondered. It was a familiar scent, just not for Quentin.

Crickets and flying insects chirped and droned. The lake's water slapped against the muddy shore as if shooing them away.

Another patrol helicopter, a Comanche, roared over him, going back toward town. Its searchlight danced across the top of the trees before disappearing over the horizon.

"Reminds me of those old concentration camp films," Jess mumbled to himself. He lifted the camouflage canoe off the truck. "Old Colonel Peterson is acting just like Hitler—bag'em and tag'em—smoke'em if you got'em."

He set the canoe down and then extracted a camouflage backpack from inside. He opened the pack and removed several tubes of grease paint. He began dressing his face. First a dark-green, then a lighter shade that he carefully blended in with a midnight blue beneath his eyes. He then removed a camouflage stocking cap and pulled it down over the tops of his ears. He dug through the backpack for his life jacket and slipped it on. He took off his shoes and stepped into a pair of camouflage aqua-shoes. After admiring his work, he began dressing his hands, arms, neck, and legs.

He glanced into the truck's side mirror and was surprised that only the whites of his eyes reflected back.

He withdrew a map enclosed in plastic from the backpack, opened it, and studied it one final time. "Northwest edge and follow Little Coney Creek," he mumbled. "Should bring me pretty darn close to highway 515. One. Two. Three. Bam. I'll be just outside the town of Yantis and on my way to Dallas before anyone misses me."

He closed the map and slipped it inside his life jacket. He checked the compass on his survival knife and attached the knife and its case to his belt. He then picked up the canoe and carried it to the shore.

The moonlight reflected off the lake, casting a glow over the small whitecaps. Its brightness reminded him of Winona's smile, but the tree stumps that jetted from the murky water reminded him of the tombstones in Quentin's cemetery.

"Damn-damn-damn."

A light breeze skipped across the top of the water, which for some reason reminded him of tossing stones as a child, counting how many times they skipped before falling into the water. He grew up near here.

He missed Winona dearly and these grunts were just a minor inconvenience.

"Love conquers all," he mumbled to himself in a song-like intonation.

A campfire shone from the east side of the lake where military units patrolling the lake were camped. Another one shone from the west side where he would pass on his way to Little Coney Creek.

The gunboats were missing. Perhaps they were patrolling another part of the lake. He didn't know and really didn't care.

"Assholes," Jess mumbled. "The Cleaners will come in and clean up whatever they screwed up when this is over. Won't be anyone alive. This town is destined to disappear off the face of the map... What the hell... of all places, Quentin, Texas, home of the Big Mouth Bass."

A fish jumped two hundred yards out. Its wake rippled peacefully toward him.

He walked the canoe out until he could no longer feel the bottom of the lake, and then he lightly paddled with one hand. His feet barely moved and never broke the top of the water.

The silvery water was cool and refreshing. He cut through it like a knife.

Music from the west side campfire began drowning out the public-address message that echoed faintly across the lake. It should overlay any sound that he could possibly make, which he knew wouldn't be much.

After forty-five minutes of fighting the undertow, he slid inside the canoe and sat for a moment. *From a distance, the canoe should look like a log drifting by, if it could be seen at all,* he thought. He took great caution in planning this trip. He studied both the map and the lake carefully.

Lying on his back, he looked up at the star-filled sky and tried to recall how long it had been raining and how long the clouds had been around. Since April, maybe March. He really couldn't remember. Even the day of the Fourth of July Celebration still had a heavy overcast of thick clouds.

The night was calm except for an occasional light northwest breeze.

The canoe drifted slightly west, rocking rhythmically with the push of the small waves.

He stared up; the only thing he could think of was holding Winona. Her warm embrace. Her dark eyes. Her love. It seemed like the only men in Quentin that cared was in love with someone and he felt as if he was starring in a movie filled with love and romance only to be clouded with Godzilla aptly named Colonel Peterson.

The canoe rocked and brought him back from his daydream. He slowly lowered a dark-green canoe paddle over the left side and began deep strokes, two on the left then two on the right. He kept his eyes on the stars to be sure he was going in the right direction. Thank God, it was a clear night.

He could almost feel Winona's gentle touch. Her small hands always seemed to find their way to his chest. He loved the warmth of her fingers caressing him. The scent of her body tingled his olfactory senses even now as if she were in the canoe with him—the scent of a woman could easily drive him crazy. He could almost see her sitting on the front bench smiling back at him, wagering that he wasn't going to make it across.

He never dreamed that Winona would win that wager.

Chapter 53.

July 28, 3 A. M.

Cameron lay wide-awake, staring at the ceiling exactly as he had for the past ten days since he had found Bernard. The terrifying image reflected against the ceiling like a picture from a projector.

The lesions were horrible. The sickly expression even worse. Cameron could still hear the wheezing of Bernard's congested breathing.

A foul taste settled in the back of Cameron's mouth, as he could almost smell the stench of Bernard's bathroom. The horrible picture still left him numb. The worst night in his ER paled in comparison, as he had never been exposed to anything as horrible as watching Bernard die like that.

He wanted to sleep, maybe fall into a wonderful dream of holding Jennifer in his arms, but the image of Bernard held him so tightly that he thought he would never sleep again. It had to be his emotional connection that made it seem worse than maybe it was...

Cameron couldn't believe the things that were happening. He couldn't believe the mass collection of Quentin's residents, or the sleepy looking soldiers who were standing on every corner in pairs. Most of them, though, did seem to be actually helping the people, certainly, the older folks and a few southern-grown soldiers took great care when the panic broke out.

Luckily, his and Mindy's blood tests had come back negative. He hadn't spoken with Jennifer, yet he believed she was okay, but to him the relationship was over. The last words that she had whispered into the telephone seemed years ago and he figured they were only out of desperation.

Four hundred and sixty-five people were found to be positive. Over one third of the surviving population was infected and was for sure going to die.

A dog barked, and sounded closer than he could remember before. He made a mental note to check on Calvin Harper's German Shepherd, Shep. Cameron couldn't recall having seen Calvin's name on the list of the infected or deceased. However, if it was, then the dog wasn't being fed and would probably die of starvation soon.

He finally got out of bed and stared out the window in the direction of the barking. It was then that he decided that the barking appeared to be more protective than from hunger.

"Probably the patrol," Cameron mumbled to himself. "Between them and the public address announcements, it's really annoying. If the virus doesn't kill us, the aggravation will."

He made his way to the kitchen that he had grown to hate and prepared a fresh pot of coffee. Then he strolled over and sat at the aging desk that he had begun to hate as much as the kitchen.

The books lay strewn over the entire top.

Mahowee's article lay pinned beneath the metal lamp, nearly hidden from sight. His research notes lay next to the lamp. A shroud of fear lay over the desk and its contents.

"Why don't they believe me?" He softly questioned himself in anger. "What damage would be caused by simply spraying? Larger cities routinely spray around their lakes anyway, why not Quentin? Why not these guys?"

Shep continued his resonating cry, which now seemed even more ferocious than before.

Perplexed, Cameron went to the side window and peered out.

The night was still. It was thick with humidity and the cry of Shep.

The lone vehicle, hidden so deeply in a cluster of pines that only the chrome around the windshield shone lightly from the moon, remained transfixed on Cameron and the rental house.

The occupant of the lone vehicle sat in the darkness as death itself, lurking in the shadows, waiting for the virus to attack Cameron.

Chapter 54.

July 28, 4:30 A. M.

Jess could sense the shoreline. He didn't have to see it to know that it lay waiting thirty or forty yards off to his right.

He could almost hear the soft waves scurrying up the sandy shoreline, and then slipping back down when they realized they had left part of themselves behind. He could almost hear the sizzle from the air-bubbles locked deep in the bodies of the combers. He'd always had a keen sense of hearing but when placed into a situation like he was in now his senses perked up, became stronger, an additional sensory perception.

He could smell the wet sandy dirt almost as keenly as he had smelled the perfume that Winona had worn the first time he held her. The first time he had kissed her goodnight and then sat in his Toyota 4-Runner for almost two hours, staring at the dilapidated four family dwelling that she lived in. The building that he secretly swore he would whisk her away from. He had the means, he was just waiting for the right time.

He pushed the painful anger down. Now wasn't the time to be angry. Now was the time to be careful, strong. She needed him to be there with her.

He peered up toward the starry sky to make sure he didn't deviate from his course. He was certain that in another hour he would be near the creek.

At first, he thought he would abandon the canoe as soon as he could. His military training didn't really include very much jungle training; he fought the war atop sand dunes for Christ sakes.

He knew that was a lie.

His training was far greater than the stories that he had made up and almost believed himself. The truth was he had been part of Special Forces. Their mission was to go in and cover up things. If that meant killing someone, such as a senator's son who had been an embarrassment to the party and take out a couple innocent by-standers, so be it. If it meant framing an innocent person so that an important government official could escape the penalty of some blunder, that was okay, too. It was for the good of the country.

Occasionally he would silently despise his orders, but he was a good soldier and good soldiers always followed orders. He took pride in most of what he did.

On one particular night, he had lost all faith in this "for-the-good-of-the-country" concept. He had been assigned to cover up a drug deal that had gone awry and two innocent police officers died. Even an ER doc had been injured and like him, the ER doc had disappeared to a small town east and west of nowhere.

"Sorry about that, Cameron. I am really sorry. We both ended up in the wrong place at the wrong time." He mumbled as he shook his head in disbelief. He sighed a ragged breath and continued in the same hushed tone, "Then, coincidentally, we ended up in the same small town of Quentin. If you only knew I was the one who shot you." He stopped, thinking. "I shudder at the thought... and you've been such a good friend... one of my best friends."

Cameron was the lucky one, Jess didn't believe in murdering doctors and placed the two bullets where he knew they would not be life threatening.

Yes, his training was far greater than what he claimed. What better way to hide yourself than to let an entire town assume you are an imbecile, an uneducated country bumpkin?

He had murdered too many to want to go back. He had repaired and covered up too many mistakes to believe that humans deserved much of anything; especially the simpletons invariably elected into office term after term. It never ceased to amaze him how those people were elected to run the country the way they did. They were far worse than the criminals behind bars were. No, there wasn't a deceased body to prove their guilt, but in the end, the evidence usually floated to the top.

Though he had considered abandoning the canoe, midway across the lake, he changed his mind. *Up the creek without a paddle*, he thought. Up Little Coney Creek as close to State Highway 515 as he could possibly get. Then borrow a car and drive like a bat out of hell to Dallas.

He had gone too far to turn around or change his plans.

He knew it—he could feel it—he would be in Dallas by nine o'clock. He would soon be holding Winona close in his arms with his hand massaging her back, maybe her butt. That was something she secretly enjoyed.

Oldies music swayed toward him like a soft breeze, breaking his daydream. As it did, he paddled to the beat of the bass and drum. Easy. Left side. Right side. Stop. Left side. Right side. Stop. Repeating until the song stopped or another took its place.

'The Temptations: My Girl', wailed. It was obvious that these soldiers were not from Texas.

The paddle stroked and pushed him closer.

Something bumped the canoe, then the paddle. An alligator gar, maybe. It felt too large for a bass. Then he wondered if gars were in Lake Fork. Lake Ray Hubbard, yes, but he wasn't sure if the Trinity River fed into Lake Fork. He supposed it did.

He withdrew the paddle from the murky water and then lowered it on the right side of the canoe and stroked.

The canoe slid across the silvery sheen with ease as the muscles in his strong arms coaxed it forward.

He really hated his life. He had disappeared from the Forces, retired, and then reappeared in Quentin. He had finally found happiness in a warm, beautiful woman and only to have it snatched out from under him as quickly as it started and it damned well hurt, damn it. It hurt so bad he just wanted to take her away and spend her last few moments alone, showing her in any way possible how much he loved her and how much he cared.

From out of the darkness, he heard weeping in the midst of 'Smokey Robinson's, Shop Around'. It was a sound that he knew wasn't part of the song.

Other voices and odd sounds accompanied the weeping and sobbing and it seemed to come in loud bursts that drowned out Smokey's satin voice midway through the song.

He must have drifted closer to the shore than he thought. He kept his eyes on the stars, and blinked only three or four times. How could he have lost his coordinates and gotten himself in such a mess? His ex-commander would have his stripes when he heard the news. If he heard the news. Officially, Jess was listed as dead. Officially, he died in the desert. His body burned beyond recognition. Officially, neither he nor the Special Cover-up Force existed.

How could he lose his coordinates? He could just hear his ex-C.O. now, bellying up to the bar, slapping him on the back and saying, "You screwed up this time, asshole. How else can you explain it?"

Jess lay deathly still. His breathing almost stopped. His ears seemed to perk up like that of a dog as it searched for the muffled sob. His second sense kicked in and he counted the voices and the scuffled footsteps. Three soldiers and one female, a young female, he believed.

"Son of a bitch," he breathed.

He rose up. Just enough to peer over the side of the canoe. "Oh, Jesus. Oh, God." Jess mumbled as he dropped back down with a soft thud. "No-no," he nearly said aloud. "Please, God. No."

He couldn't believe his eyes. Three soldiers were raping a young woman. She looked to be sixteen, maybe seventeen. Naked. Two held her down while one forced himself on her, and then in her.

The canoe coasted along with the current.

Her muffled cry became louder as he came closer to the shore. The song stopped and the disc jockey joyously announced the temperature, a commercial, and then introduced the next golden oldie. 'Walk Like a Man' by the Four Seasons wailed.

He couldn't abandon her. He just couldn't. He would never forgive himself.

He thought of Winona. "I love you, baby..." he said with a sob. "I love you with all my heart... but I just can't..."

He hated the song that now seemed amplified.

Chapter 55.

July 28, 5 A. M.

The telephone rang out, which to Cameron seemed to be about the only personal activity left in his life. Between the fears of Mindy catching the virus, Jennifer slipping out of his life, and the havoc that lay over Quentin, anything else personal was frightening.

Ironically, though all outside telephone connections had been cut off, inside the town proper, it was deemed necessary for each town official and law enforcer to have one.

Must be the Chief, he thought as he reached for the telephone.

"Hello," Cameron sleepily whispered.

"Cam?" The voice questioned.

"Marco? What's wrong?" Cameron responded as he bolted to a sitting position. *Oh, God, not Jennifer or Jasper.*

"Jess is missing," Marco snapped in a harsh Hispanic accent. "So is his canoe."

Cameron didn't reply. He already knew. He had a feeling earlier that Jess would make an escape attempt. When they were standing next to the hospital, he could sense Jess was plotting.

"I think he may have tried to escape," Marco continued.

Cameron glanced at the window and for the first time realized that dawn was breaking. The darkness was being consumed by another day of horror. In another thirty or forty minutes it would be daylight.

"Are you sure?" Cameron asked. *Now what the hell was he going to do?*

"No. But I would bet on it."

"Damn! He didn't happen to leave a clue did he?"

Marco was silent for a few minutes, and then replied, "He swam the lake once and has canoed it two, three times. He could make it." He pondered. "And I would guess it would be at the widest point where they would not be patrolling as often."

Cameron sat down on the edge of the bed, stunned. He knew Jess well enough to know that he might try. He also knew Jess well enough to know that he would go up against an armed guard. He just knew, too, that Jess was more than he pretended. Cameron also knew Winona was dying, and if he were Jess, he would want to be there too.

"Cam?" Marco questioned.

"I'm here. Just trying to think. If we alert someone, then we could conceivably cause him to get caught—"

"And if we don't?"

Silence ... Even Shep had stopped barking.

"We could get him killed..." Cameron whispered.

Chapter 56.

Jess crawled out of the canoe, into the water, and swam toward the shore that now had a burnt orange glow growing behind it. A halo of sun was peeking out across the tops of the trees in a fiery eruption.

Only the top of his head could be seen through the murky water. Every so often, he would gaze at the three soldiers. They were drunk or stoned, whatever it was he couldn't smell it yet.

The music was louder now that he was closer, ten to twelve feet, perhaps. The Four Tops wailed out 'Bernadette', one of Winona's favorites.

He came out of the water and crept toward the three men who had beaten her to a near unconscious state.

He pulled his knife.

One soldier rolled off the woman and it was then that Jess saw that she was even younger than he had first guessed. Fourteen or so. A baby. A little baby, in his mind.

Everything turned white.

He slid the knife across the throat of the first unsuspecting attacker who held her right arm. Then he shoved the knife into the back of the second one who was preparing to mount her. Then, like an acrobat, he spun around and shoved the knife into the chest of the third one. He then cradled the young girl in his arms while he searched for something to cover her with.

He looked down into her frightened eyes and murmured, "How in the world did you get yourself in this kind of mess?"

He found a blanket and her body trembled violently as Jess wrapped it around her and gently cradled her in his arms. Although his body was cool, it seemed to warm her, somewhat.

He picked her up and hurried toward the canoe.

The last thing he felt was the bullet entering his back, out his chest, and then heard it ripping through her neck.

"Winona ..."

He felt his knees touch the wet sand before the darkness consumed him and heard himself call out Winona's name one final time.

Chapter 57.

Cameron returned the telephone receiver to its cradle and at the same time somehow knew it was over for Jess. He knew he was dead. He'd wait for the phone call, or maybe help identify his body if there were room in the hospital morgue.

He lay back in bed and stared at the ceiling, fingering the bullet wounds on his chest.

Bernard's sickly face illuminated the entire ceiling, just as it had every night since his nightmare started.

The death toll climbed as the cleansing continued.

Chapter 58.

July 28, 8 A. M.

Cameron stood face to face with Colonel Orion Peterson. Their angry glares were as forceful as two rams ready to collide. Two soldiers stood behind Cameron, their weapons pointed at his back.

"You really don't believe that, do you?" Cameron complained in a harsh growl.

"Absolutely," Colonel Peterson replied, his voice fought to overtake Cameron's.

"What you're trying to tell me is that Jess made it safely across the lake, stumbled onto a young girl and decided to rape her. Then suddenly your boys see him. He kills three of them before someone else kills him. And the young girl, in the meantime, was hit by friendly fire?"

"That's the way I see it," Colonel Peterson blustered, his voice firm and harsh. His eyes locked into Cameron's gaze. Pure hatred rushed through his veins. Even if he didn't believe it, he would never admit it to Cameron.

Cameron shook his head in disbelief. "You might convince Chief Givens. And if the Mayor was still alive, you might convince him, too, but you're not convincing me with that bullshit story. Those boys raped that poor girl."

Colonel Peterson stepped closer to Cameron and glared at him with contempt, towering over him with his chest touching his, as if he were ready to pounce down on him. To accuse his men of raping a child was unheard of.

"Give me ten minutes with that little bastard you've got locked away, and I'll prove it," Cameron blared. "I'll prove to you that Jess stumbled onto them and couldn't let it go. He knew his fiancé was dying. He wanted to be there, but he just couldn't ignore what he saw happening."

Colonel Peterson turned his back and marched stiffly out of the room.

"Ten goddamn minutes, you sorry son of a bitch!"

Cameron leaned against the metal desk of Colonel Peterson's makeshift command post and cursed him and the United States Army, the CDC, USAMRIID, and any other virologist or epidemiologist that walked in front of him.

He glared at one of the soldiers standing guard and screamed as loud as he could, "You better start praying, you stupid little shit, because tonight those damn insects will be out again and they will suck on you, like you and your kind are sucking on this town. In a couple of weeks I am going to watch them burn your body, like they've burned half of the people in this town!"

His knuckles were white. His face was red. His breath was coming in short gasps. He stood and glared at the human statue as if he were the one who had raped the child and uttered, "You cold little bastard, raping a child in the middle of all of this. If the mosquito doesn't get that creep, you can bet I will." He turned and stomped out of the command center.

Chapter 59.

As Cameron left the command post and walked toward the cruiser, gun-ships roared overhead. He looked around the deserted buildings and felt helpless. He looked toward Quentin Central and felt his heart drop. He counted seven body bags tossed onto the back of an army puke green canvas truck. Seven more bodies would be cremated, their ashes probably dumped somewhere their loved ones would never find them, and where their memories would be lost forever. Perhaps dumped with the ashes of someone they had never even met.

He sat in the unmarked Ford Crown Victoria and shook his head sadly at the rambling that screeched from the radio. Fourteen more residents of Quentin were now infected and being transported to quarantine. Fourteen more bodies would join the seven he had just counted. Soon another twenty-eight bodies would be joining them and then fifty-six, until no one was left to be carried off.

A small unit of enlisted men ran in unison, away from the hospital, getting ready for the next infected group.

"They're letting the damned thing run its course. They're going to let the virus kill everyone in this town and then pray to God that it dies off..." His words trailed off into a deep whisper. "Unless the raining stops and the winds pick up, that is."

He stepped out of the cruiser and hurried to the Gray Zone. "Where's Dr. McCormack?" Cameron blurted in anger.

"I'm not sure," came a muffled reply as the Hazmat clad virologist turned to Cameron. "Hiding from you, I suspect."

Cameron glared at the hidden figure. "Do I know you?"

The figure was silent for a moment, and then replied, "No. I have been trying to stay out of your way, Dr. Nickels. Your surly reputation has grown as large as the outbreak." The figure held out his gloved hand and shook Cameron's with a firm grip. "I'm Dr. Chin. To be perfectly honest with you, the way I see this, you may be right."

Although taken aback at being addressed as a doctor, Cameron almost laughed out loud at the remark, but then continued seriously, "You know I'm right. The infected count has gone up, hasn't it?"

"Yes, it has. People who had been somewhat isolated are now infected, which means—" Dr. Chin said.

"Which means it's the mosquitoes!" Cameron interjected.

"Very possible, but no one will believe you or me. To be perfectly honest with you, I feel safer in the Level 4 lab than I do standing out here talking to you."

"What can we do, Dr. Chin? What can we do to convince these pinheads that they're walking into the midst of the killer and don't even know it," Cameron said in a frustrated manner.

"Pray, Dr. Nickels... Pray that something else happens. Something that will put an end to this nightmare and the mosquito's life span, or end this dreadful weather. Otherwise...," he hesitated as he looked around them, "someone from the outside may become infected. Of course, then they will probably believe us, but that will be too late."

Not realizing before that Dr. Chin supported his theory, Cameron continued, "You know yourself that the HIV virus is a Fila virus and is in the same family as Malaria, don't you?" Dr. Chin nodded in agreement. "And you know that a mosquito can pass Lyme disease as easily as a tick can." He nodded again. "You know that there is a new outbreak of Yellow Fever in Africa and Encephalitis in the United States. You also know that this is a new HIV virus, or that it leaped. Quentin is dead center between Dallas, Arkansas, and Louisiana, and if a strong enough wind comes by, the mosquitoes will go wherever it takes them."

"Yes, but you'll have to prove it, Dr. Nickels. Mosquitoes aren't known for migrating too far away from their breeding ground," Dr. Chin said with a nod. "Put on your white jacket and prove it.

Then maybe people will believe you. Let's face it, with all due respect, how many police officers that you know have a medical degree."

Cameron slumped his shoulders as if defeated. "I am not a virologist. I can tell you what I have read. I can even tell you what the damned thing looks like, but I can't prove it. Other than the body count, what can? Besides you and the medical staff here and at the CDC, who can?"

Dr. Chin shrugged.

"What about the mosquitoes?"

"What about them?"

Cameron glared at Dr. Chin as if his remark sparked a second burst of energy. "Has the CDC tested the mosquitoes? I've seen the traps, I'm not stupid. Surely, you're checking every damned critter and insect in this town, aren't you?"

"I have not heard the results. Even if I had, I wouldn't be at liberty to say," Dr. Chin said with a shrug.

Cameron couldn't believe his ears. Surely, they would have tested the mosquitoes. Surely, they would have found them infected with the virus. According to everything he had read it was standard procedure. Capture different species of insects and animals and test for the virus. Find the carrier as quickly as possible and eradicate.

"Or you won't say." He stopped, trying to control his anger. "The CDC knows the mosquito is infected. The RIID knows the mosquito is infected, but you're not telling anyone. You're going to let the virus run its course until it dies on its own, or can find no other hosts. The RIDD is going to keep this classified, perhaps use it as bio-warfare if that's even possible. Who's running the show, Dr. Chin? Who's running it, the CDC or the RIDD?"

"It is a joint effort, Dr. Nickels, it is a joint effort."

Dr. Chin turned and walked through the door to the Biohazard Level 2. As the door began to close, Dr. Chin pointed and shouted over the loud scraping of the closing door, "Prove it, Dr. Nickels. Prove it!"

Chapter 60.

July 28, 11:30 A. M.

Jennifer stood in front of the diner and watched while two constables hammered large nails into the plywood sheets that were now covering the windows of her dream.

Stapled to the door an eviction notice fluttered in the breeze with another copy crumpled in Jennifer's grieving-moist hands.

She turned and looked across the street to the lone courthouse, paralyzed. Closed, deserted and forgotten, and joining Jennifer's Diner in the loneliness of missing customers, the shops and boutiques that accompanied the courthouse had fallen; their owners gone or passed on, leaving the front parking spaces abandoned, giving away to twisted and gnarled weeds that had sprouted from the cracks in the cement and asphalt. Mattie's Fabrics' neon sign nervously blinked "attie's Fab". Marred and plucked apart, Talbert's Mini-Mart and Garage died along with its owner, the large glass windowpanes lay in sharp pieces in front of the entrance; a trail of old receipts, food wrappers, and trash led to the drained-dry gas pumps. Quentin Telephone looked like a command post for the United States Army. No communications in. No communications out.

"Quentin. The world's first modern day ghost town," Jennifer mumbled. She looked over at Marco. "Well." She choked back a tear. "I guess this is good bye. I'll miss you."

Marco embraced her in his fatherly arms. "Get out of here before you die." He lightly sighed. "Your father can help."

Through thick phlegm that she tried to shed in forceful coughs, she murmured, "I can't take any more of this, Marco. I just can't."

Marco held her tightly again and comforted. "Go. Fort Hood will be a new beginning." He paused. "Quentin has died. If you stay, so will you."

"What about you? What are you going to do?"

Marco grinned. "Who knows? Hide out until this thing ends. I don't know." He looked into her eyes. "For once in your life, worry about Jennifer and not the rest of the world. The rest of the world will carry on."

Jennifer backed away from his embrace and slowly doddered to her Dodge Caravan as though about to fall from the weight of everything. She sat in the driver's seat and cried, watching as chaos whirled around her.

Dark slate-gray clouds were forming like huge clenched fists overhead, adding to the gloom.

Cameron's shy smile flashed through her mind. A shy, gentle, soft-spoken man that now seemed to be the strongest and most outspoken person she had met in her life. Under pressure, he seemed to grow and thrive, and move with such calculated steps that he kept himself one or two steps ahead of both the CDC and the military. He had even run from door to door warning everyone to stay indoors, passing out flyers noting the danger of the virus and his belief that they were being passed along by the outbreak of mosquitoes. He insisted they spray, spray like they had never sprayed before. But what impressed her the most, Cameron no longer considered himself the town deputy, but considered himself a doctor that had the credentials to support his flag waving crusade.

She remembered her father cursing him. That damned son of a bitch threatened me. Do you believe that? She actually laughed as she envisioned the two bulls ramming at each other, but she knew that Cameron was right. Jess would never have committed the act they accused him of. Rape. Murder. Indeed not.

She started the Caravan and drove it out into the heavy flow of patrol vehicles rolling in the direction of Cameron's house. It was time to tell him how she felt. It was time to tell him that she really loved him, but had been afraid to admit it. Between her fear of being in love and the fear of losing her friends, she forgot her own true feelings.

Marco was right. It was time for her to start thinking of herself instead of everyone else.

She looked over at Jasper who was sleeping peacefully in his car seat and she thanked God that he had not been infected. At first, she had thought that Cameron had gone crazy when he was spraying around her house, both day and night, but now she wasn't so sure. She believed him at first, but then when everyone, including her father, disputed his claim, she began to believe that he was wrong. Now it made sense, though. The death count was still rising, but she and Jasper were fine. Neither infected.

She then thought of Mindy and wondered how she was handling the situation, especially with her father. Mindy was quickly turning into a beautiful young woman. A beautiful young woman who needed a mother.

She then thought of Mindy as a daughter. Her daughter. Not just a stepdaughter, but her own daughter. The thought of it actually began to make her feel like she really wanted to be her mother, needed to be.

A small caravan of Army camouflaged Humvees roared by. The last one carried a large red cross on its back. Each contained four soldiers dressed in Hazmat suits. Another inspection of Quentin's residents was about to take place. Those suited creatures with their self-contained breathing apparatus, helmeted mask, gloves, and boots – the entire body encased in protective gear, struck an intense fear in the hearts of the people who were already living in trepidation. The sounds of booted footsteps became everyone's worst nightmare. When they transported another infected person to the hospital to die, he/she would cry, beg, and plead to be tested again, in hopes that the test results were wrong. A mistake. A mix up. His/her name placed on the wrong tube. They test five to ten people at a time. Surely, there was a mix up. There just had to be. What had happened to America? To Quentin? To freedom?

Jennifer broke from these horrible thoughts as the Humvees screeched around the corner and sped off, fading away into the distance. She returned to her thoughts of Mindy and at how marvelous it would be to have her as a daughter. It made her smile. She looked at Jasper and listened for the shallow breathing that accompanied his sleep and thought: a girl's mother. That would be nice. Special.

When she pulled into the driveway, she found Mindy peering out from the front window. Mindy beamed, smiling so wide she nearly unleashed a "Yahoo!", and hurried to the front door.

Jennifer quickly pulled Jasper from the van and raced inside. Cameron's rule was less than ten seconds. The door was to be opened and closed under ten seconds, afterwards, they were to stop and look for any insect.

After gently placing the sleeping Jasper on the couch, Jennifer grabbed Mindy and embraced her as if she were her own lost child. "I've missed you."

Mindy pulled back, smiled and blurted, "I've missed you, we've missed you."

"He's right, isn't he?" Jennifer excitedly responded as she stood in front of the desk, scrutinizing the books and Cameron's research notes. The notes on HIV, mosquitoes, and viruses were scattered all over the desk. Mahowee's article was pinned beneath the lamp.

"Yes. All he does is read. And complain. I've never seen him like this before. He's acting like a crazy man. All night long, he rants and raves. He thinks I'm asleep, but since I can't go out during the day, I lie awake in bed listening to him talking to himself. He tries to figure out ways to get people to listen to him. Then he calls them horrible names when they laugh at him." Mindy began sobbing. "It's really horrible to see him tortured by this..."

Jennifer laughed as she embraced Mindy again. "Well, can you blame him?"

"No," Mindy answered, simultaneously laughing and crying. "He'll be so happy when he finds out you were here. He's missed you so much. He talks to the telephone. He really talks to the telephone. I hear him whispering to it. He tells it to call you." She laughed harder. "And then he gets mad when it doesn't ring, or when it rings and it's someone else."

"Do you mind if I stay?" Jennifer asked as she thumbed tears from Mindy's cheeks. She wanted to reply to Mindy but couldn't think of anything light-hearted that would make Mindy laugh and forget some of the stress she was feeling. Mindy leaped and embraced her so tightly that Jennifer nearly fell back. Her tears fell in steady rivulets as she cried, "Are you kidding? He needs you. He doesn't sleep. He doesn't eat. I need you—I need help—he's driving me crazy."

They stood in the center of the living room among the cheap rental furniture, laughing, sobbing, and embracing. A young bond between mother and daughter grew.

The imitation antique clock chimed twelve times, signaling high noon as the death toll climbed.

277

Chapter 61.

July 28, 4 P.M.

Cameron pulled into the long, dusty drive that led to Calvin Harper's twelve by twelve bungalow. The clapboard dwelling, designed as a weekend retreat that someone would rent for a couple of days, or perhaps a week, turned into a home where Calvin lived all year. He could not have cared less that the entire town wanted to burn it down. It was paid for and it was his. Furthermore, his Social Security check wasn't going to afford him a better abode and he didn't see a line of people willing to purchase or build him a new place. Especially one just a stone throw away from the lake where he caught half of his dinners.

Cameron stopped in front of the aging concrete walkway that led to the front door and peered over the collapsing chain link fence to the backyard. He was looking for the German Shepherd whose barks kept him awake every night, watching to see if its massive brown head poked around the corner with a starving grin. Those huge black eyes sometimes frightened Cameron. He couldn't tell if the dog regarded him as a friend or supper. He knew the aging chain link fence wouldn't hold back the large animal if he really wanted to escape.

Cameron opened the door to the sedan and to his surprise saw Calvin standing in front of his front door with a pistol-grip Mossberg shotgun pointed at Cameron's chest.

"What'cha want, Cam? Com'in to take me like the others tried to do?" Calvin angrily barked. "Well, screw ya all, I ain't sick and I ain't goin no wheres!" Calvin stood trembling. His knees buckled once or twice beneath his short but stout frame as he searched deep for his strength. His nerves were shattered. The Mossberg dipped down and weaved as he struggled to keep it pointed at Cameron. Anxiety cascaded from his pate and trickled down his forehead, and then slowly dripped off the tip of his nose.

"Calvin! You want to put that thing down before you blow my damned head off?"

"What'cha want, damnit? What'cha want? I ain't ask'n agin." Calvin cried out as his entire body twitched.

"Nothing, really. I just came by to see how that mangy mutt of yours is holding up. He's been barking—"

"Ain't his fault, damn it! People keep sneaking around here at night driving the dang thing crazy." Finally sensing that he was safe, Calvin lowered the Mossberg a little. "You ain't here to get me, are you?"

"No. I just told you that I came to see if something had happened to you and to make sure Shep was okay and is being fed and looked after." Cameron reached into the back seat and removed a fifty-pound bag of Purina Dog Chow.

Calvin smiled. His dark, yellow teeth peeked out from between thick, dry lips. "Should'a known better. You ain't like them damned commies. You should see the ways they're dragging ever-body from their houses and treat'n'em like pig shit."

"I already have, Cal. Believe me, I already have."

Cameron slung the bag of dog food over his shoulder as Calvin finally lowered the Mossberg completely down to his side and mumbled, "Come on inside before the skeeters get us. You knows that's the cause of this mess, don't ya?"

Cameron stopped and looked at the old man in surprise and nodded. "Yes, but only you and I believe that."

"Don't forget ol' Mahowee," Calvin interrupted. "That injun ain't as crazy as he looks."

"Crazy like a fox, I always say," Cameron replied with a smile when he stepped into a stench that practically knocked him down.

"Yes sir, that he is," Calvin answered as if thinking the same thing.

Cameron stifled a gag just as Calvin closed the door behind him. He then put the bag of dog food into Calvin's large hands and made his way to the couch, hesitating before he sat down. He thought he saw Shep's feces lying between the cushions.

Cryptosporidiosis raced through his thoughts. A picture of Bernard quickly entered his mind.

"Dang dog!" Calvin complained, dropping the large bag to the floor as he crossed in front of Cameron. He jerked a large rawhide bone from the couch. "See. Ya let a dang dog in the house and they think they own the gall-darn place. Go on—sit, sit. Ain't nothing gonna stick to ya. It's just old and looks bad."

Cameron hoped Calvin was referring to the couch and not some hidden feces. He slowly sat down as if he expected the couch to explode or expected to sit in something that he would have to wash off when he got home.

The walls were a filthy gray. The furniture was old and dusty, and newspapers cluttered the small living room in thick piles. A narrow path between tall stacks of newspapers led back to the kitchen, bedroom, and bathroom.

The stench was horrible.

The filth was worse.

Calvin sat across from him in a faded maroon Lazy-Boy recliner and laughed as he rocked back and fully extended the chair so that he was almost lying flat. "Smells like dog pee in here, don't it?"

Cameron nodded.

"Got me a mixture that'll kill ever-gosh-dang flying insect two hunnerd yards out." He laughed, coughed, and farted simultaneously. Then he let out a horrible belch. "Guess you can tell I don't get much company," Calvin mumbled almost apologetically. "Dang gas gets the best of me sometimes."

"Did they turn your electricity off?" Cameron asked, looking around the dark room.

Calvin blurted out in a laughter that quickly released more flatus in what sounded like a lions roar, "Nope. Don't want anybody stopping by un- announced. If'n it'd been anybody but you, I'd a shot'em. They're all commies. Ever blasted one of em."

Cameron smiled. "I really appreciate that, Cal. So considering everything else, how was the play Mizzus Lincoln?" Calvin gazed at Cameron with a perplexed stare, then quickly glanced around the room in total confusion. "What I mean to say," Cameron continued, "considering everything that is going on, how have you been?"

Calvin blinked, then shrugged. "Fair to mid- lin, I suppose, but it's been hell on Ol'Shep." Cameron smiled. "Shep's been going gall-darn crazy with the soldiers and that s-o-b public-add- dress system. Damned old hele-copters buzzing around worsen them skeeters. A man cain't get no decent night sleep." Calvin then wiped his eyes with thick-callused fingers that scraped like sand- paper, then ran the same-callused hand across the thick gray stubble on his face.

He picked up a bar of chewing tobacco that resembled bath soap and said, "Want a pinch?"

Cameron held his hand up gesturing no.

Calvin pushed a thick piece of tobacco into his yellow mouth and mumbled, "Suit yourself." Outside Shep began barking. "Shud-up you man- gy mutt before I feed you to the skeeters. Danged dog will drive a man to drink. If he wasn't such good company, I'd-a shot him last week."

Cameron laughed. "So you're doing okay and you don't need anything, huh? Food for you, maybe another bag or two for Shep?"

"Nope, but thanks fer asking. Stocked up just before the shit hit the fan, if'n you know what I mean. I listened to that damned old crazy injun. It's a shame all those other feeble minded buttheads didn't..." His words trailed off as if he regretted criticizing his deceased friends. A single tear formed in his right eye that he quickly scraped away with his thick sandpaper finger. "Dang shame, it'n it Cam?"

"Yes it is, Cal," Cameron answered with the same sympathetic tone. "Well, now that I know you and Shep are doing okay, I better get home to Mindy."

"Sure you don't want to stay for a cold one? Got me two six packs in the back of the commode just screaming to be drank." Calvin asked as he hauled himself up out of his recliner.

"No, not this time. If you promise not to shoot me, I'll stop back tomorrow and drink one." Cameron replied, laughing more so about the beer in the back of the commode than the gunslinger Cal was turning into.

Calvin smiled his thick yellow smile. "You're on." He then reached to open the door, hesitated and asked, "Did you trade your truck in for a new car?"

Cameron stopped and replied, "No. That's the cruiser."

"I'm old, Cam, not stupid. I mean the black Ford Taurus that I see parked at your place ever-night. Hell, that's what Shep's been complaining about. Seems like the car's there ever-night just after you get home. Well, anyways, if'n you want to git rid of that truck of yourn, I'll pay top dollar for it."

Cameron smiled as he thought about Mindy complaining about the rolling catastrophe and replied, "When I'm ready, you can have it."

Calvin released an appreciative laugh when suddenly he looked at Cameron with a quizzical expression as if hit with an idea that he had pondered for some time and said, "You might want to check out that car, Cam. Damned commies be dragging you to your grave like'n they doned to Jake and Missy across the road. Pitiful sight, Cam. It was a pit-ti-ful sight."

"Beef jerky and pork rinds, right?" Cameron said with his usual neighborly smile.

Calvin beamed. "Big'ens for Shep. Those small skinny ones ain't nothing with his big old mouth."

Cameron stepped out into an overcast day that wasn't bright but made him squint just the same. Thick clouds had slowly rolled in and began sprinkling a few small drops of rain. In the distance, he noticed skeletal fingers of lightning dancing across the sky. Claps of thunder soon followed.

"Good night, Cal. I'll see you tomorrow."

Cameron stood by the door of the cruiser and looked through the backyard and the thick pine trees to his rental house, looking for the Ford Taurus and wondering who was watching him and why.

Chapter 62.

July 28, 5:00 P. M.

Cameron sat and stared at the Dodge Caravan. His heart slammed against his chest. It had to be bad news. Why else would the van be here? Something had happened to Jasper, he just knew it.

He stumbled out of the pickup and bolted to the door. Just as he ascended the steps, Mindy yanked the door open and he quickly entered.

To his surprise, he saw Jasper sleeping on the couch. He could smell the sweet aroma of freshly brewed coffee. "Is everything o—"

"Yes," Mindy interrupted in a loud whisper, glimpsing back to Jasper. "Be quiet. He just fell back to sleep."

Cameron followed Mindy to the kitchen and beamed when he saw Jennifer holding a mug of coffee out in front of him.

"You have been a very busy, Yankee—Mr. Nickels or is it Dr. Nickels now? I understand you've changed your title in front of my father,"

Jennifer declared as Cameron blushed. "Do you want to explain why you have turned your dining room into a library?"

Cameron faltered, "I-I'm just a slob, what can I say?" and ignored the doctor remark. He was still struggling with that decision, and thought that maybe it was a good idea to trade the badge for a stethoscope.

"For starters, you could say hello. Maybe ask me how I've been. Or even better, give me a kiss."

"Hello. How have you been?"

"Lousy," Jennifer quipped.

Cameron leaned forward and kissed her softly. "I think I'm sorry to hear that you've been lousy. But not if it's because you've missed me." He leaned forward and kissed her again, but this time she passionately returned his kiss.

Mindy quickly took the mug from his hand as Jennifer and Cameron embraced and held each other. Their soft embrace tightened as the kiss lingered. The warmth of her body felt wonderful. Spears of excitement shot throughout his body.

"I've missed you," Jennifer seductively whispered.

"Missed you, too."

"Missed you more."

"I don't think so."

"Spaghetti?"

"What?"

"Would you like spaghetti for dinner? I know Mindy and I would love it."

Cameron laughed and then clasped his hand over his mouth when Mindy slapped him and pointed to the couch. Jasper rolled over, but buried his face against the back cushion.

"Spaghetti would be wonderful. Oh, God. You don't know how wonderful."

He stood in the center of the kitchen, spellbound. He knew he had to be dreaming. First, it was a nightmare. Then it turned into a wonderful dream that he did not want to wake up from; his two favorite females sharing the kitchen. Each humming a tune of her own. Jennifer's, a country and western song he'd heard maybe once or twice. Mindy's, a song that she had often sung in the shower. Something by Katie somebody, he couldn't keep up. The humming blended and sounded wonderful. It was music to his ears.

Chapter 63.

July 28, 6 P. M.

The four of them sat in the cluttered dining room, around the ratty dining table, discussing the entire ordeal. Quentin was dying. No. Quentin had already perished. Along with its residents, the economy had died. Neither Cameron nor Jennifer could see an end to the madness.

It was then that Jennifer revealed that she had lost the diner and surely would lose her home, too, before the end of the month. The room was silent. Her words trickled across the table in sullen drips. Cameron could not believe his ears. In the midst of death, economics still reigned.

"I think we're going to move to Arizona," Jennifer stated in a matter of fact tone. "I don't see how we can stay here. We're not infected and my father said he could get us out. Please come with us. Please?"

Cameron glanced to Mindy, then to Jennifer. "I think I could do Arizona if Mindy wants to—"

"Are you kidding, yes!" Mindy blurted, her eyes darting between Cameron and Jennifer. "Yes-yes and yes!"

"What does that make us?" Cameron asked, almost wishing he hadn't. Things between them were looking brighter and he didn't want to ruin it. A wrench in the gears could end what was now suddenly blossoming.

"First, it makes us survivors," Jennifer answered, "second, we move and then we decide what it makes us."

"I can do that," Cameron joked, trying to ease the tension that he felt, finding comfort in the fact that he hadn't been the only one feeling it. "But first, we try to convince these people that it's the mosquitoes. Get them to spray. Then we leave. Okay?"

"Sounds like a plan to me, Yankee." Jennifer answered with a *I knew that was what you were going to say* smile, and then nodded.

"Let me show you something," Cameron said with grief as he jumped up from the table and hurried to the desk. He picked up a map and spread it atop the spaghetti-stained plate in front of Jennifer. "Here's Quentin. This is the direction that most of the storms pass through. Here's Dallas-east Dallas. Here's Greenville, Sulphur Springs, Arkansas, Louisiana, and so on."

Jennifer followed the coloring that appeared to widen as the pattern expanded out to the East

Coast, ending at the Atlantic Ocean. "I don't understand."

"It's a weather map. The jet streams. Don't you see it? The jet stream moves across Quentin to the next spot on the map that could inherit the deadliest disaster this country has ever seen. The jet stream could force the mosquitoes to the entire East Coast."

"But that's where they came from," Mindy interjected.

Looking at Mindy, Cameron replied, "No, well, yes. First, they arrived inside the tires on the ship from the Mosquito Belt in Africa and then transferred to the truck without ever escaping. They were contained from the moment they left Africa until they spilled out in Quentin. The article mentioned that there was never an outbreak there. The shaded area is the potential path for an outbreak if the mosquitoes ride the jet stream out of here." He thought for a moment. "I don't know that mosquitoes could migrate that far, but I'm afraid they could because of the high winds."

Goosebumps covered Jennifer's arms as she traced the path with her long, slender forefinger. The area from Quentin to Florida and to the south of Boston was shaded in a pale, pale shade of red. "D-Do you think it's possible?"

"Yes. Now look at this," Cameron answered, as he opened a copy of a 'U.S.A. Today' and pointed to the forecast map. "Up until now the storms have pretty much dissipated over Quentin. The Gulf Stream pushed one way. The jet stream another. That's why we've been having so much rain. Look at the next two weeks. Rain. Rain. Rain.

Rain. Partly cloudy. Partly cloudy. Northeast winds. Northeast winds. No rain, more winds. We have just over six days to convince these people that there will be an outbreak like no one can imagine if these mosquitoes hitchhike to the East Coast. Everyone, including the President of the United States, will become infected and die. The entire East Coast from Florida to New York will become infected. My guess is that at least one third of the U.S. population will become infected and pass the virus through simple unknowingness as they jet from one coast to the other before showing symptoms."

The room fell silent.

Through the new heavily caulked windows, Cameron heard Shep's resonating howl, which made him pause until Mahowee's words, "When the rains give way to pleasant winds," flashed through Cameron's thoughts. It was then that Cameron realized Mahowee pulled Tommy and the trucker free from the wreckage. He watched as the tires catapulted into the lake and the surrounding grasses. He noticed the swarms of mosquitoes when they became airborne and he had fled to safety. More importantly, however, he had read the article.

Chapter 64.

July 29, 2:30 A. M.

Cameron stood at the window and studied the thick surroundings. The only noise he heard was the soft snores of Jennifer and Mindy asleep on the living room floor. Jasper was so silent that Cameron stood over him for a few minutes to make sure he was still breathing. He had done that many nights when Mindy had been a baby.

The night seemed still except for the droning of insects, which now floated in thick pockets toward the house. Through the glare of the porch light, he watched the plague in progress. Some of the mosquitoes appeared enormous, large enough to put a saddle on and ride, he thought, but he also knew that was a touch of paranoia and they were no larger than what he saw last year.

A clap of thunder boomed, shaking the house and illuminating the darkened yard for a mere second.

He stood gazing around the yard toward Calvin's house. For the first time he saw the dark shape of the Taurus hidden deep in the thick underbrush that filled the one acre lot between his and Calvin's place. It looked to be a standard Government Issue, but he really couldn't discern the actual type of vehicle from this distance, especially with the pulsating light of the approaching storm.

He turned and looked down at Jennifer and felt a warm feeling he had not felt in years. She was even more beautiful asleep on the floor than awake and in his arms. Her hair fanned across the pillow. Her arm draped lightly over Mindy as if protecting her. A soft snore escaped her full lips. Lips that he wanted to kiss, to taste, and maybe even nibble on. She was beautiful. She was everything he wanted and more. He had not felt like that since Amanda died.

His palms became moist with excitement and he wiped them on the butt of his jeans. He wanted to ignore the stalking Taurus, the kids, and carry her in his arms to the bedroom, and make love to her. He wanted to feel the warmth of her body lying next to him, naked; caressing each other into a simmering passion that he knew was locked deep inside her. He could tell, because he, too, kept his passion locked deep inside himself. He wanted to explode. He wanted to tell her how much he loved her, and how much he needed and wanted her.

Ignoring the overwhelming feelings, he crept back to his bedroom and went to the closet. He removed a pair of binoculars from the top shelf and crept back to the window.

The house creaked. Its mumbled groan sent a chill down his back. He knew there were microscopic holes in the walls that could allow some of the smaller mosquitoes in. When he least expected it, they could feast until their small bellies were full. Then, one by one, the crazy little bitches would sneak back out and leave his lifeless body in the darkened room until a Hazmat alien came to take him to the burning pit.

He shivered.

Standing in front of the rain-rippled window, he peered through the binoculars. He saw a figure sitting in the dark. His head tilted to the right. He appeared to be asleep.

Suddenly behind him Jennifer whispered, "Try these."

Cameron jumped, stifled a scream, and turned. "What the!"

"I didn't mean to sneak up on you," Jennifer continued in a hushed laughter. "They're night-vision binoculars. They were in Jess' 4-Runner. I don't have a clue why I stuck them in my purse." She shrugged. "I just thought they might be something you'd want..." She wrapped her arms around him in a soft embrace and kissed him.

Cameron inspected the odd-looking eyewear and slowly put them to his face. The Taurus leaped out at him. The face of the stranger slammed against his eyes like a freight train.

"Son of a bitch. Damien Butterfield!"

"Who?" Jennifer quizzed, releasing him when she reached for the binoculars.

He handed her the binoculars. "Damien But-terfield. I met him in Tommy's hospital room the other night. He told Tommy he was an insurance agent for the trucking company."

"Since when do insurance agents sleep in their cars half hidden in the woods? Unless he has someone with him, I'd say this is highly suspect, "Jennifer said as she looked out into the darkness.

Cameron continued, "No. He's government, but what in the hell is he watching me for?"

"Did you piss off Nationwide again and not renew your policy?" Jennifer whispered.

"Yeah. I went with Farmers this time," Camer-on answered. "Insured the house for four point two million. They were ecstatic."

"Hmm. If he's from the government, my guess is they think you know too much," Jennifer said. "After all, you have made quite a spectacle of yourself."

"A what?"

She smiled. Then kissed him. "And I am very proud of you. All this time I thought you were this shy quiet little man. I was so wrong." She looked at him with sorrowful eyes, and continued, "I am so sorry. All the time I thought you didn't care, but you were only doing what a man knows how to do. Fix things."

"Yep, that's me, "Cameron said in the midst of a chuckle. "Mister Handyman."

"Sometimes we—women—just want a man to listen. And all men want to do is offer suggestions on how to fix what we're talking about. But, you...

You were doing both. You were really listening all the while you were trying to figure out what was going on, so that when the time came, you could fix it."

Cameron blushed. He was speechless. Not because he was really listening, but because he didn't know what to say.

They embraced. Then kissed.

The thought of pulling her to his bed entered his mind along with the thought of nibbling on her lips. Then the thought of holding her naked body against his sent a river of warmth throughout his entire body.

"Are you going out there?" Jennifer asked after handing the binoculars back to Cameron.

"No, I don't want him to know that I know. Better to let him think he has the best of me..."

They slowly strolled back to the living room, leaving his thoughts of love making by the window.

Chapter 65.

July 29, 4:30 A. M.

Colonel Peterson was having trouble sleeping. Nightmares. Horrible nightmares that ended with sharp snaps of bright light as if hit with an IED. He usually bolted up into a sitting position drenched in perspiration. Tonight he just lay on his side and faced the barren wall while drifting in and out of a light sleep. He had finally surrendered to the fact that he was just not going to be able to sleep. There was too much on his mind. He wasn't accustomed to watching Americans die on American soil, at least not like this. This wasn't a terrorist attack that could be revenged by capturing and killing the terrorist that planned it from their caves in the mountains; this was a darkness he had heard and read about, but never witnessed first-hand.

Real outbreaks occurred somewhere else.

The threats from his superiors whirled in his mind. Their cold-hearted demands left him as helpless as a lost child, but like any good soldier, he was obligated to follow orders. Even the one final demand that haunted him day and night. An order that he would eventually have to follow. After all, he was a good soldier. A damn good soldier.

He sighed in a helpless manner.

He rolled over, glanced at the door of his makeshift barracks, and thought about getting a drink of water. The nightmare always left him thirsty. As his gaze wandered around the room, he was struck with surprise; so much so, a chill crawled across the back of his neck. Hidden deep in the corner was a silhouette of someone leaning against the wall.

Colonel Peterson sat up and reached for his pistol.

"That won't be necessary. If I had wanted to kill you, you would have already been dead."

Colonel Peterson stopped and squinted his eyes as he looked at the figure in the dark. "Do you make it a habit of entering—sneaking—into a tent uninvited?"

"Only when I need to." The figure stepped out of the darkness and handed the colonel a sheaf of paper. "Your orders—just the way you wanted them—in writing. Now level the town. There is an F-16C/D Fighting Falcon at Barksdale awaiting orders. The navigation path has already been mapped. The planned timetable is oh-four-hundred hours tomorrow. They are just waiting for your call."

Colonel Peterson held the sheaf of paper in his hand, silent. How could he drop one of the world's most dangerous thermo baric, or non-nuclear, bombs on American soil? A fuel air bomb so powerful that when it exploded it would suck in the surrounding oxygen and incinerate everything within a couple of miles of ground zero, killing everything in its path. Not only did they want him to drop one, but they wanted him to drop three at one time. Each would be reported as a gas pipeline explosion that would eliminate the entire population. Colonel Peterson pulled his pants on and then turned on the bedside lamp.

"I'd rather wait," Colonel Peterson mumbled, more so to himself.

"You don't have a choice, now turn that light off."

Colonel Peterson switched off the lamp. "Don't tell me I don't have a choice."

The darkened figured grated in a laughter that sent another chill down Peterson's back, and he never dreamed that was even possible. "Look at the signature."

Colonel Peterson glanced down at the signature expecting to see it signed by a General, but instead saw the signature of the President of the United States, embossed with the official seal. "Surely he knows we can save this town."

The darkened figure removed a fresh Cuban cigar from an inside pocket and lit it. "You don't understand, Colonel. This isn't about saving the town. This is about saving a political battle that will continue on past your retirement. We're no longer concerned with the virus. Our only concern is with political power and who has that power."

"I don't give a shit about politics."

"Certainly you do. You are a Colonel, are you not? You did not reach that rank just by kissing ass. You got to that rank through politics. And if you choose to go further, you will kiss more ass and play the political game just like the rest of us."

"Rest of us? Rest of us? You stand in the fucking shadows, pulling strings and manipulating every goddamned bastard who steps in your way. You are the political game! You are the cowards who give orders to kill, but you never pull the trigger. You and your kind make me sick. You start a goddamn war and then get someone else to do the fighting for you all the while hiding in your little rooms looking for more shat to stir. Now you want me to kill innocent people who have already lost so much because of politics. Screw you! No! Fuck you!"

The charcoal on the cigar burned a dark red as the darkened figure drew in a mouth full of smoke. Then released the smoke with a lewd chuckle. "Do you know what is going to happen when the news of this outbreak hits the networks and newspapers and goes public? There will be panic in the streets. It will be mayhem. Every homosexual will be blamed. No one will believe that a mosquito could do this."

"The CDC has already assured me that it wasn't the mosquitoes. So there really won't be a misconception, now will there?"

"They assure you only what I want them to assure you. Is that understood?"

Colonel Peterson grumbled, then swiped away the thick cloud of cigar smoke that engulfed him.

"We are talking about human rights here, Colonel."

"What about the human rights of this town?" Peterson asked as if he already knew the answer.

"They are already dying, Colonel. Everyone in this town is going to die. The virus is spreading that quickly. Everyone is going to die unless you sweep the virus and burn it to hell." Another draw of the cigar illuminated the darkened face. He detested that face. It was the face of a murderer. "We are talking about the rights of a lot of powerful people who do not want to be publicly known for their homosexual or bisexual activities. Not only political powers, but also religious influence as well. When the public realizes just how dangerous this virus really is and how easily it spreads, there will be a witch-hunt. Anyone and everyone who had spoken out about gay rights will be hunted down and murdered. Any politician who was afraid to hurt the gay community for his own political reasons will also be hunted down and murdered. Anyone who complains about an illness that remotely resembles the virus will be murdered. A lot more innocent people than the population of this town will be hunted down and murdered for no other reason than that of their sexual behavior or the similarities in their illnesses. Even if we tell them it was spread by a mosquito, people will want to know how the mosquito came into contact with the virus in the first place. Immediately they will think it came from the gay community and then, all hell will break loose. People still associate HIV with sex and homosexuals. They do not realize that is no longer the case…" There was a slight hesitation as the darkened figure toyed with the cigar, twirling it, then taking another strong draw. "Look at the reaction to the Ebola outbreak in Dallas – everyone was in a panic. No, we will not jeopardize innocent people for the sake of this town. We will not jeopardize those who cannot handle their own sexual habits because we as Christians find it openly disgusting or sinful. No sir. We will not cause an unnecessary panic just to save your conscience. You have your orders, Colonel."

"Screw you…" Came a grumble from Colonel Peterson's cot.

"And the bigger picture, which you seem to be ignoring, is that the virus will leave Quentin. Do you not understand? It's not just the mosquitoes, but it is the way the virus is transmitted? The mosquito is just spreading it that much faster."

The room became deathly silent and smelled of cigar smoke.

"I'm not killing my daughter and grandson."

"No one is asking you to. Get them tested. If they are clean, then get them out. Once they're out, level the town. Burn it to the ground, Colonel, or kiss your sorry ass goodbye."

Colonel Peterson remained silent.

"You do realize that your daughter's boyfriend already knows. And I am sure that if he knows, then she knows."

Colonel Peterson's eyes darted to where the darkened figure stood.

"What in the hell is that supposed to mean?" Colonel Peterson grated.

"He has to die. He can't leave. If he leaves, it will become difficult to kill him. Here, he either died in the blast or from the virus, either way." The darkened figure shrugged. "He's dead."

"And what if she knows?"

The darkened figure dropped the Cuban on the floor and stamped it out, then stood for a moment, not answering, turned, and left.

Colonel Peterson nervously pulled his shirt on and, while buttoning it, he moaned, "Oh, Jesus… Mary… and Joseph…"

Chapter 66.

July 31, 9 A. M.

Jennifer tried to stare her father down. She held her love for him over his head silently to withdraw it, but, being as callous as he had become, Colonel Peterson wasn't going to give into any petty demands, even from his own daughter. Spraying for mosquitoes was just a frantic last proposition. Agreeing to spray would be to admit that he believed the mosquitoes were the cause of the outbreak, which he didn't. The entire staff of virologists and epidemiologists had told him that it was impossible. He had sat in countless meetings where these people discussed probable causes, and none of them would accept that the spread of this HIV virus was due to mosquitoes. There were other hypothetical reasons tossed out on the table, but mosquitoes were at the bottom of the list.

It was impossible, but after his meeting earlier this morning, he wasn't so sure. He wasn't sure about anything except that his daughter would be murdered if he did not get her out of Quentin. The town of Quentin would be engulfed in an inferno so hot that nothing would be spared.

He quickly glanced at the three standard government clocks that were on the wall. Each was set to a different time zone. It was time to start moving his men out. It was time to have Jennifer and Jasper tested again and then placed on a helicopter and flown away. He felt she would be safer in Fort Hood, even under guard.

The clock was ticking.

The pressure weighed so heavily on him that he could hardly breathe. To think that he was involved in murdering Americans—even those infected—was unbearable.

The disaster countdown continued as his eyes drifted back to the set of clocks. In nineteen hours, Quentin, Texas would be wiped off the face of the earth. It would be listed as one of the worst disasters ever recorded. It would be even worse than the Texas City explosion of 1947 where over five hundred people lost their lives.

The hapless local natural gas supplier would, of course, be blamed. Since the president of the company would also die in the mysterious explosion and all of his worldly possessions incinerated, there would be no one for the relatives of the deceased bystanders to sue, no one for them to scream at, no estate for them to lien.

Peterson's eyes drifted back down to the map Jennifer had placed on his desk for his consideration. He chuckled. He then glanced at the newspaper that she had put next to it. It was about the only thing that was accurate in all this madness. Rain had been predicted again today.

Just like yesterday.

He looked out through the opened door of his prefabricated office to Quentin Central Hospital and watched as soldiers carried six more bodies to a waiting truck. Half the town had already perished. Half the survivors were already infected, and this time next week, he would watch their bodies thrown onto the same truck. He would hear the sobs of the soldiers as the bodies were taken to the crematorium, but only if he didn't drop the bomb.

He hated the situation in which he currently found himself. He loved his country, but hated it, too. Although he never knew it, or even realized it, he and Cameron had more in common than their love for Jennifer.

He had two choices: fire bombs or spray. Spraying was starting to look like the foremost of the two options with each tick of the damned clocks.

He looked down at the map Jennifer had given him, then to the wall that held the map of Quentin. He focused on the red circles that appeared to be the most highly infected areas.

Crystal Lakes.

The name leaped out of the fluorescent ink like the headlights of an oncoming vehicle. As he stared, like a deer, trapped, he felt it. The truth slammed into him and nearly threw him backwards.

He snatched up the telephone and bellowed to an unknown voice on the other end. "I want as much goddamned pesticide as you can get your hands on!" He waited. "I want it today. Find me as many crop-dusters as you can find." He waited again. "Call Barksdale and get their air tankers loaded up with pesticide. I don't give a damn, Sergeant! Do you hear me?" His fist pounded the desk so hard that his knuckles began bleeding. "Today! Not tomorrow, today! Get your ass in gear, Sergeant, or I'll have it on a platter with potato salad for my dinner. Do you hear me?" He waited again and smiled as he heard rummaging on the other end. "Fourteen Hundred. Make it sooner, Sergeant. Make it sooner. I need it sooner, and it sure as hell better not be later. Do you hear me?" He slammed the telephone down and looked across the room to Jennifer.

She smiled.

"Are you happy? You do realize that this is going to make me a laughingstock?"

Colonel Peterson didn't wait for an answer. He was too concerned about her safety and opened his mouth to order her and Jasper on the next chopper to Fort Hood, but before he could speak, an officer came through the door, slowing only to snap to attention.

"What is it, Lieutenant?" Peterson barked, angered for the interruption.

"Begging the Colonel's pardon, sir. T-There's been another outbreak!" the Lieutenant blurted out.

Colonel Peterson, standing behind his desk, leaned forward on both hands and loomed forward. "What do you mean, Lieutenant?"

The younger man glanced at Jennifer then back to the Colonel, hesitating before replying, "It." He paused. "It's the men, sir."

Colonel Peterson froze. Small droplets of perspiration quickly sprung to his forehead as if someone had turned off the air-conditioner. He knew the answer.

"The entire Clear—"

"Lakes," Colonel Peterson continued. "Are you sure, Lieutenant?"

"Yes, sir," the Lieutenant snapped as he stood frozen at attention.

A Humvee roared to a halt. Its occupants darted to the door with more of the same news. The entire unit that had surrounded Crystal Lakes was now infected.

The secret was nearly out.

An HIV outbreak was spreading faster than anyone could have ever imagined.

And we aren't even trying to control it.

Colonel Peterson sat down. He looked at Jennifer. "Could Cameron have been right all along?" Jennifer nodded. "Son of a bitch..."

The only salvation in this cluster fuck, as the Colonel saw it, was that the Army personnel were now infected, making it too late to firebomb.

(Or so he hoped.)

He looked at Jennifer. "Please take Jasper and go to Fort Hood. Please?"

Jennifer nodded. She rounded the desk and embraced her father from behind. "Please stop this before it kills you too," she whispered.

Chapter 67.

July 31, 11:30 A. M.

Cameron stopped in front of Mahowee's house and hesitated before opening the door of the unmarked sedan. He hadn't spoken to Mahowee since the outbreak. He had heard from the other residents that he was held up in his house and refused to leave.

He finally opened the door of the cruiser and darted for the porch. As he topped the last step, Mahowee opened the front door and let him in.

The house was amazing.

Calm and serene.

Mahowee smiled, pulled his pant legs up to expose his socks. "Same colors!"

"Turned the lights on before you got dressed this morning, didn't you?" Cameron laughed as he followed the old man to the kitchen.

Mahowee chuckled as he pulled a wooden chair away from the Southwestern style table and sang, "Iced tea or Pepsi?"

"Tea sounds refreshing, and I can use something refreshing, Pepsi will only make me want to add something stronger," Cameron said with a laugh as he took a seat. He loved sitting in Mahowee's house. The place was immaculate. The earth-tone colors blended perfectly throughout the entire house. Nothing was ever out of place and everything seemed to have its own natural place, almost like notes in a symphony. The tabletop, made of various green colored tiles, for some unknown reason, was pleasing to Cameron.

"They're going to start spraying," Cameron said as he pulled the chair further out from beneath the table and sat down with a light thump as if he was carrying the world's problems on his shoulders.

Mahowee nodded, but didn't reply.

A grimace settled at the corners of his lips in silent protest, then grunted, "There are more natural ways and pesticides than the chemicals they're going to use."

"Why didn't you tell me you pulled Tommy and the trucker from the wreckage?" Cameron asked, ignoring Mahowee's comment. He could debate this all night but didn't want to. Mahowee was right, but hell, they're spraying and asking for more would have been impossible.

Mahowee turned and put Cameron's iced tea down and then sat across from him. He looked at him for a moment before replying in a soft earnest tone, "At the time, I didn't think it was important.

Even when I saw the tires being thrown from the truck, I didn't think it was important. It wasn't until I read that article that I knew what was going to happen."

Cameron looked at his friend, but said nothing.

"I called the County Health Department and reported what I saw. They said that they would look into it, but what they were really saying, was that I was a crazy and feeble old man and they were going to ignore me..." His words trailed as he vividly recalled the conversation. "I then called the Mayor and he reacted exactly the same as the morons did at the County Health Department. So, I went to see him. He and Buster just laughed me out the door. No one listened."

"Calvin listened," Cameron interrupted.

Mahowee laughed.

"He's a bigger fool than I am. You were the only one who really listened, but by then, my good and unselfish friend, it was too late. The celebration came and the cleansing began," Mahowee said after regaining his composure.

Cameron glanced around the room, nervous and embarrassed. He tapped his fingers against the glass as he searched for something to say. "I should have done something, really, just convinced the mayor to call the whole thing off."

Mahowee spat, chuckled, and then laughed. "You are kidding, right? They would never have called the celebration off. No. There was nothing you could have done that I hadn't already tried to do. No one would listen. It was inconceivable. It couldn't happen here."

As Cameron started to speak, the timer bell that sat atop the oven sounded. Mahowee opened the oven door and removed a large metal pot from the heated cavern. He carefully placed the pot down on the stovetop and removed its heavy lid. The aroma swept across the room to Cameron's nose and his mouth quickly salivated. It was Mahowee's famous pot-roast.

"The plates are in that cabinet," Mahowee said as he pointed across the room. "We should eat. You have a monumental job ahead of you..."

Chapter 68.

July 31, 12:30 P. M.

Half asleep, Tommy tried to roll over onto his side, but the heavy cast that still embraced his leg stopped him from finding comfort in the bed that he believed would be his for another couple of weeks. He was beginning to feel like he was in prison instead of a hospital. He knew something was happening outside the dull eggshell white walls, but he didn't have a clue as to what it was. Some time back, the horrible hospital food had been replaced by MREs delivered three times a day by a soldier who wouldn't answer any questions and paused only long enough to empty the bedpan and urinal and write something in his chart at the foot of the bed. If Tommy had been able to cut the rope holding his leg in that damn traction device, he might have been able to hobble out to the hallway to get a look at all of the ruckus.

He did like the idea of having a private room though, thanks to Damien Butterfield. He was a pretty good old boy, after all, Tommy thought.

Damien Butterfield stopped by every day to see how Tommy was feeling, and to make sure that he had plenty of magazines and snacks. He kept close contact, keeping an eye on him. Tommy was careful not to ever let Butterfield know that he felt well enough to be discharged. He was already thinking about filing suit against the insurance company and the trucking company since it didn't appear he was going to be arrested for DUI.

Then the sad feeling that had crept over him last night, returned. He just knew Arlene had abandoned him. He figured she had run off with the manager of the Stop'N Go. It had been about six days since she last stopped by to visit. He couldn't remember for sure. Every day seemed like the last one. They all seemed to be one long ribbon of days and nights. When she did come, she just complained. The house needed repairs. The neighbors were busybodies. The weather was miserable, just like his drinking, and now they were almost penniless. She just didn't know how they were going to pay this month's rent. With Tommy in the hospital and she only earning a meager paycheck from the Stop'N Go, she was sure they were going to lose everything. He never thought he would miss her bickering and constant babbling, but now, lying flat on his back and being bored completely out of his mind, he did.

He could sure use a cold Coors. Maybe a shot of Jack chased by the Coors.

That thought made him wonder why he was still here.

He seemed to nap more now than when he had first arrived at the hospital.

He stared at the blank television and felt a queasy feeling come over him. It must be from the lunch, he thought. He lay back deep into the pillow and stared at the ceiling. Suddenly he cringed as a sharp pain sliced through his stomach like a knife. It felt hot. He felt hot. Sweat ran down the sides of his temples.

"What the hell?" Tommy gasped. His entire body trembled as he ran his hand across his stubble-bearded face. His chest rose and fell in quick breaths. He felt like he was dying. He tried to remember who was in his room last, but he couldn't recall anyone, except the soldier who had brought his lunch. He didn't remember her name, but he damn sure remembered her cleavage. He tried to remember if maybe he had heard someone else in the room. That may be the reason he had awakened from his nap.

His heart began pounding ruthlessly against his breathless chest. His face began turning red from the nervousness. Although he had eaten lunch only thirty minutes ago, he now suddenly felt famished.

He tried to sit up, and when he did, he began vomiting. His entire body trembled.

He fell back against the pillow and chills raced through his body.

He lay in a cold sweat staring at the eggshell white ceiling and listened to the shuffling of feet that swept past his door.

Finally, he closed his eyes.

The death toll climbed.

Chapter 69.

July 31, 2:30 P. M.

Cameron stopped in front of Calvin's place. This time he left the cruiser without hesitation and darted for the front door. As he ascended the top step, Calvin opened the door and let him in. The method was the same for those who knew it was the mosquitoes.

Cameron nearly fell back from the stench; his breath came in jagged gasps and breathed only through his mouth.

As Cameron handed Calvin the bag of snacks, he took the bottle of Coors beer that Calvin held out in front of him and made his way to the couch. He hesitated but then sat down without a second thought. The last thing he wanted to do was get Calvin upset like he had yesterday. Calvin was simply an old man who lived alone who also happened to be a hoarder.

"I just knew you'd be here," Calvin cackled in a loud roar. "I just knew it. I tol' old Shep that you'd be bring'n him some treats, too. He's jus' gonna love ya fer it, I jus' know he will."

Cameron took a small drink from the cold bottle, hoping he'd get used to the stench. "Everything still okay?" Cameron asked, nodding.

Calvin threw the bag of pork rinds in the recliner and started for the back of the house. "Yep, and just got better. Wait till old Shep gets a whiff of this bag o' treats."

When Calvin disappeared to the back of the cabin, Cameron stood and walked to the window that faced toward his house. From this position, he could see where the Taurus had been parked. Except for the flattened brush where the tires had rolled and then rested, nothing else seemed to be disturbed.

When Calvin returned, Cameron turned to him and asked, "Any clue as to who is sitting in the car?"

Calvin hesitated for a moment, as if he was seriously pondering the question, and replied, "Nope. He just sits there and stares at your place. He never leaves the car. He never eats or drinks. Never anything. He just sits and watches like he's wait'n on somethin'."

Calvin spat a thick stream of tobacco juice toward a Maxwell House coffee can, but missed with a shrug, and then dropped down into his Lazy-Boy recliner. He quickly pulled the handle, lay back, and ripped open the bag of pork rinds.

Cameron sat across from him on the couch, took another drink from the cold bottle, and watched while Calvin shoveled a hand full of pork rinds into his tobacco stained mouth.

"I watched yesterday," Calvin garbled. "He showed up about five, maybe ten, minutes after you did, and far's I can tell, leaves about ten minutes before you do. He drives old Shep bark raving crazy."

Cameron laughed, but he knew he had someone worried. The question was who and why? Who was this Damien Butterfield and why was he keeping such a close eye on Cameron?

Chapter 70.

July 31, 7:30 P. M.

Cameron and Jennifer sat close to each other, looking out of the back bedroom window.

Rain slashed against the windowpane in huge drops. The backyard blinked in quick strobe-like flashes of light. The roar of the storm and crashing of thunder shook the bungalow in accord with the strobes.

They traded a kiss occasionally, but rarely pulled their eyes from the lone vehicle that sat in the semi-darkness and stared back at them.

"Friend or foe?" Jennifer whispered.

"Foe," Mindy quickly answered. She and Jasper were lying across the bed, sneaking a peek through the fog-laced window.

"Could be friend," Cameron answered, although he really didn't believe it.

"Did you call your friend in Washington?" Jennifer asked.

Cameron kissed her and replied, "Yes, he's looking into it."

"I thought the phones were dead?" Mindy asked.

"Not at the station. Although, I was surprised I could dial outside of Quentin." Cameron then chuckled and continued with a thick Texas accent, "I guess studying Buster's voice came in handy after all."

"And all that time, I thought you were trying to impress me by losing that Yankee accent."

They laughed at Jennifer's comment and continued to peer out of the window into the rain-soaked darkness.

She squeezed his hand and lay her head on his shoulder.

The warmth of her body was nudging him toward the edge.

The telephone rang with good news.

Chapter 71.

August 1, 5 A. M.

"I'm not going!" Mindy shouted from her bedroom doorway.

"You have to," Cameron replied, his voice choked with sadness as he timidly entered her bedroom.

"I'm not leaving you here alone—"

Cameron embraced her, kissed the top of her head, and whispered, "I need you to keep an eye on Jasper. Please?"

She pulled away and went into her closet, removing a Nike carryall and slamming it down on her dresser. "Who's going to watch you? You can't even work on your truck without me."

Cameron went to her and held her again, caressing the back of her head as she cried in his arms. "I can't chance anything happening to you. I just can't, but I can't abandon everyone else, either."

She pulled slightly away and looked at him. He cradled her face in his hands and wiped the tears from her cheeks with his thumbs and smiled when she said, "You promised mom that you would never leave me alone..."

"And I'm not. I'm sending you to safety until I can figure out what's going on around here. That's all," Cameron said as he choked back tears. He paused and cleared his throat. "And for you to keep an eye on Jasper. Jennifer really needs to know he'll be in good hands."

They both stood in front of the small bed, each putting a piece of clothing into the carryall. Each hesitating, as if this would be the last time they saw each other.

Their silence was broken by the roar of a helicopter overhead.

"I love you," Mindy said, but Cameron barely heard her beneath the roar of the helicopter.

"Me, too," He crooned in his own little way when he wanted her to really do something for him.

She broke into a nervous laughter, which she normally did when he answered her that way. "You love yourself, too?"

He hugged her. "It's going to be okay. Two, three days you'll be back home complaining about summer camp. Before you know it, you'll be complaining about school. Then when we get to Arizona, you'll have something new to complain about, and can start all over again."

"Just like mom, right?" Mindy replied, her sobs coming in harsh waves.

Cameron embraced her again. "Just like your mom." He kissed the top of her head as he held her. "I love you."

"Me, too." Mindy mumbled.

Chapter 72.

They walked toward the Huey, which Cameron was beginning to hate, because their camouflaged bodies swarmed like dragonflies over Quentin, frightening the residents. It was bad enough that the death count was now three-quarters of the town's population, but then those who survived had to live in fear.

He watched as Jennifer strapped Jasper to the seat. Jasper held his tiny arms out, screaming as Jennifer tried to get in and sit next to him. His small hands and arms fluttered about in fear.

Two soldiers in full field dress, stood erect with their automatic weapons pointed upward, and their faces frozen. A third tightened the strap on Jasper and began to inspect the one on Mindy, cinching it tighter.

Deciding to go along, to make sure everyone was out of Quentin and safe, Cameron climbed aboard and sat next to Mindy, across from Jennifer. He stared out of the helicopter door as it ascended. The town looked ghostly. Roadblocks still blocked the major thoroughfares. Military units still marched through and around the dense woods that engulfed it. Gunboats still patrolled Lake Fork and Lake Quentin. Cameron knew how lucky they were, there wasn't even an attempt to airlift those who were not sick, had shown no evidence of contracting the virus, and unbeknownst to Jennifer, Cameron knew what was coming.

Not one television crew stood on the banks trying to get the scoop of the century. The military bombing of a civilian population in East Texas would go unnoticed. This would disappear in time, and in time, all would be forgotten. How the government and the military had kept this a secret was beyond him.

It was sad, something that he could imagine happening elsewhere, but not here. Not in the U.S. and certainly not in By God Texas.

The suicide rate had doubled. Travis came to his mind. His body lying against the back of the couch. Cameron and Travis, friends from the day they met, would be missed. Just as well as the others that had met every morning. Bernard, Chauncey, Monica, Amy, Claude, Shauna, and Brett. They all were gone. Marco, he was just a matter of time. Claude had sneezed one too many times.

Then he thought of Shauna's ex-boyfriend, Chet. He hadn't been at the celebration, and he lived outside of Quentin proper. But, he had died last week. He, like Bernard, was found lying in his bathroom, but unlike Bernard, it was much too late and he had died alone.

How? How could he have been infected?

As the Huey banked left, going southwest, he could see Dallas engulfed in a heavy brown haze.

The winds and rains failed to disperse the pollution that hung over the Metroplex.

Thick rain clouds rolled eastward. Another day, another storm. It would be only minutes before it pounded Dallas and possibly an hour before it rolled over Quentin. An hour before it could conceivably push the mosquitoes farther east into Arkansas or Louisiana.

He glanced back down and witnessed the mist of insecticide being sprayed from both the air and the ground. Colonel Peterson's orders were being taken very seriously, even if Cameron's words had been ignored. *Nothing, and I mean nothing, will ever hurt my baby again,* echoed in Cameron's mind. As much as he hated to admit it, he was beginning to like the old man but he still held reservations.

Other than the squawking from the Huey's radio, silence filled the wingless craft. Sorrow accompanied the foursome as they escaped the intensity of the deadly virus, not knowing if they would ever return to collect what few possessions they still owned.

Cameron looked at Jennifer, and stirred a slight smile before saying, "We'll be back before you know it."

She returned his smile briefly, cutting it off as she held Jasper next to her.

A Transavia PL-12/T-230 Skyfarmer flew next to them before it seemed to sink beneath the horizon. A thick plume of insecticide trailed behind it. Cameron saw two more off in the distance. Every inch of Quentin, doused with the spray, covered in a fog that looked like a horror movie. He shook his head, thinking, it's about damned time...

The remainder of Quentin would survive. In time, the soldiers would leave. The Hazmat alien creatures would climb back into their helicopters or unmarked vans and disappear with samples of the virus, new strain which was much worse than the type 'O' that had been discovered recently. This strain took only weeks to kill its host.

The Huey banked again and Cameron saw the Ford Taurus parked in the hospital parking lot between Colonel Peterson's personal jeep and the truck that took away the dead. It glittered from the rays that snuck between the dense clouds and insecticide fog.

"I'll be back for you, Mister Damien Butterfield," Cameron whispered to himself. "I will be back for you..."

Chapter 73.

August 5, 1 A. M.

Colonel Peterson sat in front of the USAMRIID epidemiologists discussing the outbreak. All agreed that it had ended. All were shocked to learn that the Anopheles was more-or-less responsible, however, very debatable, for the HIV outbreak. They also agreed that such information should not become public. All of the documentation should be sealed, made top secret, and locked away.

This particular HIV strain had been categorized as a level 4 biohazard virus and searching for a serum was now top priority. If it happened once, it could happen again. If it happened in this small town, it could have just as easily happened on the East Coast where the original shipment had arrived.

"The President is pleased with your findings," a Presidential Advisor commented. "He feels you men and women have done an incredible job and commends all of you."

The Advisor walked to the front of the room but, before leaving, stopped at the door, turned and said, "The bombers have been ordered to stand down, Colonel. The President wants to commend you in person, at your earliest convenience. It was you, along with our soldiers who saved this town and its remaining residents." The Advisor smiled and continued, "Good job, soldier, good job." He started through the doorway, stopped, and reentered. "Before you leave, brief the replacements."

Colonel Peterson nodded.

The Advisor finally disappeared into the darkness of Quentin. His helicopter was waiting to carry him to Fort Hood. Then his next stop, Washington D.C.

All those at the table smiled as congratulations spilled. No one admitted that it was one man and one woman who had led the crusade against that which could have crippled the entire United States.

No one, except Colonel Peterson.

Chapter 74.

Colonel Orion Peterson watched as the epidemiologists left. Their happy moods and high spirits left with them. Colonel Peterson wanted to be as excited as they were, but he knew there was more to come. He knew deep inside that he could not prevent the next war where there would be just one casualty.

Cameron Nickels.

"You poor bastard," Colonel Peterson breathed.

"Yes, he is," came a sudden remark. A remark loud enough to startle the Colonel.

Colonel Peterson turned and stared in anger. "What the hell are you doing here? It's over. Go crawl back under that rock you slithered out from under."

Ignoring the contemptuous comment came a reply, "It's time to make everything disappear."

"Why? Why can't you just leave well enough alone? The man saved over five hundred people. He should be a decorated hero."

"That would be nice, Colonel, but we already had this discussion. We certainly don't need another hero."

Colonel Peterson sat staring at the far wall, the map that Jennifer had given him, recalling their argument, and then recalling his other option. Cameron and Jennifer should be decorated as heroes, but Colonel Peterson knew that would never happen. Cameron was a beacon of horrible news. News that could never become public. The virus was going to continue to spread at its current rate, doubling each year until they discovered a cure or its host eventually isolated. The methods of transmission would remain the same; unprotected sex, shared needles, untested blood, bodily fluids, or inherited from an infected mother. All other methods of transmission discovered would disappear along with the proof that the Anopheles Mosquito could spread the virus to the whole world.

"The list?"

Colonel Peterson slid a sheaf of paper across the table. Its corners flapped up like the sail of a boat.

"There are only three names on this list." Colonel Peterson said as he looked up at one of the most despicable people he had ever met.

"That's right. Cameron Nickels, Calvin Harper, and the old Native American man by the name of Mahowee. We can't find a last name, or maybe a first name, on him. No birth records, no records anywhere.

"Everyone has a last name."

"Well, not this one—he's from some reservation—I don't know. You have all the fucking connections, look it up your damned self."

"You're forgetting one."

"No, I haven't. If you touch her, I will kill you."

"Is that a threat, Colonel?"

"No. That is a promise."

"Being a colonel, you should know better."

Colonel Peterson glared at the figure sitting across from him. "You being a major you should know better."

Lighting a Cuban cigar, the Major replied, "Now you know I no longer carry military rank. I lost that when I retired and joined the Federal Emergency Management Agency. My charter has since changed. So let me remind you, we are an independent agency for the government reporting directly to the President. Our mission is to reduce the loss of life and property and to protect our nation's critical infrastructure from all types of hazards."

The Colonel was speechless for a moment and then said in a sarcastic tone that he hoped would draw blood, "Like how you handled Katrina and Louisiana. That was a cluster fuck if ever I've seen one."

"FEMA and Homeland Security has ultimate authority over all jurisdictions and with the way our charter is written, we can take over the country, without warning, at the President's pleasure," the voice said, totally ignoring the cut. "So you just remember that. I call all the shots anytime and anywhere. All I have to do is say it is against the silent enemy, a virus, and I have full control..." a pause, a smile, "...and I can put your name on that list any time I want, so don't fuck with me, Peterson. I'm not in the mood."

Chapter 75.

August 5, 8 A. M.

Flying over Quentin was exhilarating. Cameron was eager to land and find out what had happened to his friends since he had left. From the air, Quentin still appeared very different. The roadblocks were still in position, but now they appeared to be cordoned off by road construction and natural gas line crews instead of by Army barricades. Of course, he knew there were still Army personnel handling the isolation, but at least, now it didn't look quite as dire as it had the day they flew out.

The helicopter pilot had warned Cameron before they took off, no one in, no one out. He was to pack their personal possessions and fly back to Fort Hood that evening. He assured them that the Army would make certain that their furniture and vehicles were transported to wherever he and Jennifer were going.

As he leaned against the window, Cameron recalled how he had very much enjoyed meeting Eleanor Peterson, Jennifer's mother. She and

Jennifer were so much alike that Cameron had almost mistaken her for Jennifer one night when he had sneaked into the kitchen for a glass of tea.

She had a wonderful sense of humor and her love for Jasper was remarkable. Like Jennifer, she was a very wonderful and caring woman. She had taken a back seat to the Colonel's career. Cameron thought she was much too precious for a man like Colonel Peterson and could not see what she might have seen in him.

As soon as the Bell 205 touched the ground, Cameron left it in awe. The town was languid, almost lifeless. A tomb. It was as if a bomb had exploded and all human life had disintegrated. Other than a few military types, no one was visible on the streets. Five days had swept by, virtually unnoticed, and the residents seemed to have disappeared with them.

He hurried to the Department of Public Safety and was taken aback; it was locked and abandoned. One naked light bulb shone in the middle of the narrow hall that led to Chief Givens' office.

He peered through the front windows and saw that whatever had happened, happened quickly. Shirley's Texas Tech University coffee mug sat in its normal coffee-filled position. Normally, before she left for the evening, she would wash the coffee mug and turn it upside down on a napkin until the next day. Today it sat upright. He knew she was still alive; at least she had been this morning, because he had spoken with her on the telephone.

Cameron walked to his cruiser and tried the door. It was locked also. He quickly drew his keys from his nylon windbreaker pocket and tried the lock, but the keys no longer fit the door.

"What the? ..."

He glanced at the sedan for a moment, puzzled, and then left for the hospital.

As he got closer, he discovered that the bio labs were no longer there. He stopped in front of the entrance to Quentin Central Hospital and gazed at its surroundings. The infection tents had vanished. The barbed wire that had encircled the hospital was gone also. Quentin was slowly changing, but to what he didn't know. He felt as if he had landed in another town. A town without a pulse.

"It's over," Cameron breathed. "I can't believe it... it's really over."

When he walked to the door that led into the hospital, he was surprised to find it open. He hurried in and stood in the small main lobby. Its presence was warm; not like the chaos that he had left five days ago. As the thought occurred to him, he realized that the entire room had been redecorated. The aging floral wallpaper grotesquely stained with blood and feces had been replaced with a new, more modern covering. Distinctive rainbow colors brightened the room in a very comfortable and pleasant tone.

He stared at the furniture in disbelief. It, too, had been replaced. Two white IKEA tables sat in the center of the room with various magazines neatly stacked on top of them. Six matching IKEA chairs sat in a semi-circle around the tables.

"Something I can do for you?" An older woman, maybe in her late sixties, asked. She stood behind a white Formica reception counter acting as though none of this nightmare had ever happened. She was just performing her mundane task of welcoming a visitor to a typical, small town hospital.

He was stunned.

He didn't recognize the room, nor did he recognize the woman. Her bluish hair sat neatly atop her head, teased high in the good ole Texas style. Hidden behind a thick layer of eye makeup in an attempt to hide the years that had crept up on her and strangled her face were fierce green eyes that watched every move Cameron made as he strolled around the room. He almost expected her to reach beneath the counter and pull back a shotgun.

"Good morning. I'm Deputy Cameron Nickels."

Cameron had never used the word deputy the entire time he had lived in Quentin and wondered why he used it now. Perhaps he was expecting something to happen. Maybe two or three armed soldiers would bound down the hall and shoot at him, or perhaps she would pull that shotgun and shoot him in the face. He didn't know what to expect, but he knew this was not the same hospital he had left less than a week ago.

He thought about Monica and Chauncey. A chill swept through him.

The woman cast a pleasant smile. "Is there something I can do for you, Deputy?"

"No… No, thank you. I believe I can find my way around." Cameron answered, hoping that he was hiding his confusion.

She gave a bright smile as she sat back down and continued reading an old Better Homes and Gardens magazine.

Cameron darted around the corner and made his way to Tommy's room. When he pushed open the door, to his surprise, the room was empty. Tommy had vanished, too.

Cameron glanced around the empty room and as quiet as he could be he stepped inside, looking for evidence that might have been left behind. "Nothing," Cameron mumbled. "No clothes, no magazines. What the hell? …"

"Excuse me, sir!" The hospital security guard blared.

Surprised, and taken aback at the forcefulness from the rugged voice behind him, Cameron—with his hand on his Glock— quickly turned and, not only was he surprised at the forcefulness but even more so when he didn't recognize the guard, but then again, the hospital had never needed a guard. Cameron knew almost everyone in and around Quentin. It was his job to know everyone.

"I'm looking for Thomas Johnson. Have you seen him?" Cameron asked, disturbed.

"Are you family?" the large man said, then hesitated for a moment before continuing, "Visiting hours aren't until six."

"No, but I am the arresting officer and I have the right to know where he is."

"Arresting officer?"

Cameron pulled his badge and wallet from his jacket pocket and held it so the guard could see it. "Yes. I arrested him for driving while intoxicated. He was in an accident... That was why he was here."

The guard hesitated as he glanced at Cameron's badge, and then over a sheaf of paper fastened to a wooden clipboard. "I'm sorry, sir, but there isn't a Mr. Johnson listed on the admittance ledger."

Cameron, numb, his mouth slightly ajar, didn't know what to say.

"Are you sure that's his name?" the guard continued.

"Yes." Cameron said as he took another look around the room, more perplexed than he could ever imagine. He looked back at the guard. "He was here only a few days ago." Cameron paused, thinking. "Did he check out?"

"I really wouldn't know if he was released, or not, sir," the guard answered in the same abusive manner. "Maybe before I came in, but...," he flipped to another page, "...his name is not on the discharge list."

"Then what would you know?" Cameron asked, following the guard's tone and manner. The guard didn't reply. "Where's Dr. Jeanerette?"

"Who?"

"Dr. Jeanerette, the doctor who runs this place."

The guard looked at him with a confused expression. "I've never heard of him. Can I help you find your way out of here, sir?"

"No!"

The guard eased his hand to his pistol and when he did, Cameron quickly followed his move.

"Really?" Cameron asked. "You really want to do this?"

The guard stood stoic, no answer.

"I don't think a shoot-out in a hospital is necessary. Do you?" Cameron continued. "If I win and you live, you will go to jail, and if I lose, you'll still go to jail."

The guard removed his hand. "I'm just doing my job, sir. DPS or not, I don't know who you are, or the people you're looking for. If you were me, how would you react?"

Ignoring the guard's question, Cameron blared, "Have a little more respect for the police, and quit fucking calling me 'sir' and tell me who's in charge!"

"That would be Dr. Alistair. Francis Alistair." the guard grated in heated anger.

"Take me to him!"

"Dr. Alistair is a *she*, sir."

"Then, take me to HER!"

The guard led Cameron down another hall that led to the administrative offices.

Every room was empty. The patients, gone.

Cameron was relieved that the outbreak had ended as quickly as it began, but he couldn't understand what was happening. He knew that Dr. Jeanerette was alive when he left. He stood face to face with him and talked with him fifteen, maybe twenty, minutes before he and Mindy boarded the helicopter. Now, it seemed that he didn't exist at all.

When he stepped through the double doors to the administrative unit, Cameron was astonished. He did not recognize any of the medical staff. It looked as if there had never been an outbreak. It was like Quentin had been moved and another new town had taken its place. If he hadn't seen the landscape from the helicopter, he would believe that he had arrived in some other town.

An attractive woman in her early-fifties or so looked at him. "May I help you?"

Cameron hesitated. He felt paralyzed.

"Dr. Alistair?"

"Yes."

"I-I'm Deputy Cameron Nickels."

With a warm, pleasant smile, she said, "Yes, Deputy, what can I do for you?"

"I was hoping I could see Dr. Jeanerette," Cameron answered in a tone that made him feel as if he were going crazy. This woman seemed to command authority that Cameron wasn't sure he wanted to give, nor did he understand why. Who was she?

The smile quickly faded. The warm glow in her light brown eyes quickly disappeared. She placed her arm across Cameron's shoulder, comforting him, and politely led him away from the guard.

"I'm afraid Dr. Jeanerette has passed away," she whispered.

"That can't be. I just spoke to him, it's not possible," Cameron stammered.

Dr. Alistair pulled him lightly toward the administration desk, removed a death certificate from a manila folder, and handed it to Cameron.

Cameron, putting on his MD hat, studied the certificate for a moment. "Yesterday? He died yesterday?"

"Yes, he was cremated last night. Unfortunately, once it became public that he was homosexual, he took his own life. Dreadful thing for a man to do. Simply dreadful," she whispered.

Stunned, Cameron fell against the counter, almost relieved that she hadn't used the word infected. He rubbed his eyes as if trying to wipe away a tear. "Damn ..." He paused. "Where's Tommy Johnson?"

"Tommy Johnson? I'm sorry, deputy, but I'm not familiar with that name."

"That's impossible! Tommy was admitted into the hospital before the outbreak!"

"Outbreak?"

Frustrated, Cameron slammed his hand down on the counter. "Yes, outbreak! I want some goddamned answers, lady!"

Dr. Alistair stared at the ceiling, showing that she was losing her patience. "I am sorry, I don't have answers to your questions. I've never heard of this outbreak. Have you notified the county?"

"Look, lady, I don't know who you are, but I'm getting awfully damned tired of this song and dance you're giving me." Frustrated, he turned from her, moving toward the middle of the room. "You and this guard... I don't know... You two seem to be screwing with me. I know if you were shipped in by the state, you'd have to know what happened and why you were brought in."

Dr. Alistair stepped away from the counter. "I don't recall giving you my dance card, Deputy Nickels and you will call me DOCTOR Alistair." Then in a frozen intonation she continued, "You'll have to excuse me now. I have work to do."

"May I escort you out into the hall, sir?" The security guard interjected, his hand resting on his pistol.

Cameron glared at the large man.

"No, thanks. I can find my way." Cameron snapped. "It's a small hospital, and unless someone fucks with you, it's hard to disappear."

Cameron stepped through the double doors in the direction where the emergency room was located. At least, where it used to be located. Like the front waiting room, the emergency room had also changed. The large plate-glass window was now a white wall. The room had been sealed and in time, would be forgotten. He stood looking for something familiar, but recognized only one wall that looked like it belonged there. Even the linoleum tile had been replaced throughout.

From what he saw, there had never been an outbreak. From what the doctor just said, there never had been an outbreak, or even a Thomas Johnson.

He walked through the doors across from those that used to lead to the emergency room and he fell back against the wall. A new room had been constructed. It looked exactly like the old emergency room, except it was now on the opposite side of the entrance. He knew it was. The last time he had looked through those glass doors with the plastic curtains, the room had been on his left. Now, it was on his right.

Confusion shrouded over him like a heavy metal lid on a pressure cooker, keeping his thoughts whirling and building to a near explosion. Was he losing his mind? Could he have been wrong? Could he finally now be infected with the virus and dementia slowly taking control of his senses? Were the doctor, the guard, the woman at the desk, and the waiting room just figments of his imagination?

He fell against the doorjamb that led to the emergency room waiting area trying to catch his breath. His heart slammed against his ribs in panic.

He stumbled out of the door, trying not to look back.

Chapter 76.

Outside, the air was crisp. A slight breeze blew across the parking lot cooling the perspiration on his forehead. The breeze felt great but it was only then that he realized he'd been sweating.

He had to pinch himself to make sure he was awake. Surely, this was a bad dream. A nightmare. There was no one here who could tell him what was happening, or what had happened.

He knew he wasn't infected. He didn't feel or act like Monica and Chauncey. Or, at least, he didn't think so.

He stared at the hospital in disbelief.

A slight tremble swept over him.

He headed to the rental house and his truck. He had to find someone who knew what was going on. He had to find someone that could at least make things normal... normal to him.

Chapter 77.

As much as he hated it, the rental house at the end of the driveway was now a welcomed relief. Parked where he had left it, the Ford F150 even made him chuckle; the right rear tire was going flat. That he remembered. He had a slow leak and was thinking about replacing it before the outbreak had occurred but had opted filling the tire with air every week.

He stopped next to the truck, peered in through the driver side window, and grinned. He inserted the key, expecting the lock to be changed, and smiled when he saw the dome light blink on as he pulled the door open. Hesitating, he pulled the door all the way open and then stepped back as a blast of heat and humidity slapped against his face. He lowered the window and shut the door.

"So far, so good. At least something is still the same," he said aloud, then paused as another thought crossed his mind. "And the frigging truck didn't explode..."

He glanced around the yard and then sauntered to the front stoop.

Something didn't feel right.

He felt someone watching him.

He looked around the yard expecting to see the Taurus, but saw nothing, and then unlocked the front door. He eased it open and slowly, *very slowly,* he entered.

Silence.

At first glance, everything in the place appeared as they had left it; Mindy's socks left near the couch, a glass on the table, and stale coffee in the pot that he could see through the doorway from the living room. However, as he made his way to the desk, he felt a punch to his stomach; the desk, stripped clean of all his research notes, books, and Mahowee's article, left him nauseated. He knew he had left everything out, he remembered thinking that he should hide everything for this very reason. Now that thought gnawed at him as he held the lamp to his forehead, fighting the urge to heave the damned thing across the room.

He sat the lamp down and then took a seat in front of the desk and breathed in defeat. He knew, but didn't want to admit that a cover up was in process. Any evidence, which could prove that something had happened in Quentin, had disappeared. Those infected, of course, were dead, but those who knew, would have to be eliminated as well.

The only comforting thought that whirled through his mind was that he knew he wasn't infected.

A cover up had begun.

He thought of Jennifer, Mindy, and Jasper.

"Oh. Shit..."

Chapter 78.

August 5, 12:30 P.M.

It took nearly an hour to get the pickup started. Mindy was right; he missed her when she wasn't there to help him turn the key or pump the gas pedal. He missed her teasing and banter when the truck acted up.

He wanted her by his side. He wanted his whole family by his side. He wanted to drive to Fort Hood, pick up his new family, and continue west until the old pickup died or they found a new home, but he couldn't. He just couldn't allow himself to abandon everything and act as though it had never happened. If this outbreak had occurred once, it could occur again, but the next time the results could be even more devastating.

The pickup backfired, shimmied, and coughed as he turned the motor off and stepped out.

He had made a mental list of the people he needed to talk to and Chief Givens was his first. Out of all the people remaining in Quentin, Buster would know what was going on. Cameron wasn't sure if he would tell him, but it was a start.

Cameron pressed the doorbell, and then impatiently knocked.

Buster opened the door and tried to conceal the surprise.

"Cam. Welcome back, son. Welcome back."

Buster moved out of the way as Cameron stepped into the foyer, uninvited.

"Just wanted to let you know the station is locked," Cameron said, clearly irritated.

"Well." Buster hesitated, drawing a rough hand down the front of his face, then reluctantly replied, "As you know we're still under Martial Law and there's no reason for us to be getting in everybody's way."

"Gave everyone the week off did they?" Cameron said.

"Yeah, I guess you could say that. Somehow, I didn't think you would be back." Buster said with a good grin that said a day off was better than a day writing tickets.

"Alive, right?" Cameron said with an impatient look before regarding the large cluttered living room. Buster hadn't been out of the house the entire time Cameron had been gone.

"I'm not sure I follow," Buster said as his smile gave way to a blank expression.

"Sure you do. Everything is being covered up. The outbreak didn't happen, and anyone who knows or is expected to say so, is going to be dealt with. Right?"

Buster shook his head and laughed. He walked back to the living room. "I'm not sure I quite follow what you mean, Cam." He sat down on a long canvas covered futon couch, picked up a tin can and spat into it. Then he turned his attention to the twenty-six inch color television and the Texas Rangers baseball game. "Sounds like you're looking for something that isn't there, Cam, and I'm telling you there's nothing going on. Go on back to Fort Hood. Go back to that beautiful gal of yours." He paused. Spat into the tin can. Then continued, "Go on back to your family, son, and take advantage of the time off."

"The entire hospital staff has changed. Slowly, but surely, everything will disappear, won't it?"

"The State stepped in, what can I say. The County is running the hospital. The State is handling all public safety. Consider yourself on vacation, and if I were you, I would take it. Go on, son. Go on back to Fort Hood. Stay a week, hell, stay two. By that time everything will be back to normal." He spat again and said, "Hell, son, you deserve this break more than anyone."

Cameron paced Buster's living room like a caged animal. Pent up fear and frustration kept him on edge as he fingered the bullet wounds, kept him wondering what was going to happen next, to him, Buster, Jennifer, the list of names went on.

He glanced at Buster and softly spoke, "I've always liked you, Buster. I've always had a lot of respect for you, too, but if you don't tell me what the hell is going on around here, you just might force me to do something that I'll regret for the rest of my life."

Buster stared at the baseball game, silent.

"The damned hospital is not admitting to an outbreak. The new doctor acted as if she didn't have a clue about it."

Buster remained silent.

Cameron turned and walked to the front door and as he reached for the handle, Buster called out, "Nothing is being covered up, son. The State just wants to help put everything back... I'm not the Chief anymore. I'm just a working stiff like yourself." He met Cameron at the door. "That's the truth. They still want people off the streets until they can be sure that the mosquitoes are dead and gone. The last person who died was Alex Jeanerette. Best-goddamned friend I've ever had. He killed himself when he discovered he was infected..." A tear sprang to Buster's strong eyes. "I'm being honest with you, son. As far as I know, there is not a cover up."

"The new doctor or administrator said Jeanerette took his life because it was discovered that he was homosexual."

Buster looked at Cameron with a blank response, and after a few labored breaths he mumbled, "No, he wasn't."

"So, why can't the truth be told?"

"I suspect they don't want to cause a panic. You were right. It was the mosquitoes. The Army thinks they've got everything under control. So, why cause panic?"

Buster leaned against the doorframe and stared outside, fighting back frustration, and thinking about Alex. Buster knew Alex better than anyone in Quentin and knew Alex liked women as much, sometimes more than, any man, and wondered who would dream up some cockamamie story and why.

"The Governor said he wanted two more weeks before opening up Quentin. Two weeks ain't long, son. Hell, we have been through worse, wouldn't you say?"

Cameron didn't reply, he just looked at him. He believed Buster was telling him the truth; at least, as far as what Buster knew. Perhaps he didn't want to know. Perhaps he really didn't know. Perhaps Cameron was wrong. Paranoia brings about very strange ideas when it comes to a person's ability to think straight.

But why the different stories about Dr. Jeanerette?

"Someone broke into my house."

"No kidding? Take very much?"

"Only my notes and the books that I had," Cameron answered sarcastically.

Buster stared directly into Cameron's eyes and honestly said, "Well, it's for sure somebody doesn't want to see documented proof. That much I'll say. Besides, you did make quite a few enemies—" he chuckled, "I honestly believe that's it, though. I honestly believe that it's over."

"Yeah, maybe you're right," Cameron said while looking down at his shoes, embarrassed. "Guess I'll go on home, pack up some things, and head back to Fort Hood." He held out his hand and the two-shook hands goodbye. "See you in a few weeks."

"Say hello to Jennifer for me," Buster said with a distressing smile.

"Will do."

Cameron stepped out the door and listened as a Transavia PL-12/T-230 Skyfarmer flew overhead. A light pesticide dust escaped from behind it like a thin contrail.

He still believed there was a cover up going on, but if so, he really didn't expect anyone to tell him.

Chapter 79.

August 5, 2:30 P. M.

Cameron parked the pickup next to Jennifer's Dodge Caravan and allowed himself a slight chuckle and smile. He wondered if Jennifer would fly back to Quentin so the two of them could drive her van back to Fort Hood, together. It would give them time to be alone. They could maybe stop off for the evening and have a nice quiet dinner. Or maybe stop by a Cineplex on the way and see a movie. Anything to get his mind off what had happened. He should start his vacation off right. Discuss their plans for the future. On the other hand, he thought, maybe they could just spend the time at the rental house; pack their things and then move.

Anything.

As long as they were alone. Together.

After all, she had brought up the idea, and he really wanted to be alone with her.

He walked to the door, stood for a moment, and listened to the silence. The public address announcements had stopped. Peaceful silence replaced the droning of mosquitoes and helicopters, something he now cherished.

There were no screaming jeeps, nor residents clinging to the back of the Humvee's trying to escape with their lives dangling on the edge of disaster. Only a peaceful silence.

He stood and listened. Nothing.

He opened the door and walked into the living room. It was the same. Other than his notes missing, everything was as he had left it. If Jennifer had been here at this moment, it would be perfect.

He picked up the telephone, dialed Colonel Peterson's telephone number, and to his surprise, heard ringing on the other end. Even the telephone service had been restored.

Chapter 80.

August 5, 6:30 P. M.

Jennifer left the helicopter with as much enthusiasm as Cameron had earlier. Other than the empty courthouse, to her amazement, everything appeared near normal. However, when she glanced at the diner, a knot quickly rose in her throat.

Cameron met her at the helipad, hugged and kissed her as he slowly led her to the pickup. He considered her expression and knew he had to get her away from the diner as quickly as possible before she broke down; the diner was her life dream.

"How was the flight?" Cameron asked.

"Much better than the flight there." Jennifer answered in a somewhat cheerful but exhausted manner. "Nice to see the military has packed up."

Cameron returned her smile, kissed her again, and then opened the door to the pickup and waited until she climbed fully in before closing the door.

That odd feeling engulfed him again.

He glanced around the empty parking lot and then up toward the rising helicopter, that feeling of someone watching caused the hair on the back of his neck to stand on ends.

The helicopter disappeared over the top of the courthouse, but the feeling remained.

"Paranoia at its finest..." Cameron mumbled as he rounded the back of the truck.

He angled himself in and behind the wheel, looking around, trying to find whoever it was that was watching him.

"How about we have dinner? I'm assuming we can leave and then come back," Cameron said while inserting the key to start the engine. "Then... I don't know." He paused, smiling. "Pack everything and leave for Fort Hood."

Jennifer leaned against him. "How about I cook dinner? We can have a nice quiet evening alone. Then tomorrow we can pack and leave."

Cameron loved that idea. He kissed her and as he keyed the ignition he replied, "That's an even better plan... assuming I have anything edible in my pantry.

Chapter 81.

August 5, 10:30 P. M.

An empty '14 Hands' wine bottle stood in the middle of the dining table between two smoldering candles. The dishes remained in front of two empty chairs. One linen napkin lay across one chair, the other beneath the table.

Jennifer stood in the bathroom, hesitating as she tried to gain enough courage to abandon the small fortress. She glanced at Cameron's shirt and wondered if she looked acceptable. The past few weeks had been horrible for her, and she knew the stress was still evident on her face. She glanced into the mirror and brushed her hair into a ponytail, then checked her makeup. She sighed. It had been over two years since she had been with a man and she was frightened.

What if he doesn't like me? She thought as she flipped her ponytail across her shoulder. Looked at it. Then flipped it back.

She ran her hands over the front of the shirt, trying to smooth away the wrinkles. She unbuttoned the top button and opened the collar, exposing a small trail of cleavage. Then she quickly buttoned the button. She repeated this three times before she decided a little cleavage would be allowable, maybe even a little sexy. After all, she was still young and attractive. Surely, the stress hadn't aged her that much that she was no longer appealing.

She breathed a nervous laugh.

She glanced over her shoulder to see if the tail of the shirt covered her buttocks and quietly laughed again. She never really realized how large Cameron was.

She heard the radio turn on, and then quickly go off. Music from an 'Aaron Neville' CD then filled the room.

When she reached to open the door, she realized her palms were moist. She wiped them with the hand towel, sighed a deep breath of courage or, perhaps, resolution, and then pulled open the door.

The bedroom lights were off.

Night-lights that she had never noticed before reflected along the floor in a soft ambiance.

The two candles were now on each end of the rental dresser glowing softly across the ceiling and creating a halo in the mirror.

She breathed deeply. Her knees trembled. It wasn't until now that she realized how much she really loved him. She hated to see him leave this morning, and began missing him only thirty minutes after he had left, but now she felt a heaviness in her chest.

Damn him.

She looked at the bed, then at him lying on it. His smile embraced her as she stepped around to the foot of the bed and slowly sat down.

Damn him and his innocent ways.

She eased close to him, and as he reached up to kiss her, he mumbled, "You are the most beautiful woman I have ever seen."

They kissed.

Her lips were soft and full of passion. Her tongue tasted of mint and felt wonderful as it caressed his. She was even better than he had ever imagined she would be.

She trembled. So did he.

He caressed her shoulder and then tightly held her next to him. An embrace that he wanted to last forever.

She gingerly kissed his neck. Then his ear.

Chills rushed down his arms.

Crickets chirped.

Aaron Neville was singing, 'Don't fall apart on me tonight'.

An incredible wave swept over him as she lightly pushed him back and began kissing his chest. The passionate kisses, quickly replaced with chilled air, forced new goosebumps to leap across his chest. Her tongue left a small trail as she moved lower.

She stopped and sat up on her knees. She untied her hair and let it drop across her shoulders, and then she unbuttoned her shirt and opened it.

The soft warm glow of the candlelight covered her.

She let the shirt fall from her shoulders and stayed still for a brief moment, as if frozen in time.

He sat up and kissed her breasts, and then gently pulled her back down with him. Her breasts felt firm against his chest. Warm. Velvety. Soothing. She felt even better than he could have imagined.

They gently rolled over to their sides, exchanging more kisses as their hands explored each other's bodies.

Her hand glided across his thighs.

His fingertips gently glided across her breasts.

Shadows of candlelight danced across the ceiling in rhythm to the music that gently filled the room.

He kissed and caressed her neck, her arm, her breasts, and then her stomach.

His breath came in stuttered cadence as if he were making love for the first time.

His fingertips gently massaged her stomach and legs, and then finally entered her.

She moaned and pulled him up to her, searching for him, massaging him in the same gentle abyss that they had fallen into.

She was moist.

His readiness ached.

She rolled, trying to climb on top.

He did the same.

They laughed like two awkward teenagers who were trying to make love for the first time.

To him, it felt like the first time.

She lay back down as he slowly edged his away atop her.

She thrust up as he entered her.

He moaned as he felt her warmth surround him.

"I love you so much," Cameron whispered.

"I know," Came her reply.

Their bodies thrust in rhythm. First slowly. Soft and gentle. Then faster, and faster. Finally, they exploded merely a second apart.

A new melody filled the room. It was softer. Slower.

He remained atop her as though he never wanted to leave. She embraced him as if she felt the same. They exchanged softer, more loving touches and kisses, neither wanting the night to end.

The act had ensured their love for one another. An act that both had thought might never happen. An act he had been sure would never happen.

He moved from atop her and lay tightly against her. His hand massaged every inch of her neck, breasts, and stomach.

Then a bullet crashed through the bedroom window, slamming into the headboard, only inches from their heads.

In sheer reflex, Cameron rolled off the bed pulling Jennifer with him.

Another bullet ripped through the window and crashed into the mirror above the dresser. The mirror exploded from the caliber of the bullet and glass rained down and across the top of the dresser, knocking the candles to the floor.

Cameron pushed Jennifer beneath the bed and groped for his pistol.

The ER flashed. Once. Twice. Pulling anger from deep inside him.

He crawled to the window and cautiously peered out.

Darkness lay over the yard in silence. Nothing moved. Nothing made a sound. The onslaught seemed to have frightened the crickets into silence.

Another missile ripped through the window, hurling shards of glass at him as the bullet embedded in the top drawer of the dresser.

Cameron dropped down on the floor and waited. Just as he started to get up and move back to the window, Jennifer handed him the infrared binoculars.

He looked at her, then around the room and realized that she had extinguished the candles and night-lights.

"Stay down," Cameron whispered. "I haven't a clue who they are, where they're at, or if it is a they."

She jumped to the other side of the window and dropped down as another bullet whistled past Cameron's head.

They waited.

Time seemed to stand still as they listened for any movement. Cameron knew the gun had been equipped with a silencer, and could not calculate how far away the shooter might be.

Nothing more happened.

He slowly looked out the window through the infrared binoculars, nothing. There was no lone Taurus, nor a gunman. Only darkness.

Shep began barking.

Jennifer looked at Cameron. "Who did you upset?"

"I'm sure many people, including your father," Cameron answered with a chuckle. "Although I think he'd use a missile launcher."

"Well, you shouldn't have seduced his favorite daughter," Jennifer said, continuing the nervous banter.

"I guess I should have seduced his not so favorite daughter, huh?"

"You wouldn't like her."

"No?"

"She has small breasts, and you look like a breast man."

Cameron laughed out loud. He couldn't believe they were joking in the midst of an ambush, but he loved it. For some strange reason it was making him feel more relaxed.

"We need to make a list of possible suspects first thing in the morning."

Cameron looked around the darkened yard and replied, "How about within the next few minutes? I think whoever was shooting at us has run out of bullets."

"That will work, too."

"Oh. By the way, I do like your breasts."

"Thank you. I like yours, too," Jennifer joked.

"Men don't have breasts. We have pecks."

"Well, I like your pecks, and I really like your butt."

Cameron glanced down at his nakedness and then back at her, shrugged, and then looked back out the window. He looked toward Calvin's and saw Shep lying on the back porch. He knew the gunman was gone. He also knew he would be back.

He turned to Jennifer and kissed her.

"Sure added a lot of excitement tonight," Jennifer continued.

"This was the best date I've ever been on," Cameron replied. "I can't wait until the next time."

Chapter 82.

August 6, 6:00 A. M.

Cameron stood on the front stoop of Calvin's cottage. He had been banging on the door for the past ten minutes and was ready to break the door in when he heard Calvin calling out.

The door edged open and Calvin smiled. "What in the blue blazes are you doing here so early?"

Cameron turned to the pickup and waved for Jennifer to come. Calvin opened the door as the two rushed in.

"Someone paid us a visit last night," Cameron answered. "I was hoping maybe you saw something. I think Shep must have scared off whoever it was."

"Nope. Didn't see a thing." Calvin said in hesitation as he looked around the room.

Cameron stared at Calvin, thinking they got to him. "You didn't see a thing?"

Calvin hesitated. "Nope." He walked into the kitchen and sat at the small Formica and chrome table. "Slept pretty much all night."

Calvin began rubbing his eyes in an odd fashion, using his thick forefinger as a pointer. He stopped, and then rubbed his eyes again, pointing at the telephone.

Jennifer caught the signal and asked, "Can I use your phone?"

Calvin hesitated, pointing forcefully. "Ain't workin."

"Sure it is. All the phones are working," Cameron replied, not realizing that Calvin was trying to signal them.

Admitting to defeat, Calvin groaned, "Is it a local?"

Jennifer smiled. "Well, no, I was going to call my dad. I know this isn't the proper time, but you know how little girls are."

"I'm sorry, but I can barely afford the fee to keep the dang thing ever-month. I know I can't afford a long distance call." Calvin answered in a joking manner.

Calvin stood and walked toward the bathroom, waving for them to follow. "You'll have to excuse me, but I gotta get a shower. I got me a chore, or two to do today in town."

They followed Calvin to the bathroom and waited while he turned the shower on. "The phone is bugged," he whispered,

Cameron looked at him in surprise. "What makes you think that?"

"Heard'em talking through it last night."

"What?" Jennifer blurted nearly aloud before Calvin was able to catch her attention.

She looked at Cameron in total amazement. Exasperation engulfed her otherwise pleasant appearance. She honestly could not believe what she was hearing. It was horrible that someone was trying to kill Cameron—them—but to be monitoring innocent people? People who have no idea what is happening in the world today. People so dirt poor that they spend their entire life trying to make ends meet. She was fuming, angrier than she had ever been in her life.

"Dang Ol'Shep knocked the blasted thing off the stand," Calvin whispered, "When I picked it up, I heard voices. Heard your name, Cam. Better'en be careful son." Calvin scratched at day-old whiskers before finishing, "They's want you deadt. Real deadt. I hadn't heard talk like that since dub-dub-two."

Stunned, Jennifer and Cameron left the bathroom and went into the living room.

Leaving the shower running, Calvin joined them.

"I'll keep an eye open tonight, but I cain't promise nothin. Been sleep'en harder'en hell lately," he said with a wink, still playing the game but not caring who was listening. "Why, with the virus gone, and the public-add-dress system gone, it's been kinda nice, ya know? If'n you said Ol'Shep was a barkin, then I gots to believe you," he paused for a breath, "Tell ya what, doe. I'm gonna lock'em inside tonight."

"Well, whoever it was, I don't think they'll be back. Besides, we're going to be leaving today."

"Where yaw off to?"

"Fort Hood," Jennifer answered. "Vacation."

"Thas nice, real nice," Calvin said, bobbing his head.

They stepped outside, and although warm, the air felt pleasant.

"By the way, the truck's yours," Cameron said.

Calvin smiled, thinking they were still playing a role of unsuspecting victims and asked, "How much?"

"Nothing. Just take good care of her."

Calvin looked at Cameron and realized that he was not role-playing. He smiled. He then pulled the door shut and walked them to the pickup. "You be real careful, hear?"

"We will," Jennifer answered, and then kissed him on the cheek.

"I'll drop off the truck before we leave."

"I always... always liked you, and never could unnerstand why, bein' a Yankee and all. But, now I know. Thanks, Cam. You'en's be real careful, they want you real deadt."

"You be careful, too," Cameron replied. "They know that you know and I'm sure they'll be wanting to talk to you as well."

Calvin shrugged a 'who cares' shrug and held out his hand.

After shaking hands, Cameron and Jennifer waited and watched as Calvin lazily strolled back to the front door, stopping to pick up a newspaper that had already faded to a dark yellow.

"Can they do that?" Jennifer asked.

"What?"

"Bug the phones like that."

"You bet they can... I'm sure that's how they knew where we were last night. I'm sure the truck's bugged, too. And no doubt your van."

They turned toward the pickup and Jennifer blurted, "You mean to tell me, they heard us last night?" Cameron laughed. "It's not funny! Is there no privacy left in this country?"

She babbled, complained, and struck at the air, hitting at an invisible figure. The more she complained and fought, the more Cameron wanted to laugh. Maybe the outbreak had changed her. He didn't know. What he did know was that he liked it. He hoped the change would never go away.

Furthermore, and somewhat surprising, she looked damned exciting with her ranting and raving and carrying on like an out of control lunatic. If they survived this, he promised himself that he'd never forget this moment, a mental snapshot moment.

Each stood on the opposite side of the pickup and looked around the area. The boughs of the tall pines swayed easily in the light breeze. It softly patted against their cheeks. The sun poked through the thickness and warmed their arms.

Cameron could feel danger.

The gunman was nearby.

A high-powered scope sighted in on one of their foreheads.

"Where to?" Jennifer called out with her eyes still scrutinizing the surroundings. Her anger, although somewhat subsiding, still simmered. Discovering that someone had violated her privacy angered her as much as losing her dear friends and extended family. Knowing that some hidden branch of the government was ready to murder those who knew what was going on disturbed her even more.

"I don't know... home, maybe?"

"Let's go to Jess's."

"Jess's? Why Jess's?"

She looked around the empty driveway and then across the hood of the pickup. "I promised Winona, before she died, that I would get and keep their rings for her." She choked. A tear edged its way to the corner of her eyes. "I can't believe they were going to get married..."

Cameron jumped into the drivers seat and started the truck before Jennifer could continue her thoughts. He suspected that if she continued, she could fall back into a depression and now wasn't the time for that. He needed her new enthusiasm. Her new attitude. Her.

She sat across from him, babbling on about the marriage. Then suddenly she slapped his shoulder. "Don't go thinking I'm losing it. I'm not. But she wants us to use their rings, if that's okay with you?"

Cameron, blushing, smiling, and almost flushing with a nervous laughter, blurted, "Yeah... Yes-yes." He slammed the truck into reverse and sped out of the driveway only seconds after she closed the door. He swung the truck around and then slammed it into drive, spinning tires, and throwing up rocks as they sped away from Calvin's.

Marriage.

He couldn't believe it!

Chapter 83.

August 6, 7:00 A. M.

They slowed, and then coasted to a stop in front of Jess's shingle-sided bungalow. The A-frame was nestled deep in thick pines, barely visible from the pine needle road that led to the front drive. From the outside it was immaculate and in much better condition than Calvin's place, but much, much smaller. Two windows faced the front yard and one was on the right side where the bedroom was. Another faced the back yard from the kitchenette. Cameron had never been to Jess's house before, but from what Jennifer had described on the way, it was very nice. He believed it, but was still surprised.

The bungalow did not fit the country-boy personality that he had believed Jess to have. However, his recent bravery and honor had also surprised him just as much.

They walked to the front door.

Jennifer reached down into a dirt-filled flowerpot and removed one of the smooth rocks similar to those often found on the lakebed of Lake Quentin.

She turned the rock over and slid the bottom off, exposing the door key. She removed it.

Cameron smiled. "Looked real."

Jennifer nodded as she unlocked the door.

Inside it was almost as immaculate as Bernard's house had been, although the furnishings were not quite as expensive. However, the taste and quality were still very appealing.

Cameron released a near-silent whistle. "Nice."

"They were in the process of remodeling. Winona picked out the furniture."

"Very nice," Cameron mumbled.

They crossed into the darkened living room, and Jennifer snapped on the overhead ceiling light that extended beneath a Casablanca style-ceiling fan, and then continued back to the kitchenette.

Exposed high-glossed-finished oak beams stretched down from the peak to the floor. Antique farming utensils hung from the end beam in the kitchenette.

The sink was clean and free of dishes.

A two-piece china and silverware setting accented a round oak dinette table with two matching chairs. A pale blue honeycomb candle seated in a silver candleholder stood in the center. It matched perfectly with the light-blue straw place mats.

Swans decorated a small bookshelf that stood against the wall. Two of the swans surrounded a matching picture frame that held a picture of the romantic couple holding each other in a tight embrace.

Soft music escaped from the only bedroom.

"Small, but really quaint," Cameron continued. "Just who in the hell was this mystery redneck?"

"Country people have taste, too, you know?" Jennifer responded, laughing.

Cameron started to apologize, but couldn't find the right words to explain how he was feeling. It was impossible for people who earned meager wages as Jess and Winona did, to afford this place and the décor. The furniture, although not terribly expensive, was not inexpensive. Even though he was discovering another side of Jess that he had never seen before, he failed to see how that other side matched the quaintness of the structure he was standing in.

They made their way to the bedroom and stopped at the door. An envelope with Cameron's name on it lay on the pillow, as if Jess had expected him.

"What the?" Cameron said in a near whisper.

He picked up the envelope and tore away the sealed flap, then removed a note and read it while Jennifer searched for the rings. When she found them, she stuffed them into her front pocket, and turned to Cameron. "Found them..."

The note held a heartfelt apology for shooting Cameron.

Chills raced up his arms. His hands trembled.

He suddenly recalled the drug war that turned an already busy hospital into chaos.

The shooting and the yelling.

A senator's son, shot three times at close range and nearly thrown from the gurney he was lying on, cried out for God.

Then an orderly, shot in the back of his head, execution style, fell to his knees. Then shot again in the face by a second shooter, before falling over on his back.

In hindsight, the shootings were intentional, a professional hit.

Although Cameron didn't see the shooter, or shooters, running through the ER, he must have been considered a witness, just before he felt the impact, he heard the shooter apologize as he pulled the trigger and shot him in the chest. The figure then stood over him and mumbled, "Don't move, they'll think you're dead." He felt a second bullet hit him seconds before the gunman fled the hospital.

He now recognized the voice.

The voice of the man who shot him.

Jess's voice.

Cameron looked at Jennifer, repeating what he had read.

Silent at first, she mournfully whispered, "I'm so sorry."

Cameron dropped the first page of the letter on the bed and continued to read the second. It explained his attempt to escape Quentin and be with Winona during her remaining days. If Cameron was reading the note then his attempt was unsuccessful and he obviously didn't make it. Perhaps Winona didn't make it, either. He prayed for her.

After a long moment, Cameron looked up at Jennifer. "It's a letter of warning. He's saying he's sorry, but he's also warning us. His letter says that there is a non-official military unit responsible for covering up disasters. They call them 'The Cleaners'. A secret group spun off 'Operation Northwood', a black ops group..."

Jennifer, her eyes soft and warm, stared at him in a sorrowful gesture.

"The unit is comprised of soldiers, Marines and Seals thought to be deceased. Each man enlisted in this unit is believed to be dead. These were men whom the government felt could not be placed back into society, unmonitored. Murderers. Hard core murderers. Their leader is a—"

"Not my father. Please don't say it's my father," Jennifer said with a gasp.

Cameron shook his head.

"According to this, it's a major stationed in Washington. Somewhere between the Pentagon and the C.I.A, but I think I met him. He was here just a few days ago. Although Jess didn't mention his name, it had to be the one and only Mr. Damien Butterfield."

Following the instructions in the letter, Cameron walked to the bathroom off to the right of the bedroom and opened the door to a white sink and vanity cabinet trimmed in gold.

Taped to the back of the bottom of the sink was a bulky package. He removed the package, returned to the bedroom, and handed it to Jennifer.

While he continued reading, she emptied its contents onto the bed. Seven stacks of unmarked one hundred-dollar bills, wrapped in plastic, tumbled out first. Then an unmarked, unregistered .22 caliber Beretta Jetfire pistol (the same pistol used on Cameron) thumped down on the bed. Lastly, there was a note that listed the assassins. The cover-up unit.

"There must be over a couple hundred thousand dollars here," Jennifer whispered, mostly to herself and in total amazement.

She picked up the note, read the names, and then noticed that on the back was a list of hits that they had already supposedly done. Cameron's name was there. The Star of David was penciled in next to his name, which meant that the hit was identified, but was not necessarily a kill. Most of the others had a regular star and some had two or three. She didn't know what that meant other than it didn't appear to be a good thing.

"What he is basically saying is that, because of the outbreak, one of two things will happen. They will either firebomb the town, which we know they didn't do, or they will kill everyone who knows how the outbreak started. He goes on to say that since I was so outspoken about the mosquitoes and if that proves to be true, I'll certainly be murdered."

The room was silent, except for the soft music coming from the radio.

Jennifer asked, "Does it say anything else... like how to get the hell out of here without being murdered?"

The radio beckoned them with soft alluring music.

"We need to get help, Cameron..." Jennifer whispered.

The radio softly called to them.

"I mean this list could save our hides..." Jennifer continued, looking at Cameron looking at the radio.

The radio.

The radio finally relayed the message that was intended, Cameron grabbed Jennifer's arm and dragged her down to the floor.

Enveloped in Aaron Neville's, 'Don't fall apart on me tonight', Cameron heard their voices from last night.

Outside a bird chirped. A car or truck backfired.

Without warning bullets ripped through the window. An onslaught began, which seemed to last at least ten minutes or more.

Dust, smoke, and glass exploded throughout the room.

The radio played another Aaron Neville's tune, then, although the conversation barely recognizable, their voices.

Cameron grabbed the contents of the envelope, along with the note, and shoved them back into the envelope and then stuffed it into his pants at the small of his back.

"Stay as low as you can, but we have to get the hell out of here. That radio is probably a bomb—"

"What?" Jennifer shouted with panic. "Then they know about the envelope, the note, the list, the money."

"Quiet," Cameron excitedly whispered as he tried to keep Jennifer down close to the floor while leading her across the bungalow.

She glared at him for being told to be quiet. Then she realized that they were already close to the front door. They had already crawled across the bedroom floor and through the kitchenette into the living room. She didn't realize that they had moved that far, because she seemed to be moving in slow motion. Time was ripping past her while she stood still.

Another barrage of bullets ripped through the bedroom. The inner walls were being chipped away.

A cloud of drywall dust followed them into the living room as the pounding continued. Chips of the wooden support beams rained down like confetti at a New Year's Eve dance.

Cameron led Jennifer to the fireplace.

The radio played another song that Cameron knew. All the songs were the exact same songs that he had played last night while he and Jennifer made love. It wasn't a radio station, but a recording of their lovemaking.

Jennifer heard herself moan.

She looked at Cameron, surprised. "That was me from last night." Chills raced up her arms. "They're playing last night back to us, the son of a bi—"

"Be quiet."

Jennifer looked at him and in a stern voice through gritted teeth uttered, "If you tell me to be quiet one more time I'm going to knock your block off."

In the midst of everything that was happening, Cameron laughed.

"I mean it!"

Cameron pulled her into the fireplace and before she knew it, they had stepped through a brick wall. They were enclosed in a hiding place, surrounded by bricks and steel. A panic room.

Dry and free from odor, they sat together silently listening for another onslaught. Cameron was hoping that the gunmen would think they were still in the bedroom, perhaps dead.

The bedroom exploded. Its explosion rocked the bungalow. The panic room, where they sat close to each other, rocked and swayed. Mortar dust rained down from the ceiling. A spider web rocked and swayed, but its owner remained hidden.

Cameron stood up and helped Jennifer to her feet. He kissed her. First softly. Then harder, embracing her as he had never embraced her before.

"I love you," he whispered.

"Me, too, as long as you stop telling me to be quiet."

Another blast followed the first one and Cameron felt the impact against his back. Two bricks fell from the ceiling, inches from their heads.

"How did you know about this room?" Jennifer asked.

"It was in his letter. He recommended we hide here in this place until things blew over."

Cameron wasn't sure the little sanctuary would hold up through another barrage. He silently prayed that was the last one.

Chapter 84.

August 6, 10:00 A. M.

Three unbelievably long hours crawled by. Three hours, while a fire blazed throughout the bungalow.

They could hear the crackling as the fire raged. They could smell the smoke as it escaped up the chimney.

They could hear the voices of men searching for them.

Nervous, Jennifer wanted to laugh, but the voices lingered near the opening. They seemed to be just outside the fireplace opening. She heard men wondering aloud how the two of them could have escaped. All sides of the bungalow had been under surveillance with each man positioned so that every window and door was within someone's sight.

From what Cameron could tell, the bungalow had burned completely to the ground. The smell of smoke and ashes surrounded them, but the concealed room had been constructed solidly enough to withstand such a blast, as well as keeping the room from being engulfed in smoke and debris. Well trained, Jess had been prepared for something like this.

Sweat beaded. Their oxygen was running low. Their bodies were tired. The battery to the lights were running low as well and the room grew grayer as the time ticked on.

Cameron looked at his watch and could tell that it had stopped again.

"What time is it?" Cameron asked in a raspy voice.

Jennifer held her wrist up and answered in a tired and raspy voice, then nearly laughed. "Ten o'clock. Do you think they heard us?"

Cameron almost laughed. "Would we be standing here, if they had?"

She hit him with her elbow. "Do you think they're still here?"

Cameron listened as muffled voices complained. "Yes, but I hope they leave soon—I'm getting hungry."

Jennifer covered her mouth and giggled, "Me, too."

Their reactions surprised them both. Perhaps it was that they were with each other or maybe it was that they had been through the hell of a deadly virus outbreak only to be confronted by an assassination attempt. Who knows? Maybe later they would hold each other and figure it out. Now was not the time.

Cameron removed the .22 from the envelope and checked it for cartridges. It was loaded. "Ever use one of these?" Cameron whispered as he handed it to Jennifer.

She grinned and said, "My father is a Colonel. I learned to shoot before I learned to walk."

"Have you ever shot anyone?"

She elbowed him in the stomach and mumbled, "No, but if you yell at me one more time you'll be the first."

Cameron smiled, kissed her, and then removed his own pistol. "I'm going out first. If we're lucky, the back of the fire place will be blown away."

"Did you ever think that there might be a back door?"

Cameron stared at her in shock. The thought had never occurred to him. If Jess were intelligent enough to build a secret room, certainly he would have been ingenious enough to build an escape route.

They heard a crash from outside somewhere, the bedroom maybe, someone was shouting about the envelope. Surely, it would have burned. It was then that Jennifer realized why they left it; they were going to kill them and burn the place down.

Cameron squeezed past Jennifer and began pressing on the walls until finally he saw a slight seam in the steel wall. He slowly pushed it and the wall hesitated, but then moved. Bright sunlight flooded the small passage.

Jennifer smiled facetiously. "You should have asked sooner, especially when they were blowing the place to smithereens."

Cameron shrugged and then dropped down on his stomach. He pushed the wall opened a little farther and crawled out.

The yard was empty. Voices came from the other side of the fireplace. A gray shadow that lay across the ground revealed the front and bedroom sides of the bungalow were gone. Skeletal beams of the roof stretched up, but disappeared into a charcoal of smoldering flame. Spider web fissures stretched across the outer wall of the fireplace.

They were very fortunate.

They darted across the smoke filled yard and into the thick pines.

Chapter 85.

Racing down a ravine and into the thick brush, Jennifer's heart pounded against her chest. She wanted to stop, but the fear of the men behind her kept her going. She knew that it was just a matter of time before they found their hiding place and then be in hot pursuit.

Cameron glanced back, stopped, and then ran back to help her.

Covered with mud, and exhausted, she finally fell against a tree, gasping. "I can't go much farther," Jennifer spoke in between the gasps.

While she sat in ankle deep water, Cameron surveyed the surrounding woods, looking for anything that moved, especially anything coming after them.

They didn't hear the shot, but a bullet zipped past Jennifer's head and lodged in the tree she was resting against.

Jennifer screamed, "Oh, God," and bolted to her feet. Another bullet. Then another. Then two ripped past them into the dense foliage up ahead. "How could they have caught up with us so fast?"

"They're trained for it. Come on!"

Jennifer followed closely behind Cameron this time. They dropped down into another ravine before darting off to the left. Cameron knew this section of the woods because he and Mahowee had been here before, collecting bottles, cans, and anything that was recyclable. He knew, or at least he thought, that Mahowee's cabin was over the next ridge. Not far, a quarter to a half a mile.

"Through those trees and on the other side of the ridge is Mahowee's—get going," Cameron said while pointing in the direction that he wanted her to go.

"And where do you think you're going?"

"I've got to try and stop them. If not, we're dead."

"Oh, no. I'm not leaving you!"

Cameron looked at her with pleading eyes and a sorrowful grin. "You have to. We have Mindy and Jasper to think about."

She turned, hesitated, and then trudged through near-waist-deep water into the dense foliage that hid the border of Mahowee's land.

All she could think about were the men chasing her, and snakes!

Chapter 86.

August 6, 12:00 P. M.

Soundless, Cameron lay against a muddy wall that rose out of one of the small lakes around Quentin. Getting the idea from a movie he had seen, Cameron covered himself in mud. He hoped that it would work as well in real life as it had in that movie. He knew it was a foolish idea, but he thought any idea right now was worth the effort. Too young for Desert Storm and being a single parent he was not able to participate in the Iraq and Afghanistan conflicts, Cameron never had military training so anything he'd do now would be something he had seen on TV or at the movies. Camouflage was certainly not a talent of his, but he felt he knew people and these people were here to kill them.

Two men, clad in camouflage, slunk past him. Both were carrying Enfield MP-45's equipped with a slightly longer barrel and a silencer. Although they were semi-automatic, Cameron knew they could fire those weapons as fast as any automatic weapons that he had ever seen.

Removing his Glock, Cameron knew that he would get only two shots. If he missed, well, at least he knew Mindy would be taken care of.

The two men stopped as if they sensed his presence. Both turned toward the muddy wall and looked in the direction of Cameron. The one furthest away from him grinned a predatory grin. His dark eyes peered from beneath thick black eyebrows. His eyes were as dark, if not darker, than his brows and they shone even brighter atop a grin that engulfed Cameron with fearful chills that made him shiver. Cameron knew immediately that this predator killed for pleasure. Perhaps only for pleasure and that he would love to take his time and watch the person suffer a long agonizing death.

The other man had the same grin and jokingly stepped closer to Cameron until he was about a foot away. He was the only thing between Cameron and the other predatory grin that still peaked over the man's shoulder.

Stunned at the arrogance, Cameron knew they had seen him as he squeezed the trigger.

While the man standing in front of him, wide eyed, took the first bullet and began falling away, Cameron moved to the right for a clear shot at that other grin.

He took it, and watched as the other man fell backwards.

Both men lay in front of him, dead.

Cameron stood up, breathed until he stopped trembling, and started toward Mahowee's. He didn't know how many men were behind these two, but at least now there were two fewer. If the others were the same as these two, he knew he would probably be caught and killed. These types stalked their prey for enjoyment.

He feared that grin. It burned into the back of his mind.

Chapter 87.

Jennifer stood about thirty to forty yards from Mahowee's back door.

The cabin held a macabre silence, which also seemed to feed on its surroundings. Nothing appeared to be alive around the house, not even a flying insect.

Crouching while clutching the .22 pistol in both hands, Jennifer ran to the back wall and lay flat against it.

She waited.

Were they aware that Mahowee had known about the mosquitoes? Surely, they were. They had to have known.

She slowly edged her way to the back door and hesitated before she ascended the wooden steps on the tips of her toes, trying in desperation not to make any noise. She knew her footsteps would echo in the silence and be heard around the entire house.

Peering through the back door windows, the house appeared to be unoccupied.

A loaf of fresh baked bread sat on the table.

Her stomach groaned.

She turned the knob as slowly and as silently as she could.

The door latch opened with a faint click.

She opened the door just a sliver and peered inside.

The loaf of bread was sitting on a cutting board next to a plastic container of butter and a jar of Mahowee's homemade apple-butter. A knife gleamed its razor edge like a silvery ribbon. A carafe of coffee, still warm, sat on the counter across from the table. Its aroma beckoned her in.

Her stomach groaned again.

A coffee cup filled with water sat in the sink.

Her throat was parched. Her tongue, thick. She could barely swallow the small amount of saliva that surfaced from the thought of eating.

The house was silent.

She didn't know Mahowee as well as Cameron did, so she couldn't tell if he was home or not. In Quentin, it wasn't uncommon for doors to be left unlocked.

Had the killers been there?

Had they murdered the elderly man who tried to save the town?

There was no sign of a struggle, at least not in the kitchen.

Clutching the .22 caliber Beretta in both hands, she went in.

Only two silent steps in the door, she stopped and looked around the kitchen, then peered down the hall to the front door, and finally, through the aperture that led to the living room.

Nothing.

The silence frightened the hell out of her and she nearly jumped out of her skin at the sound of her own harsh breathing.

The room was comfortably chilled. The air swept over her like a cool shower. It was a welcome relief.

Her muddy hands trembled as she held the pistol in front of her.

A chair, pulled slightly away from the table with a large fluffy southwestern designed cushion made her knees weak. Her legs ached. She wanted desperately to sit down, even if it were for only a few seconds. She really wanted a hot bath in which she could soak her aching body.

She took another silent step into the kitchen, one-step farther away from the door. The door that would allow her the chance to escape if she had to.

The bread and apple-butter looked inviting. The cup of water even more so.

Her hands shook.

She stepped to the sink, and with her back to it, picked up the coffee cup. Visualizing Claude and Marco, and the horrible way that the virus had spread, she poured the water out. She fumbled with the faucet as she swung the Beretta from side to side in front of her. Each door and each aperture was a potential danger.

After filling the cup, she slowly sipped it while keeping herself on constant guard of everything around her.

She filled the cup again, this time in a little less of a frenzy.

She heard popping behind her. Gunfire. Cameron. Oh, God. No.

As she turned toward the back door, the pantry door opened.

She felt someone grab her around her neck.

As she tried to spin around to see who was there, darkness overcame her.

Chapter 88.

Cameron clambered up the next muddy wall on his hands and knees, losing his left shoe in the mud. He wasn't sure how far back the black ops members were, but he had heard them calling out moments after the last shot. He had thought about taking one of the semi-automatics, but then decided against it. He had heard stories where weapons were booby-trapped, and he sure wasn't going to go down because of his own stupidity.

Three or four bullets zipped past him in sequential flashes. At least they seemed like flashes when they ricocheted off a rock that lay in the narrow path he was following.

Damn. He couldn't tell from which direction they were coming. He didn't know if they were directly behind him or closing in from the sides. Worse yet, he didn't know how many shooters there were. He wished he had read that list, or even better, had seen the team before they opened up on the bungalow.

He fell.

Slamming against the trunk of a heavy boughed pine, he saw sparks—stars.

Dizzy, he clambered to his feet, staggered a few steps, and then fell to his knees.

Another shot, so incredibly close that he felt the pressure, zipped past him.

He stumbled down the last ravine, and then clumsily staggered up the other side, sliding down twice more before his feet gripped into the thick muddy wall as he thought of Mindy growing up without him. Mahowee's land was on the other side of the clump of trees. Then there was an open field, (old farmland that had produced nothing two years in a row) before another dense patch of pines.

Cameron felt a stinging sensation on his forehead. He ran his fingers across it and saw blood when he brought his hand down. He wasn't sure if that last bullet had grazed him or if he had hit his head when he fell.

Another shot. This time the bullet ripped through his pants and grazed across his right thigh.

He fell and rolled before stopping on his side.

He grabbed his leg with a sharp wince of pain and knew it was over. The footsteps were too close. He could hear rustling just over the slight incline.

Another shot. This time it landed just inches from his face.

Mindy came into view with her soft smile, her slightly turned up nose that wrinkled when she was confused, and her thick auburn hair that shone even brighter than her mother's. No, he wasn't going to stop. Not now, not ever. He rolled to his stomach and, almost blind from his own blood, pointed the pistol toward the footsteps.

He pulled the trigger.

The shot rang out in a dull pop, which was quickly followed by another dull thud.

He thought he had been shot.

Silence.

Realizing that he hadn't been hit, he wiped the blood from his eyes. In front of him, he could see a gunman only five, maybe ten, feet away, lying dead. Cold granite eyes of death stared back at him in surprise. The bullet had entered the man's forehead. He had died instantly.

Cameron lay for a second, breathing deep gulps of air. His heart pounded against his ribs so hard that he thought they would give way.

He looked at his leg and saw a small gash. It was superficial, but it hurt like hell.

When he got to his feet, he fell. The pain in his leg got worse. He stood more cautiously the second time and began a slow limping jog toward Mahowee's. He didn't hear any footsteps or voices, only the sounds of his own breathing in heavy gasps.

A black bird cried out.

Chapter 89.

Cameron crept to the edge of the pines and stopped just before the thick carpet that stretched from Mahowee's back door to the beginning of the back woods.

No Jennifer.

Surely, she had to have made it by now.

Cameron sensed something behind him and, raising his gun, spun around, but except for the woods, saw nothing, and knew his paranoia was getting the better of him. He knew there was at least one more shooter looking for him, had heard him call out after Cameron shot the one who shot him, but he didn't see anyone.

He crept along the tree line until he came to Mahowee's shed where Mahowee had stored his collectibles; cans, bottles, papers, recyclable products that would bring in a few pennies were neatly stacked inside. The modified Kroger's shopping cart stood parked next to the door as if Mahowee had been getting ready for another round of collecting.

Cameron looked at his wristwatch, stopped again. "Damn. I should have listened to Mindy."

He tried to guess the time. It was too early for collecting. Mahowee never walked the streets in the afternoon. The temperature was usually too warm.

Something wasn't right.

He crept closer to the shed's door, hesitated, and then bolted across the openness to its entrance. When he approached the last few feet, he dove into the darkness.

Chapter 90.

It took a long few seconds before Cameron's eyes adjusted to the shadowy room within the toolshed. He lay on his stomach, exhausted, searching for movement, searching for someone who might leap out of the shadows shooting at him.

Nothing. No lone predator standing in the shadows laughing at him, and the shed was too clean to house a rodent or snake.

He was amazed that he had been able to elude the black ops team so easily. "They're toying with me, the bastards. They wanted me here..." Cameron mumbled, cursing at them and himself, for allowing things to turn out like this. At how he allowed them to control everything.

He checked his thigh and groaned as blood seeped through the laceration.

He looked around and after spotting one of Mahowee's bandannas, he struggled across the dirt floor.

He grabbed the bandanna and wrapped it snug around his thigh, and then crawled farther to the back of the shed, deep into the darkness where he collapsed, exhausted. He needed to rest and regain some energy, before proceeding into Mahowee's house.

He knew something had happened to Jennifer, he sensed it, felt it.

He rested against a stack of newspapers and let his eyes roam the darkened corners where predators of any type could hide, and as he searched, his eyes grew tired.

The darkness fed him a serene sense of safety.

Exhausted, sleep overwhelmed him.

Chapter 91.

Cameron had no idea how long he had dozed, but night had already settled outside the shed door.

He struggled over to the entrance and peered across the empty yard to Mahowee's house where the kitchen light shone like a large spotlight. It illuminated two long rectangles of plush Bermuda grass that extend along both sides of the back door.

His leg throbbed. His head ached with a horrible pounding. He was so hungry and thirsty that he was shaking.

Leaning against the doorjamb, he pulled the clip and checked his Glock. Three bullets were spent, thirteen shots were left and, although he was a fair marksman, he didn't think thirteen bullets were enough against these guys and he didn't have a spare clip. The possibility of a gunfight had never entered his mind.

He crept along the darker side of the shed until he was in total darkness. Then he sprinted in an agonizing limp across the open yard to Mahowee's back door.

He stood wincing from the pain. Then he dropped down and crept toward the front of the house. There was no way he was going to enter the brightly lit kitchen directly into the hands of a killer.

Lodged between the thick Azaleas and the cabin, Cameron crept silently to the front porch.

A tranquil breeze slipped between him and the cabin wall, cooling the nervous droplets of perspiration from his forehead.

The only light was from the kitchen. The moon peaked over the crest of the roof, but Cameron hid from the pall of the moon.

Up on the porch, he quietly turned the knob and pushed the door open; something that he knew was unusual, Mahowee had always locked his doors, even when he was home.

He crawled across the threshold and then spun to his left and lay tight against the sofa. Fortunately, Cameron knew Mahowee's cabin as well as his own place.

After resting for a moment, he crept toward the kitchen, stopping every so often to listen for movement.

In the kitchen, he felt an emptiness that engulfed him. Jennifer was nowhere to be found. He heard himself cry out.

His echo rushed across the open backyard before it disappeared into the thick pines.

Chapter 92.

August 7, 1:00 A.M.

Standing in front of Jess's bungalow (where he had left his pickup) and looking at the destruction from the earlier attack didn't affect Cameron as much as he thought it would have. Losing Jennifer and Mindy meant everything to him and was the only thing on his mind.

Although he had taken an oath when he became a doctor, that oath didn't mean anything now, these men were going to die.

The words of the social worker, *You will lose it and kill someone, someone close to you,* resounded as if the ruthless wench were standing behind him again. Only this time, he didn't care. He knew someone was going to die, but it wasn't going to be someone close to him. At least, not by his hands.

He climbed into the Ford F150 and started it. It shimmied and backfired, but this time with shattered nerves, which made him laugh a pathetic laugh. He slammed the truck into gear and sped toward Calvin's.

Hatred and anger replaced his usual calm.

Chapter 93.

Standing outside of Calvin's house, Cameron was surprised that Shep hadn't barked when he pulled up. He painstakingly crawled over the fence, hobbled to the back of the bungalow and froze when he saw Shep lying across the back steps. Dead.

As he got closer to the animal, he saw two bullet holes in his head and one in his thigh. The one in his thigh was obviously fired from a distance, because drops of blood led up the steps to where he now lay.

Cameron ascended the steps and opened the back door. They had been here, but now the question was whether Calvin was still alive or left outside somewhere like Shep.

He entered the kitchen and limped to the living room. Then he went back to the bedroom and bathroom. There were signs of a struggle but, obviously, Calvin had lost; drops of blood trailed out of the bedroom.

Seeing the Mossberg pistol grip shotgun laying hidden between the La-zy-Boy recliner and sofa, Cameron picked it up and loaded the chamber.

It was a powerful shotgun with minimal spray, but it would work wonders on a human at close range.

He took one final look around the dusty house, searching for extra shells. If the shotgun was full, then he would only have five, maybe six rounds. He wanted more. As he made his way to the back door, he glanced around the kitchen and saw a box of shells on top of an even dustier refrigerator. Things were looking up.

He grabbed the box of shells and emptied them into the pockets of his slacks.

Time was passing much too fast to suit him, and the longer he stood here at Calvin's, the more time the predators had to play their games.

He rushed out the back door.

Chapter 94.

He sat at the entrance of Quentin Central Hospital, the place he believed held all of the answers. The place where you could easily hide someone if you wanted to.

He left the truck and boldly limped through the glass doors to the emergency room.

He passed the admittance desk and continued down the narrow hall to the administrative offices as if he belonged there. He wanted to see the records. He wanted to see the autopsy reports. He wanted to see the death certificates. He wanted to see Jennifer and the men who took her.

Pissed, his white knuckled fist strangled the grip of the Mossberg. His finger played with the trigger. His cool was gone but not his calm.

He was ready.

Chapter 95.

Mahowee's black hair lay in thick strands across his bloody face. Nose broken, lips swollen, and one eye swollen shut and flooded with tears, he sat rigid and straight as another blood-wrenching punch landed across an already swelled cheek. Blood and saliva splattered against a far wall from the brutal impact.

"Where would the son of a bitch go?" Ricardo shouted in a thick New York Puerto Rican accent. "Where is he hiding?"

Ricardo stood six foot two at around two hundred and twenty pounds with arms as thick as Mahowee's legs but that had not frightened Mahowee. In fact, Mahowee had laughed when Ricardo threw his first punch.

"Only a frightened and weak man would attack a man half his size," Mahowee said moments after he hit the floor..., "only a frightened and weak man would attack an old man such as myself..., and only a fool would pretend to be a strong man of character as he throws his weight around. You are nothing more than a piss ant."

Mahowee looked at the man who was beating him and mumbled incoherently, "I don't know where he is." His head slumped down to his chest. "I'm neither his father nor his keeper…"

"We found the bitch at your place, so we know he was heading there," came a belligerent reply before another brutal slap.

As the hand raised back to strike Mahowee again, a voice called out, "Leave him alone, the Major wants us back there now."

The torturer looked down and said, "Old man, your fucking days are numbered. When I get back here, you better have an answer or the bitch will be next."

When the door slammed shut Jennifer called to Mahowee, "Tell him that Cameron is at your place, hiding in the shed."

"No!"

"You have to or they'll kill you," Jennifer pleaded.

"They'll kill us anyway, and what if he is hiding there?" Mahowee responded softly.

"He's not. I can tell. I can sense him moving around searching for us. He wouldn't stay there." Jennifer looked at Calvin, his face badly beaten, bleeding, and she mourned, "They'll kill all of us unless we tell them something."

Calvin looked at her through swollen, red eyes. "No. They'll jus keep beatin us. If theys wanted us deadt, then they'da kilt us afore this— they kilt my Shep." His head drooped down to his chest as he began sobbing. "The sons of bitches kilt my Shep…"

Jennifer looked up at the ceiling and shuddered. She strained at the binds that held her hands behind her and prayed that Cameron would come soon. She knew he was nearby.

She then looked across the room and cried as she looked at her father, lying on his back, unconscious. He, like Mahowee and Calvin, had been beaten so badly that they had nearly killed him.

He didn't know that his daughter was sitting across from him, sobbing.

Chapter 96.

Cameron hurried through the doors to the administrative office and as the guard turned toward him, Cameron pointed the Mossberg at him and pleaded, "Please, don't. I've had a really bad day. My head hurts. My leg hurts even more. I haven't eaten since last night, and I've lost one of the three people that mean the most to me in this world."

The guard's gaze never left the Mossberg. His hands lay limp at his sides, but the horror of what the Mossberg could do to him, raced through his mind.

Cameron walked up to the guard as if he were going to talk to him, and slammed the Mossberg against his head. The guard dropped back and fell against the counter, then down to the floor, unconscious.

Today three men lost their lives. To Cameron that was three more than he had ever wanted to kill in his entire lifetime. The thought chipped away at him like a sculptor with stone. It also chipped away at the hatred he had felt since that night when a supposed gang war had opened up in his ER. But this hatred was larger than he was and more would have to be chipped away before all of the pain would subside.

Cameron slipped quietly down the hall to Dr. Jeanerette's office where he had to break in. Once inside he dug through the files strewn all over the desk.

He found and read Tommy's chart and blurted, "Son of a bitch, insulin overdose. I knew he wasn't infected." He then read Dr. Jeanerette's chart, "Inoculated with infected blood."

The blood drained from Cameron's face. Chills crept across his scalp. "They were experimenting on these people and then documenting the results." He slammed his fist down on the counter and grated, "Those bastards. Those assholes. They're worse than the damned virus."

He then wondered if the incident had been planned. Could they have known the mosquitoes were on the truck, hoping to infect the Dallas-Fort Worth area instead of a small town in the middle of nowhere?

While Cameron stood over the desk reading the other charts, Chief Buster Givens entered with his revolver drawn and pointed at Cameron's back.

"You had to come back, didn't you?" Buster said with a slight tremor in his voice.

Cameron slowly turned, the Mossberg pointing down to the floor.

"You should have stayed at Fort Hood. You should have kept your big mouth shut."

Cameron's glare sliced through Buster like a laser beam. "Tell me, Buster. Did they pay you off or just decide to let you live?"

"Both," Buster answered. "And you had your fuckin' chance to disappear, but no, you had to be an asshole hero and come back. And now you're still digging up shit—"

"Buster!—" Cameron tried to interrupt.

"Shut the fuck up!" Buster continued. "It was the fuckin' insect that scared those people into doing what they did. Cain't you just let it go?"

"You should know me better than that, Buster. I can't let this drop any more than I can let a person die in my ER," Cameron said in a manner that took Buster by surprise. He then shook his head in disbelief and uttered, "Go home, Chief. Go home. There will be no more killing in this hospital. These people have killed enough."

Cameron glanced around the dimly lit office thinking about Alex. Thinking about how he must have felt when he described their friend's symptoms to him and Jennifer the night everything started. His chin trembled as he fought the pain of losing another friend.

Cameron mumbled, "They killed Alex. They injected the virus into him and documented the time it took for him to die... just, go home."

Buster stood frozen in confusion. He didn't know and couldn't believe that they had murdered Dr. Jeanerette. If he had known, perhaps they would have already murdered him. He slumped against the wall, revolver still pointing at Cameron. "They couldn't have..."

"They did. It's here in black and white. The time they injected him. His reaction to being locked in the basement. His reaction to the virus. And more importantly, how long it took him to die. They even made a note regarding his fear level, with an additional note stating that they would have to do the test again. It appears that this one was inconclusive because the fear he had was because he knew that he was infected and was going to die. The bullet was placed in his head after he died, damn it!" Cameron threw the chart at Buster. "Read it for yourself. The same people, who paid you off and want to murder me, murdered your friend."

Buster read the report and, as he did, his large frame appeared to shrivel as it slid down the wall to a sitting position. Tears sprang to his eyes. Tears so thick that he didn't see Cameron leave. His sobs so loud, he didn't hear Cameron's footsteps.

Chapter 97.

The last of the black ops, the 'Cleaners', stood in front of the cabin that Jess had used to hide his Toyota 4-Runner.

Small whitecaps licked peacefully at the shore. The murky water became even murkier as the breeze skipped across the top. The prosaic odor of the lake wafted across the beach and into the pines, surrounding the cabin.

Four men stood listening to their leader. A leader who bore a camouflage that was much better than theirs. The men stood nonchalantly listening to the final plan.

All but one had been captured; here they would stay. There would be no more abuse. No more broken bones. These would be the bodies of those who would be reported missing. These would be the last people that the virus had attacked and left to die.

Why these four were found together would be a mystery. Unless, of course, Cameron escaped. Then he would be accused of their murder, and, of course, be accused of spreading the virus by secretly inoculating people or by other nefarious means and blaming it on the mosquitoes. As far as the country, and even the medical profession, was concerned, it was both improbable and impossible for a mosquito to pass the virus. Insects, more specifically the mosquito, could not pass the HIV virus. There were just too many scenarios to prove it was impossible and only this small town that said it was possible.

The major walked back into the cabin and pulled a chair next to Jennifer. "He's coming here, isn't he?" The major said with a smirk.

Jennifer didn't reply.

"You don't have to answer. We know it as well as you do."

"How can you do the things you do and sleep at night?" Jennifer asked.

"Easy. I don't care," the major answered, and then stood over her. "Frankly, I don't care who lives or dies."

Jennifer looked away.

"That's okay. All four of you will be infected and left to die. Your boyfriend will carry the label of mass murderer, accused of killing the entire town of Quentin. Your remains will be the last found, in skeletal form, and the story will blossom into a love story that went awry. He was mentally unstable. You rejected him. He couldn't handle it and found a way to murder you. It's perfect. A mass murder to cover up the one he wanted to commit in the first place."

"So cliché. I thought you guys were pros, is that the best you can do?" Jennifer said. She then turned to the Major and continued, "People won't believe it," she shook her head, "the town knew how he felt about me, especially those close to us."

"People will believe anything. You don't understand the big picture. We don't want this news to leak out. We don't want mass hysteria. People will accept the fact that he murdered everyone before they will believe a mosquito did this. Besides, the mosquito will never be mentioned. A news leak of infected blood being stolen from a blood bank in Dallas will make it easier for people to believe," the Major said as if she already believed her own lies.

The Major stood and stretched.

"HIV will always be thought of as a disease that you catch from homosexuals, unprotected sex, drugs, or infected blood. Always. People won't believe that it could be passed by any other means. They don't want to believe it. It's too frightening. They don't want to know that they can catch it so easily. You have to remember, Jennifer, things only happen to the other person. It never happens to us as individuals. It's always the other guy, not me."

Jennifer wept as she shuddered at the words she heard. She knew what the Major was saying, was true. Horribly true. She knew that no one believed Cameron in the beginning, so why would they believe him now? If the Major's plans were successful, Cameron would be hunted down and murdered. His life would never be safe.

Chapter 98.

The pickup weaved and fishtailed as Cameron sped down State Highway 154 toward Lake Fork. The left front headlight blinked off and on as he slammed into thick ruts and deep potholes. If Calvin survived this ordeal, he would be spending a lot of money replacing the shocks and springs, the truck bounced and weaved like a boat lumbering through a storm.

Cameron slowed the pickup for only a few seconds as he passed Mahowee's. Traveling at eighty-five miles an hour, he would be near the fishing lodge in less than ten minutes.

He piloted the pickup to the left side of the road and rushed through thick foliage until the truck disappeared from the road. From here he would walk.

As he stumbled down the narrow path that Winona had crawled on that horrible night, he could see lights in the cabin; although hidden, the interior lights shone like a distress beacon.

Suddenly he froze; off to his left was the stalking Ford Taurus. It was parked beside the dirt road that led down to the cabins.

He just knew Damien Butterfield was the Major. That frail, clammy grip was a facade for a murderer, a murderer who would probably kill his own mother given a half-assed reason.

Cameron crept closer to the Taurus and it was then that he saw one of the guards, barely hidden to the right of the front door. As Cameron got closer, between the Taurus and the cabin, he spotted another guard on the left. Then the flame of a match, sparkling like a faraway star, exposed another guard on the back left side. Cameron now figured that there was a guard positioned on each corner. That meant that there were possibly four men standing between him and Damien Butterfield.

They seemed so relaxed. Surely, these men were more intelligent than that. Surely, they knew that Cameron would be coming for Jennifer. Could they be so confident that he wouldn't succeed?

Cameron crept closer to the cabin, scrutinizing the surroundings. With his pistol, he could hit one guard from this position, but he would have to be closer to use the Mossberg.

Then the door of the cabin opened.

Cameron froze.

Dr. Alistair stood in a glowing eminence like a guardian angel.

Sweat beaded before cascading down Cameron's temples.

Something droned past his ear. He nervously swept it away.

What was she doing here?

Cameron edged closer, trying to hear what she was saying, and watching the men as they became alert to her presence. Cameron then moved more swiftly as they surrounded her like bees guarding their queen.

The Queen was the Major?

Cameron couldn't believe it. She was giving orders as if she were in charge.

"We'll inoculate them. By the time someone finds them, it will be too late."

"I want that son of a bitch," Ricardo snapped and then punched the pillar. "No one takes out half our unit and lives."

"He'll surface. And when he does, he'll be arrested. I promise you, then you will have your day." She grinned a horrifying grin that sent chills across Cameron's neck. "Just make it a slow, agonizing death."

Cameron raised his Glock.

A dull blast reverberated around Cameron within a half a second after the bullet entered her left shoulder and hurled her backwards. She hit the ground hard as the four men raised their weapons and began firing in Cameron's direction.

Cameron lay as flat as he could as bullets zipped inches above his head. Pine needles felt like shrapnel when they flew up from the barrage of bullets. The missiles continued to rip past him. Three and four at a time, all came close to hitting him.

Their Queen was down. She screamed in pain.

Cameron rose up, aimed his Glock again, and pulled the trigger. Ricardo fell back against the cabin before dropping to his knees, and then falling flat on his stomach.

The other three scurried off into the thick foliage, hiding from and searching for the gunman.

Cameron, disappointed, holstered his pistol. From here, he would have to use the Mossberg, which meant they would have to be closer. Too close.

Cameron looked at the cabin and watched while Dr. Alistair stumbled through the door. The Queen was injured, but alive. He had to get in there before she could inoculate them, before she had the chance to kill them. He rolled over, then stumbled to his knees and went right.

The pain in his leg burned.

Chapter 99.

Jennifer watched and almost laughed as Dr. Alistair crashed through the cabin door. The Major looked weak. She looked as though the bullet had ripped the arrogance right out of her very soul. Her condescending attitude bled away into a horrifying scream. The God complex she wore like a crown was left in a crimson stain where she fell.

Alistair stumbled across the room as she tried to remove her jacket. She bled profusely. Her knees quivered, and then buckled. She fell against the small wooden dresser. It rocked and then banged against the wall. She fell to the floor.

"What hurts the most? The bullet or realizing you're human like the rest of us?" Jennifer asked as she stared down at the wounded woman. "I hope that hurts like hell."

Alistair stared back as the room grew dark. She complained in faint whispers. Her left arm quivered in spasms. Her fingers opened and closed as if she were a robot testing a new hand. Tears welled and blinded her, as the room grew darker. She tried to sit up, but her shoulder, connected only by thin threads of flesh, fell limp. She fell back down. Her breathing slowed, and then came in harsh gasps.

"The virus w-would have been a w-wonderful weapon. You don't realize the j-jeopardy you have placed your country in."

The crimson spot spread across her chest and down her side. She moved her right hand and exposed her horrible wound. Jennifer could clearly see the cartilage and bone. The bullet had literally ripped her shoulder and arm away from her torso.

She pointed at Jennifer as if trying to say something then fell silent.

"I bet that hurt like a sum-bitch," Calvin said.

Jennifer wanted to laugh, but the whole thing nearly made her cry. Not because of her death, but because of the fact that this woman was going to use the virus as a weapon.

Mahowee, barely awake, mumbled, "It will not stop here, in this room, unless someone does something about it. The cleansing will continue."

Chills ran up Jennifer's spine.

"The cleansing will continue until the Breath Maker has found no one else to take…"

Jennifer sobbed. Where was Cameron? Had he been killed in the hail of gunfire? Who would look after Jasper and Mindy?

Chapter 100.

Cameron hid in a dense patch of underbrush, watching the predator close in on him. He raised the Mossberg and waited.

Twelve feet away. The predator could sense Cameron was near. He walked straight toward him, his gun pointed directly at Cameron.

Unexpectedly a flash appeared out of the darkness. The flash was accompanied by a silent puff, the sound of a weapon with a silencer. The predator fell in a thud. Quick and clean.

Cameron turned toward the flash and watched in amazement as Damien Butterfield walked out of the darkness, his weapon pointed at Cameron.

"I'll lower mine, if you lower yours," Damien whispered.

For some inexplicable reason, Cameron lowered the Mossberg and then nodded toward the cabin.

"The men are dead."

Cameron, stunned, stood up and said, "Who the hell are you?"

"Damien Butterfield, like I said. Your friend, Captain Zollor, thought I should come and keep an eye on you."

Cameron relaxed.

"He's running for chief of police, did you know that?"

Cameron nodded, but didn't reply. *In shock* did not begin to describe his mental state.

"Oh. I forgot to tell you. I'm with the FBI. We've been hunting for these people for a long, long time. Now I see why. They're invisible. But like Zollor said, if anyone can bring the light of day on a mystery, it would be Cameron Nickels."

Cameron smiled. Then chuckled. His friend had answered his call after all.

Butterfield helped Cameron stumble to his feet and then helped him walk toward the cabin, as if they were old friends.

"I'm glad you called but can you do me a favor?" Damien whispered.

Cameron looked at the man who stood mere inches taller than he did. "What's that?"

"Disappear. Just disappear and don't let anyone know what part of the planet you fell off, because it really isn't over. There are others, higher up than Alistair, and they may very well want to come looking for you. This outbreak has got to be kept a secret."

"Why?"

"Well, mostly because of politics and religion. You would be very surprised. I know I was when I learned the truth."

As soon as Cameron entered the cabin, he hurried to Jennifer. His heart stopped for a brief second, and then was flooded with gratitude and a depth of love that he had never experienced.

While untying Calvin, Damien Butterfield looked down at Alistair and quipped, "You know what I liked least about her?"

"No, what?" Cameron asked turning to him.

"Those cigars. I don't know what it is, call me what you want, but I sure hate seeing a woman smoking them. I know it's a fad, but it's a fad I just can't get used to."

Jennifer looked at her and felt nothing but hatred. She honestly believed the woman had gone mad. Wanting to use the virus as a weapon frightened Jennifer beyond belief. What kind of human could experiment with mosquitoes to see how fast they could infect and kill everyone in a town?

Another test.

Another weapon.

As Cameron stood in front of Mahowee, tears sprang to his eyes. His good friend had been beaten so badly he hardly recognized him.

Mahowee smiled between bloodied and broken teeth and looked down at his socks, he murmured, "Missed again..."

Cameron untied Mahowee and let him slump against him. "Black and dark-blue... not a bad miss."

Mahowee chuckled, and then breathed, "The cleansing has not yet stopped." He struggled for air. "It has only begun."

Between tears, Cameron answered, "I know." He then lay Mahowee down in his lap, and watched as his good friend joined a Spirit Guide and passed through to the Other Side. The Other Side that Mahowee had spoken about from time to time. It was a place where you waited until your life could be judged. You could wait a mere few minutes or for a mortal's lifetime, but there you waited.

A silence filled the cabin.

As Mahowee waited, Cameron sobbed, "It was this man who saw the future and what it had in store for us. It was this man who said the Breath Maker was angry, but had hoped that he would be spared."

"Why him?" Cameron screamed out.

Cameron hugged his friend and rocked him until Jennifer laid her head on his shoulder, wrapping her arms around him.

"He's resting now, Cameron. He's okay."

Jennifer looked into Cameron's eyes and for a split second witnessed what she had always believed. He was the most compassionate man she had ever met.

Chapter 101.

November 22, 1:00 P. M.

A cool breeze swept down from the mountains and filled the yard with a pleasant freshness. Jennifer, nestled in Cameron's arms, smiled as she watched her father chase after Jasper. A new life had begun and she was happier than she had ever been.

She peered around the clean, clear sky of Sedona, Arizona, and silently thanked Bernard for the inheritance and Jess for the money he had left behind. That, along with the money that she had received from the government for her house and diner, assured them a pleasant existence. After a short three months, Cameron received his license and the required paper work, and began looking at the local clinic to start a practice as a doctor. Although he'd keep an eye open for an assassin, he felt safer than trying to be an officer of the law.

Cameron never made it clear to Damien whether he would say anything about the Quentin outbreak. He did promise that if anything ever happened to his family or to Calvin, then his war would not be over.

The small craft shop that they had bought would provide enough income to lead a comfortable life until Cameron could establish himself. Her father gave the cabin to Cameron for saving his life. The two rams actually began getting along. Jennifer knew that they really liked each other more than either would admit.

They planned a June wedding and her father gave Cameron his blessing. Jennifer was surprised that Cameron actually asked him for permission. She didn't think that men did that anymore. It was, well, it was romantic. Underneath the shy caterpillar exterior, was a romantic butterfly that she loved and adored.

She snuggled closer into his warm embrace and smiled at her mother and Mindy.

Sipping from a mug of hot chocolate, Mindy smiled back.

Off in the far distance an assassin listened for his orders. His headset sat beneath a chocolate chip, camouflage stocking cap that matched his face, hands, and fatigues. Invisible, he hid inside a clump of creosote bushes that he had assembled for the clandestine assignment. The desert backdrop assured his ability to be a ghost.

Cameron's forehead was centered in the crosshairs of his high-powered rifle.

"Negative," came a near-silent reply.

" كرر,", repeat, the assassin, whispered in Farcie as if he had not heard the command correctly. Surely, they would not call off the hit when he had the target in sight.

This was too damn easy.

The entire family.

"Stand down," came another command. "Abort—abort."

The assassin lowered the rifle and sighed. It would have been a perfect hit.

"القـــرف!", shit!

About The Author

John J. Smith (who also writes as Jonathan Black) is an award-winning author of paranormal suspense, mainstream, and romance. He has written five novels and ten screenplays. His most recent paranormal novel, Jester, received an Honorable Mention during the 2008, 77th Annual Writer's Digest Magazine contest. He also received a Writer's Digest award for his romance, Delayed Flight during the 2007, 76th Annual Writers Digest Magazine contest, and awards for other works during 2003, 72nd and 2004, 73rd Annual Writer's Digest contests.

John is a member of the Cambridge Who's Who, for his life's accomplishments. He works full time in managing computer performance and availability for an international bank.

John lives in Plano, Texas with his two Shitzu's, Charley and Benny. His passion is writing and most of his work is set in the Dallas area. He is an unrepentant coffee addict.

Join John at:

Twitter at JohnJTheWriter

Facebook at John J. Smith

Website at: WritersAlcove.com.

Other titles by John J. Smith

Two former childhood sweethearts realize that their love or each other never died. Veronica realizes that it was her own father who had twisted her dream into a nightmare.

A young man's sister becomes missing, and while he ventures out to find her, he falls in love and stumbles onto the zany, insane, and criminal world he never knew existed.

New to the Dallas Homicide Unit, Detective Krisztina Peters discovers that she is chasing a serial murderer that is going to be more difficult to apprehend than she ever imagined until she becomes the killer's next target.

Other titles by Jonathan Black

Jester has a history of seeing ghosts. So ma
ghosts that it drives him to the bottle, to murd
to jail, and then finally to a mental institu
where he disappears from everyone. At lea
until a brilliant and methodical serial killer is
the loose and Detective Kristina Peters of t
Dallas Serial crime Unit stumbles onto him.

When Pararescue jumpers board a yacht ap
named the "Loose Change", they are met with
deadly adversary beyond all comprehension.
order to save the lone survivor, Shari Kelly- w
has been imprisoned on the family cruiser and
near death-they must first learn how to defeat
Wrongful Wish that has stalked her since chil
hood.

Aberrant Endings is a collection of eight sho
stories that will draw you into the insanity
their worlds and betray you with their aberra
endings.

CPSIA information can be obtained
at www.ICGtesting.com
Printed in the USA
FSOW01n0122281015
12658FS